D0229787

GRINGA

GRINGA

JOE THOMAS

Arcadia Books Ltd
139 Highlever Road
London W10 6PH

www.arcadiabooks.co.uk

First published in the United Kingdom 2018

A catalogue record for this book is available from the British Library.

ISBN 978-1-911350-24-8

Typeset in Garamond by MacGuru Ltd
Printed and bound by T J International, Padstow PL28 8RW

ARCADIA BOOKS DISTRIBUTORS ARE AS FOLLOWS:

in the UK and elsewhere in Europe:
BookSource
50 Cambuslang Road
Cambuslang
Glasgow G32 8NB

in Australia/New Zealand:
NewSouth Books
University of New South Wales
Sydney NSW 2052

To Rachel Mills;
and for Georgia, Clemmie, Mack, Jed

For what will it profit a man if he gains the whole world and forfeits his soul?

Matthew, 16:26

Even God cannot change the past.

Agathon, from Aristotle, *Nicomachean Ethics*

São Paulo

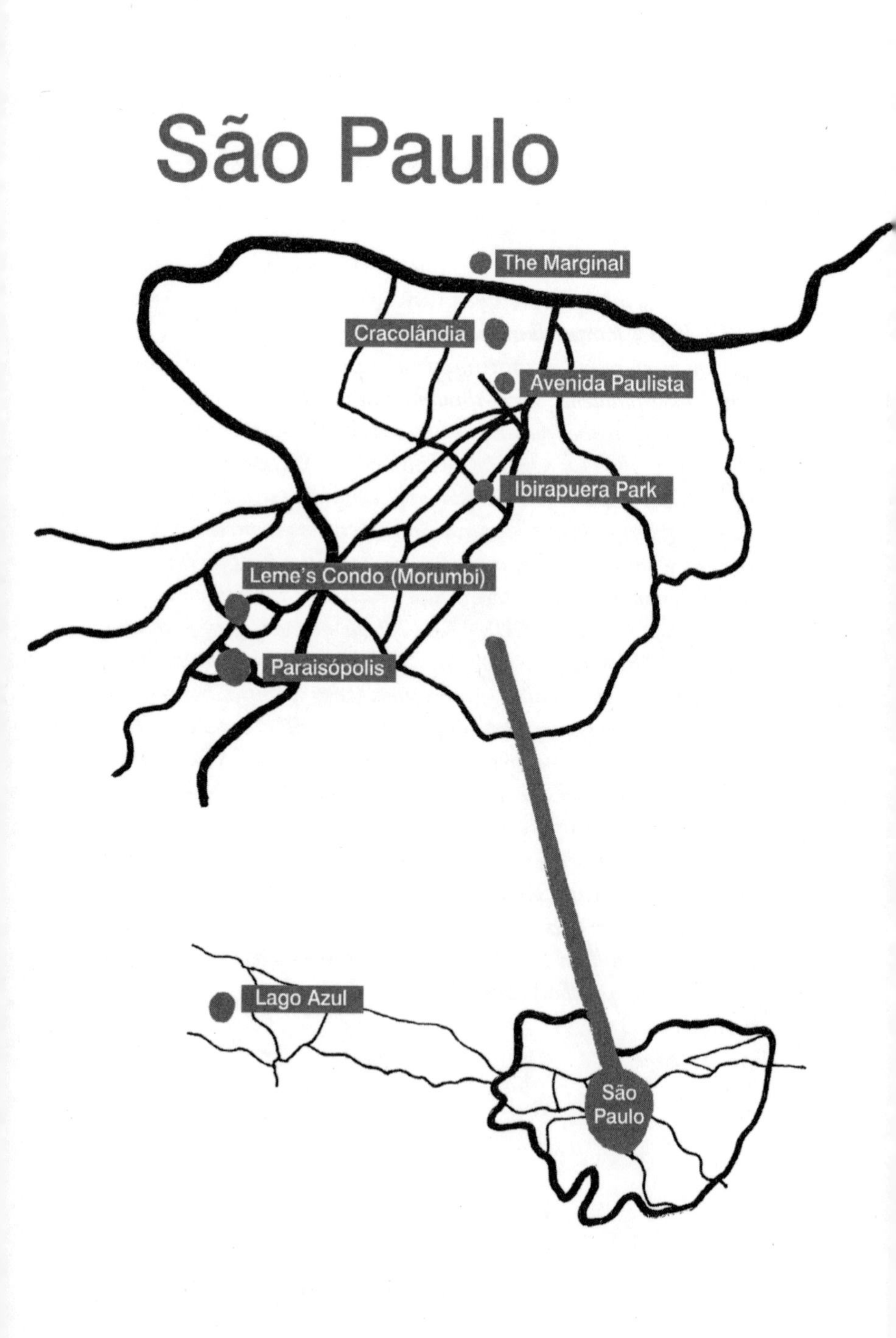
The Marginal
Cracolândia
Avenida Paulista
Ibirapuera Park
Leme's Condo (Morumbi)
Paraisópolis
Lago Azul
São Paulo

Home

*Cheap bars, bottled beer, rich students; lounges, cocktails, piano music; pushy playboy pussyhounds; Gay pride, World Cup, Olympics – *FUCK RIO*; Parque Ibirapuera, spunking fountains, rollerblades; meat-eating, year-round tennis; Itaim galleries, big business, Saturday nights in Vila Madalena, street-throbbing heat; fucking, drugs, ambition; 5 a.m. sushi at the seedy end of Rua Augusta; sex tourism, LOVE STORY, CAFÉ FOTO; OSCAR NIEMEYER; Liberdade, B.R.I.C., CRIME, TRAFFIC; Workers' Party corruption; "não existe amor in SP", they sing; largest number of pizzarias in any city, anywhere; ten people arriving every hour – to live; construction, gentrification, favela slum-bum resident removal; the Mostra film festival; restaurants; markets; the Pinacoteca; ROUBA MAIS FAZ – steals but gets things done – ORDER AND FUCKING PROGRESS; violent storms, mud slides, petrichor; the colonial centro, pockmarked with graffiti; the world's largest street-lighting system; Rita Lee; Socrates; spiral-cut spicy sausage; acrid, fetid river stink; theatres; fireworks in the favelas at every goal; clubs in disused butcher's, baker's, oven-maker's; soap operas; aspirational fireplaces, never lit; exercise in manicured, faux-forests; feijoada; roof-top pools and barbecues; kitsch camp of the pet clothes stores, the pet hairdressers; tiny, sweaty Samba clubs; hot-plate grilling on the pavements – cat barbecue: filet Miaow –*

São Paulo: 21 million people, 7 million cars, 900 street markets, 350 theatres, 54 parks, 4 Tiffany stores –

My city now –

My new home.

Paraisópolis Favela, Central São Paulo

Late spring 2012, a little after midnight

Dragging a piece of shit favela-fuck dealer out the back of a car through Paraisópolis for a few minutes didn't, it turned out, kill him. There were six of them in the ride along. Five military police and this guy Leme, a detective with the civil lot. Two vehicles. The driver of the first – a young recruit – pulled over. The car behind did the same.

The young militar driver kept an eye. Wing mirror. There he was, the little fuck – pulled out from behind the second pimped-up SUV. Alive, yes. Just.

Shaking. Groaning. Swaying all over the place – light-headed, dazed. Poor cunt.

Gold tooth glint. Dreadlocks. Cheap, dirty T-shirt. Shorts.

Mate, you are well and truly, entendeu? the young militar thought.

The other five bounced – engines killed, doors slammed.

'Vamos, caralho!'

The dealer was muscled inside.

They were high up in Paraisópolis – a militar favela safe house. Dust and brick. A hollowed-out Beetle in front. Corrugated doors squeaked shut. The lights around them dipped and throbbed as the electricity growled down illegally tapped cables. Cicada-silence. The slum bumped down steep either side. Circled by condominium-wealth, balconies and pools, barbecues and tennis courts.

The young militar nervous – scared by what he was seeing.

'Stay down here, certo?' Carlos – his senior in the military police. Could be a bit of a nasty bastard, old Carlos.

No argument.

What next?

He didn't want to know. He'd sit tight and keep an eye.

They hustled the kid into a favela shack.

That Polícia Civil stooge Leme – Carlos's friend – went too.

What next?

Nothing but keep your finger on the trigger of an automatic and hope to fuck no boys from the PCC drug gang appear out of the slum gloom.

Eyes – peeled. That's all there is to it.

Nada mais. Do what you're told.

The young militar waited. He scoped the favela. They were there because of Leme, Carlos's contact. Leme's wife had been killed by a bala perdida, a stray bullet, a year before, he'd heard, and Carlos had a tip – the unfortunate little fuck they'd just bundled into the shack. Two birds situation, then, right? Running a favour for a friend and ridding the favela of one of their less productive, less civic-minded residents. The old middle-class attitude to heavy-handed policing: menos um – one less crook.

The young militar didn't care to know exactly what was going on in the shack above him, but it didn't sound like great fun for old Gold Teeth. Maybe they were just going to put the frighteners on him, send him away, into the city proper, exile on fucking Main Street, entendeu? That was how old Carlos always described it. The young militar didn't get the reference, but he got the gist.

He heard water splash, muffled thumps, the sounds of a struggle. He knew the drill. Plastic bag over the head, filling with his blood. Bucket of water to bring him back. Then the bag again. And whatever else they could find. In a shit-show like the empty shack they'd picked out, he imagined broken furniture. Chair legs. Collapsed shelves. Kitchen utensils, if there were any lying around. Can do a lot of damage with a spatula of a certain size. Porra, the young militar thought. When did this get so fucking routine, eh?

Routine, but still scared. One thing to normalise a beating, but another to be the guy making sure you're not caught doing it. There's your fear: flip-flops and assault rifles snaking up the favela, and, in a shudder, a flash, it's done, acabou, ciao.

So he kept an eye. And waited. He counted – seconds, blows, rounds of violence.

Fuck this, he thought. Vamos, Carlão, let's go, ne?

His finger tight on the trigger.

His eyes tight. His chest tight. His mouth tight.

Come on, caralho.

This Leme character had better be grateful. Polícia Civil pussy, needing us to sort out his little domestic.

OK, he thought, chega. Two minutes and I'm going up there. This ain't worth the risk.

Then: a door slamming. Old Carlos skipping down steps.

'Drive, porra,' he barked at the young militar.

Carlos and Leme in the back. The young militar checked the wing mirror. The others coming down more slowly, checking the perimeter, loading up the second SUV.

'Vamos, ne, caralho.' Carlos was leaning back, looking behind him.

The young militar gunned the engine, lurched forward, then left, aimed the SUV at the bottom of the favela pit. Lights off. Ghosting down the half-roads in a fast creep, smooth, in and out of the corners, avoiding the pockets of activity at this time of night: one or two bars still open, the odd drunk yelling injustice, the odd playboy popping into a boca de fuma to score, the odd puta whore winding back home after a house visit up the hill. Eyes – peeled. Nada.

It was quiet and dark. The half-houses closed up for the night. The window-gaps in the brick half-filled by dirty blankets – bedtime. The air still thick with the stale smell of stewed beans and cheap pork. No rain that night and the air heavy, not yet ready to crack.

The young militar knew a quiet route out, straight into the thick vegetation at the edge of the favela. A road half-buried under yawning, aching trees and shrubbery. No one there even during the day. The SUV popped, and there they were, out, and round the corner from Leme's apartment building.

He eyed the rear-view mirror. Carlos and this Leme were talking quietly. Old Carlos had his arm round him. Reassurance. Leme sat stoic – said nothing. Eyes down – face downcast.

Carlos kept up the quiet chat – nodding. Leme – nothing.

The young militar pulled into Leme's condominium building and waited for Carlos to give him instructions.

He thought: what's with this Leme pussy? Some kid-dealer gets ironed out and he's got a fucking conscience? The same kid-dealer put a bullet in his wife. What goes around, bitch, entendeu?

Whatever. The young militar was breathing, and at this point that's all that mattered to him.

He heard Carlos say: 'It's over now, you can move forward. And you can trust my boys, sabe? Good kids. Staunch as fuck. This goes no further.'

The young militar nodded to himself. *That* much is certainly true.

Leme hopped from the car and dragged his feet home.

Carlos watched him. Satisfied Leme was through the doors, Carlos turned.

'Embora, cara,' he said. 'Let's get a fucking burger. We've earned it, ne?'

The young militar gunned the engine, smiling.

PART ONE

Single Gringa

São Paulo: 15–17 October 2013

São Paulo, Marginal Freeway

15 October, morning rush hour

Leme's phone yapped. He checked the traffic ahead and behind. His borrowed car was landlocked on the Marginal. Boxed in – tight. He leaned forward, unstuck his back from the leather and fished his phone from his bag.

Text message from Ellie, the English girl:

I know you're following me, detective ;) xx

Porra. Ellie was right though: he *was* following her. He could see her head through the taxi's back window, a few cars in front.

She was too busy enjoying herself to turn around and wave. Leme concentrated on the road.

The traffic flexed and settled, stopped, black exhaust belching from trucks. He lurched forward alongside the river.

River –

More like an open sewer, dark, ghostly men fishing out rubbish –

Industrial waste baked in the heat, the stink drifting in through his open windows.

No air-con – hot as fuck inside this rust bucket, Leme sweating something fierce.

He'd bummed this piece of shit car from a funcionario kook who worked in his building.

The kook loved to help when Leme was on a case. Leme fed him stories.

Leme told him: 'Always good to rotate cars when you're looking for a dead body.'

'Bit hot to be looking for a corpse,' the kook said.

Leme agreed. The very idea of it, decaying. *Melting –*

Migraine-heavy.

Leme popped two aspirin, dry.

He was angling out towards São Paulo's international airport, following the English girl, the journalist. She had a tip she'd said, a contact she was meeting, and she wanted him there –

You never quite knew with her.

The traffic eased and Leme floored it, keeping the taxi close. He passed the cavernous all-you-can-eat meat restaurants, the love motels with their discreet entrances, their Greek statues and their heart-shaped advertising boards, the Evangelical churches, like neon-lit, God-sponsored aircraft hangars.

And everything you need:

Meat, sex and religion

Order and progress

No surprise the gringos loved it here so much. And Ellie was one of them.

The taxi bent right and into the city, round towards Lapa and the crawl back into the centre. Leme followed and there was Ellie, waving this time. Moving her head from side to side as if she were laughing at him, opening her mouth, he thought, delighted by all this.

'Puta que pariu,' he muttered and grinned.

Leme loved this girl. She was a hoot. Menina louca: real wild-child type.

He had met her, what, a year earlier? A young journalist – twenty-two? Twenty-three? He wasn't sure – working for one of those cultural magazines that had started to delve into investigative political reporting now the World Cup and Olympics were coming up, not to mention the election. She'd been a friend of the victim of Leme's last murder case. And Ellie had been helpful. She was nuts, for sure, but she was well-intentioned and surprisingly resourceful for a gringa who'd been here only a year and a half.

His phone. Ellie again:

Try and keep up, querido xx

She seemed to think it was her right, her duty as a journalist or something, to pester Leme at his office in the delegacia, as if by getting involved in whatever he was doing, *she* would be helping *him*.

And another message buzzed in:

We're stopping.

Leme watched the taxi roughly pull into a parking spot by a small, neighbourhood lanchonete restaurant. A few manual workers sat at the bar and tut-tutted in appreciation when they saw Ellie's white legs swing out of the car.

Leme breathed heavily –

Here we go.

He wondered what it might be this time. Too often with Ellie it was a hurricane in a glass of water. But there was something about her that always made him sit up –

You never did know.

He saw her take the table furthest from the bar and position herself so as to keep an eye on the entrance and exit.

Leme went to the bar and ordered a coffee. He felt the looks of the workers slide off him. 'Policial, vai se foder,' he heard someone whisper. *Old Bill, you can go fuck yourself.* He stared at the bar, challenging who'd said it to meet his eye.

No one did. More tut-tutting, tongue-clicking –

Leme caught sight of himself in the mirror behind the counter. He did look like a fucking cop. He sipped at his coffee, deliberate, slow. He looked straight ahead. He felt sweat prick at the back of his neck. He was nervous but couldn't work out why exactly. Anticipation or anxiety, being in a strange place with strange people.

A young man came in and paused before heading over to where Ellie was sitting. Leme studied him in the mirror. He was handsome. He was cheekboned and tanned, relaxed. He wore expensive soft leather shoes. He was dressed in navy blue cotton trousers and white shirt, rolled up to the elbows.

He wore a middle-class uniform –

Playboy masquerading as a cuntman:

None of the shiny, cheap polyester of the boys from the favela who had managed to land a job in an office. There was confidence in the way he sat and ordered.

And his hair: it wasn't styled or sculpted –

Just an expensive-looking cut.

This was rare in the young men Leme had any contact with. He thought: pretty style king.

The workers rubbernecking, twisting on their stools trying to get a look.

Ellie and the man chatted for a few minutes. Once or twice she caught Leme's eye in the mirror and opened her mouth and eyes wide as if to say, 'Gosh, aren't I naughty!' Leme looked away each time. The man didn't notice. The angle was such that he couldn't have.

He drank his coffee in one go, and pushed a piece of paper and what looked like a Carteira de Trabalho, the official employment document, across the table to Ellie. He kissed her, ran a finger along her arm and bit his lip, stepped out of the lanchonete, lit a cigarette and got into his car.

Leme noted the number plate. The car was a Ford, a Fiesta, Leme thought, and it looked old: the windows weren't tinted and it needed a clean. Normally, if you could afford a car like that, you added in the precautionary blacked-out windows, and you had it cleaned every couple of weeks.

Or you had your maid do it.

The car didn't quite match the man, and Leme thought that it was probably deliberate.

'Hello, stranger,' Ellie said in English as Leme sat down at her table.

Dust kicked up from the road as a truck shuddered past. Ellie waved for more coffee. Angled her cup at Leme in a question. He nodded. She lifted two fingers and snagged the barman, who, in response, raised his eyebrows. The barman shrugged, and smiled. She had that effect on men –

Leme was coming to realise this.

'You're hardly a stranger, Ellie,' he said.

The coffee arrived. The barman placed Ellie's in front of her, tucking a napkin under the saucer. He dumped Leme's on the table so that it spilled slightly and stained the sides of the cup. Leme used his finger to stop it dripping onto the table. He licked it. He looked at the documents on the table and nodded at the door through which the man had left.

'So,' he said, in Portuguese. 'That was your contact, then. He didn't look very threatening.'

'Not quite, querido.'

Leme looked at his watch. Still early. His partner Lisboa wouldn't be at the delegacia for another two hours at least. He could afford this, even if it came to nothing.

'So who *was* the kid then?' Leme asked.

'Kid? You jealous, detective? He's the one giving me the contact's details,' Ellie said. She shifted in her seat, serious now. 'He's a lawyer, but, you know, one of those humanitarian ones, not like that corporate hussy girlfriend of yours.' Leme let that pass. 'And he's been working with a social housing group, trying to help the residents in Cracolândia.' She paused. Made a face that said *gosh, danger*. 'You know about that, right?' she said.

Leme nodded. Of course he did. Crackland. The isolated blocks in the centre of São Paulo where the addicts – the *noias*, as they were known, the paranoid hophead fuckheads – and down-and-outs lived.

Ellie was right to make that face: it was not a place to visit.

Leme had been there as a young recruit and it was how he imagined the end of the world might look. Hollow-eyed, desperate, emaciated, toothless addicts slumped in the doorways of broken-down shacks with plastic sheets for roofs, lying on corners.

And then the prowling, sharp-eyed young men carrying guns in their belts, barking instructions –

Every man for himself and God for all.

Leme had a cop friend who took a spark there, way back when: shivved, whacked up something nasty. Tetanus and other shots were the thing: you didn't know where that knife had been.

Leme touched the table. 'And these?' Meaning the documents.

Ellie picked them up. 'The *details*, detective? Just a name and an address.' She showed Leme the paper. 'Leandro Bastos. And a phone number, his, I assume. The address is in Paraíso.'

Leme nodded.

'And this is his Carteira do Trabalho,' Ellie said. 'Which he gave me to prove Leandro's credibility, you know, prove he's a good contact, that he does actually work at the company. They keep them at work, for these intern types. So he says. Can't think why.' She pushed it across the table. 'I have to give it back.'

Leme could think why. It helps control them.

Leme flicked through the passport-sized book and found the photo of Leandro. He was a young black man of about twenty with a thin goatee beard and a serious expression on his face. Leme turned the pages until he found the employment records. One job only. And still doing it, according to the book. Leme checked the salary amounts and holiday allowance. Fuck all. It wasn't quite slave labour, but it wasn't far off.

'You know this company?' Leme asked, showing Ellie the name in the Carteira.

'Uh-huh,' Ellie said. She jerked her thumb towards the door. 'The lovely Fernando works there too. Rather more senior, entendeu?' She smiled.

The lovely Fernando, Leme thought. He said, 'And how do you know *him*?'

'You know,' Ellie said.

Leme thought he could probably guess –

The first time he'd met Ellie properly, she'd told him about her latest boyfriend.

'And I said to him,' she'd laughed, '"Thank God for that. My last boyfriend's cock was so big I had cystitis pretty much constantly."'

She'd laughed louder.

'I'm kidding, caralho.'

Then she'd paused, drunk down the rest of her beer, and said, 'Well, sort of. You know.'

Leme liked her a lot.

She had an electric and restless enthusiasm that kicked something off in him that he hadn't felt for a while: a desire to work.

She was efficient, but playful, didn't seem to take anything too seriously. This was very important to Leme; it made dealing with the sorts of crimes he did bearable.

More bearable.

'Então,' he said. 'Why am I here? You seem awfully relaxed.'

'Ah,' she said, with impressive Brazilian intonation, 'I don't know exactly what we'll find, to be honest. I called you for – what? – protection, entendeu? As young Leandro here is going to show me something. Which means – as you're following me, you *weirdo* – he's going to show you something too. We're going to his place. Know it?'

Leme nodded and looked back to where he was parked. 'I do. Thing is, your taxi's gone.'

Ellie arched an eyebrow. 'No, it hasn't,' she smiled.

She slid a ten reais note under the bill and secured it under the napkin dispenser.

'Called multitasking,' she said and she stood and grabbed Leme's hand.

'Come on.'

They feathered their way towards the city centre, the traffic lighter.

Ellie sat in the back. 'In case anyone sees us,' she'd said, 'you're my driver.'

Leme knew she just enjoyed playing, talking to him when he couldn't properly examine her face as she spoke. She enjoyed the proprietary dynamic. Why not? This was a better morning than he'd had in a while.

Not for the first time he wondered what the fuck Ellie was really doing in São Paulo.

She did seem to like it though, he thought, seemed to thrive on the chaos, on that tension and violence where luxury meets despair. He remembered her saying something like that herself. He'd dismissed it as a writerly affectation: she wasn't a war reporter, though she apparently thought she was.

The magazine she wrote for was in English, and not widely circulated. It was aimed at expats, and Paulistanos who felt superior enough to buy English press. But, as Ellie remarked, the website was part of the global publication brand, and so, theoretically at least, millions of people had access to her articles.

'Doesn't any website create that potential?' Leme had said.

'Not quite what I mean, stupid,' she'd replied. But she didn't bring it up again.

They cut towards Avenida Paulista up the hill from Pacaembu stadium, passing rich students who flirted in cafés.

Ellie scoured the pavements, wound down her window.

'Looking for someone?' Leme asked.

She closed the window. 'How's … *Antonia*?' she said.

Leme eyed her in the rear-view mirror. 'She's very well.'

'Very well? Oh. How nice. Must be nice to have, you know, a *girlfriend*.'

'It *is* very nice.'

'Yes, it must be.'

'It is. We're moving in together, actually.' Leme smiled.

'Like I said…'

Ellie tap-tapped on her phone. 'How long, do you think?' she asked.

'Fifteen minutes. Depends.'

She nodded and carried on tapping.

They reached Avenida Paulista, back in the heart of the city. She could have asked him to meet her here instead of teasing him into tailing her halfway out to the airport. Though she had no idea, presumably, where this Leandro lived.

Paraíso. Where the fantasy of São Paulo – the wealthy, brimming capital of Latin America – disintegrates. It starts at the end of the slick, glass-fronted corporate strip of Avenida Paulista.

And disintegrates is the right word.

It's not even an especially poor neighbourhood.

But the contrast is sharp –

It falls away, either side of the hill, down from the main drag and into the burrows of the city.

Swank Jardins to one side, the American bars and cruising streets of Augusta and Frei Caneca on the other. Streets Leme knew he was lucky never to have to work again.

He crunched through the gears, doing an illegal turn to get off Paulista. A motorbike courier slapped his bonnet and swore. Leme ignored him.

He *knew* Paraíso. He grew up across the way in Bela Vista. When he was a teenager he called the place by three names:

If he was with a girl, he lived in Jardins, played posh.

If he was with a student, a hipster-type, he lived in Bela Vista.

If he was with a mano, a brother, it was Bixiga.

Bixiga: the bladder of São Paulo.

Eye-talian canteens and rent-boy botecos.

'Just here, I think,' he said, aiming the car down a tiny side street off a steep hill.

Ellie stretched and yawned like a cat. She smiled at him in the mirror. 'Just pull round in front and wait for me,' she said. 'Five minutes and I'm back for you. Don't want to scare young Leandro off too early, now do we, entendeu?'

Leme jammed the brakes and pointed at a rusting, narrow gate, the number painted in a wobbly script. 'That one. I'll wait in the car.'

Ellie winked and skedaddled.

She knocked on the door. There were plastic bags of rubbish sweating to one side. She pushed a toe into one of them and it gave. She held her nose in an exaggerated gesture for Leme to see. Rubbish been there a while, he thought.

She knocked again. No one answered –

She turned and shrugged.

Fucksake, Leme muttered. She knows this guy, he works with her boyfriend.

'Try the handle,' Leme mouthed at her.

She formed an ironic 'O' with her mouth and tried the handle. It was open. She pushed it wide and gestured so Leme could see inside, waved, and walked confidently into the dim, damp-looking corridor.

He unbuckled his safety belt, pushed the seat back into a reclining position and waited.

Leme playbooked it:

Ellie had said nothing about meeting this Leandro before last night. Ellie needed proof of Leandro's credibility as a contact. Ellie was dating Fernando and he was giving her a story. Or a lead. Ellie wanted Leme there, *just in case*. The whole thing might be a game.

Ellie liked games.

Yep. Ellie *liked* games. And it had worked. Leme had come after her, after all.

Leme listened to the sound of a beeping truck, warning him that it was reversing. He turned and saw it at the end of the road. His mouth was thick and bitter from the coffee.

He cleared his throat and sucked saliva from the insides of his cheeks. He looked at his watch.

He'd been waiting for five minutes or so.

This was a different sort of morning to those of a year or so before, when he'd sit in his car in Paraisópolis, in the place where Renata was killed by a stray bullet in a righteous fire fight – police, dealers and thieves. Hopeless work, but if he didn't do it, he'd feel empty, wrong. He'd moved on from that, at least. Just.

This morning, though, might be another form of hopeless work. He was at something of a dead end in the Polícia Civil, he knew that. Twenty years' service, now do one, thanks. Got to get inventive, keep busy, *act*. That much was crystal. And keep your head down, and try not to get stitched up.

What a motto.

Where the fuck was Ellie?

He straightened up and looked at the front door of the house. It was open. Had she left it open? He frowned. Yes, he thought she had. He looked up and down the street again. It was deserted.

He breathed out. Fucksake, he said again, and left the car, putting on a pair of plastic gloves, out of habit.

He speared the door. The corridor was damp, he was right about that. It was a little wider than his shoulders and a threadbare blanket covered the concrete floor. Well, it covered *bits* of the concrete floor.

Leme made out two rooms leading off from the corridor, and a back exit, though in the darkness – there were no windows, apparently – he couldn't tell where it led.

He called out, 'Ellie.' And again. 'Ellie.'

Nothing.

The quiet was settled, like there hadn't been anyone in there for a long time. He knew this was illogical – he had seen Ellie walk in minutes earlier – but the emptiness was tangible and the air seemed heavy and undisturbed.

He cracked the first door down the corridor. It opened reluctantly, with a whine. It was a concrete box, the wall ridged and flaking, shedding gravel pellets when he lifted a hand to touch it. There was the skeleton of a sofa against one wall. There were several empty sacks, dusty and scrunched in the corner. They were folded like old yellowing books onto a forgotten shelf.

No sign of anyone.

He called out Ellie's name again.

The other door, he could now see, was open.

He stepped towards it, thinking only now of his gun, safely locked in the glove compartment of his car, which was parked in the garage of his condominium. He doubted the kook he'd borrowed the car from this morning had a similar arrangement.

He moved into the room. There was a tiny window, a hole really, in the wall at the back of the house. It afforded a little light. Not much. But when Leme scanned the room and saw what he did, he was grateful for that.

A young black man with a thin goatee beard was tied to a chair, his head rolled forward but his eyes looking up, thick, coppery red blood crusting around his mouth and neck, which had been opened up, Leme thought on first look, with a blunt, jagged knife.

He gagged. He stepped back.

The room was otherwise empty. He felt queasy.

Where the fuck was Ellie?

He fumbled for his phone and dialled her number.

As he waited for it to ring, he ran through the next steps in his mind –

Call the emergency line at the delegacia, arrange for forensics, uniforms; then Lisboa, get him straight here; figure out how he would explain to Lagnado, the superintendent, why exactly he was here at all. He'd have to tell the truth, that Ellie had tipped him off on something and he'd thought it worth pursuing. That was no problem, was it?

Fuck, he thought, this morning has taken a fucking turn.

Then he realised something. Ellie's phone was ringing. A noise mimicked the rhythm. He held his phone away from his ear. Yes. That was her ringtone. There, on the floor: Ellie's bag. Inside: Ellie's phone and underneath it was Leandro's Carteira do Trabalho.

He tried to open the door at the end of the corridor –

He couldn't.

But there was no lock.

He pushed at the top and it gave a little –

Same at the bottom.

Padlock:

Locked from the outside.

He kicked at the door, smashed his shoulder into it, and it splintered and cracked.

He pushed through –

At the end of the tiny, concrete yard, an iron-wrought gate lay broken on the ground, opening up a tiny passage between the houses.

Leme paused. Caralho, he thought. The fuck? If this *was* one of her games, he would not be best pleased. And if it wasn't?

Fuck.

He scanned the yard, turned back to the house, checked the corridor again.

Porra.

She was nowhere to be seen.

Leme leant back against the car he'd schnaffled. He smoked. He watched the teams of men he'd called go to work. The road had been cordoned off and he had a chance to examine it properly.

It was like an afterthought in between two more significant avenues. The houses – though not favela shacks – looked constructed from old and discarded materials, as if they had existed before, fallen into disrepair, and had then been divided up into smaller units to house more families, with little thought as to which rooms went where.

This would explain what Leme saw inside. No kitchen as such, and no real bathroom: a gas stove and a tap in the tiny backyard.

Once again it occurred to him that in São Paulo space was filled in the same way a sponge soaks up water. The difference was that the city kept finding more gaps to fill and would never become saturated.

He watched as men dressed in white traipsed through the narrow doorway. A couple of them grunted at him in a resigned greeting. They were going to have to strip the place, study every inch of it.

One of the medical team came out to speak to Leme.

'Puta que pariu, eh?' he said. '*Not* a pretty sight. That guy kicked it something nasty. Fucker's been strafed.'

Leme glared at him. 'Então?' he asked. 'Straight up, right? Don't fucking mug me off.'

The guy nodded as if understanding there would be no bate-papo today, no pleasantries. 'So, I can't be sure,' he said, 'but the victim's been dead for twelve hours or so, I think. State of the blood and temperature of the body, though that is only an estimate. We'll get him in and carry out the tests. Shouldn't take too long.'

Leme nodded. That rules Ellie out, he thought, and then felt a pang of shame for thinking that at all. But it *was* important: she might have gone – and that was *not* cool, game-playing gringa ingénue or otherwise – but she couldn't be a suspect. Which gave him some time. And Leme didn't want to make her one. He had to figure her whereabouts, and without any intra-departmental fuckery. Which meant he'd chase her solo.

And he'd found her phone and the Carteira identified the body: Leandro Bastos.

Leme figured the play. 'We done?' the medic asked.

'Yeah, you jog on,' Leme said, half-smiling in apology.

'Relaxa, I get it,' the guy said, and mooched.

Leme lit another cigarette. He fingered Ellie's phone in his pocket. He needed the forensics to hurry up so he could get back outside and have another look around. He shouted at a uniform and told him to pass on the message.

At either end of the street life continued as normal. Deliveries were being made to a lanchonete and a pharmacy; brown faces hung from the buses that ferried them into menial work in the centre; men in suits carrying leather portfolios exited the smarter cafés shaking hands, vibeing each other's cut-and-oiled hair; students ambled towards the college buildings just off Paulista futzed on dope, stamping on joints when they noticed the flashing lights of the police vehicles.

Leme caught it all in a glance. He shook his head and it was gone.

Where the fuck was Lisboa? This, Leme reflected, was becoming a little too much of a refrain.

It wasn't like him to be late, you know, relatively speaking, but things had changed over the last year or two. The two of them went back a *loooong* way. Lisboa's old man had persuaded them both to join up. Teenagers and men together: not a bond easy to keep, actually, but if you did, it's one that's near impossible to break. It was Lisboa who took care of Leme after Renata died. Like a parent, really. The parent he had just become. Unconditional love, no judgement – bathing him, feeding him, cleaning him up. Lisboa had made Leme a priority; Leme wasn't sure he could ever really reciprocate. After the initial weeks, when Leme had clung to Lisboa like an infant, it had been work that saved him, pulled him back out of himself. While Lisboa went back to tending to his family.

Leme knew he couldn't argue with that. But, he wanted to.

He wished Lisboa had the same attitude.

Then Lisboa nudged Leme. 'E ai,' he said. 'Foda, ne? All this.'

'Jesus, where'd you come from?'

Lisboa's reassuring bulk leant heavily against the car, his arm squashed against Leme's.

'I'm like a fucking ninja,' he said. 'You'll never hear me coming, and then,' he made a sweeping movement back and across his neck with his fingers, 'swish, swish. Entendeu?'

'Christ,' Leme said. 'Grow up.'

'Yeah, well. Fact is, amigo, if I don't have to see another no-mark with a slit to shit throat for the foresee-a-*fuck*-able, I will be one feliz and dandy motherfucker, entendeu?'

Leme grunted a grim laugh. Staunch as fuck, old Lisboa.

They stood in silence. They watched as forensics signed at each other and spoke indecipherable code from beneath their facemasks.

It had a surreal quality, Leme always thought, this business of murder.

Here were teams of experts dedicated to cleaning up a mess that was likely as avoidable as anything else you could think of.

Leme once said this to Renata, that the thing about murder is exactly that, it's *avoidable*, there's never any *need* for it.

'Querido,' she'd replied, 'there's very rarely any *need* for anything.'

'It's human then, I suppose, isn't it? Creating a need.'

Lisboa turned. 'The fuck?'

'Nothing. Sorry. Thinking aloud.'

'At least you're thinking.'

Leme ignored this.

'So you going to tell me how the fuck you ended up here first?' Lisboa asked.

'That girl, it's her fault.'

'Which girl?'

'English girl, Ellie. You know, *Eleanor*.'

'Right. Her.'

'Yeah, her.'

'And?'

'She called me last night.'

'Oh yeah?'

'She sent me a message last night, and told me she was meeting a contact in the morning. She was worried. She told me to, no, she *suggested* I follow her. So I did. Turned up at her house early.'

'You know where she lives?'

'You know I do.'

Lisboa smirked.

'Slow down, babaca,' Leme said. 'And fucking grow up.'

Lisboa made a face. 'Go on,' he said.

'So I tailed her out to Lapa where she met up with a guy called Fernando, works at the same place as the victim.'

'We better talk to him.'

'You going to let me finish?'

Lisboa nodded.

'He gave her the victim's address and Carteira do Trabalho. Then we came here together.'

'She knew there'd be a body?'

'No.' Leme paused. 'No, no fucking way. She told me there was a contact, someone she wanted to talk to about a story she was working on, but she was cagey, sabe? You know, she's nuts, full of shit. Said something about protection, but I'm sure it was nothing. She had no idea.'

Lisboa raised his eyebrows. 'Coincidence, then.'

'Yeah,' Leme said. He paused again. 'Coincidence.'

'Right.'

'You don't think so?'

'Don't be a cunt, Mario.'

Leme nodded.

'So where is she?' Lisboa asked.

'Well that's the thing,' Leme said. 'She's gone.'

'Gone?'

'I was waiting for her in the car. She knew the guy's colleague so I figured it'd be OK. She wanted to talk to him first before bringing me in, sabe, not scare him. I've waited five minutes like we planned. She doesn't come back. So I've gone in to look for myself. I find the body but Ellie's not there. I find her bag which has her phone and the lad's Carteira.'

'So she either left on her own, locked the door, or…'

'Someone else took her.'

'Or…'

'The two of them left together.'

'Exactly.'

'And her bag? What was it, dropped?'

'Think so. Make it look like she's been taken, ne?'

'It *does* look like that.'

Lisboa nodded. 'True, and that's what we'll have to assume, *officially*, for now at least.'

'Yeah,' Leme nodded.

'The coincidence though, bothers me. That's my point.'

'Yeah.'

'But we *had* better try to find her. We can start by getting hold of this Fernando guy.'

'The lovely Fernando,' Leme muttered.

'Eh?'

'Nada.'

'You got his details?'

'Easy enough to find them.'

'OK. You want me to do it?'

'Make a change,' Leme muttered, again.

'*That* I heard.'

Leme gave him the name of the law firm where Fernando worked – but the name as it was in the Carteira, which was unlikely to be the name by which it was known – and the registration and make of the car. That would be enough. Lisboa wandered away to call the delegacia and have the details looked up.

Leme fumbled in his pocket for a cigarette and, as he did, Ellie's phone started vibrating, flashing, the ringtone louder this time, more insistent.

Leme swiped the screen to answer it. 'Quem fala?' he said.

'Who is this?' A woman spoke in English. 'Ellie? Who's speaking, please? I need to talk to Ellie, it's very important.'

'Fala Portuguese?' Leme asked.

'Sim, claro,' the woman replied in heavily accented Portuguese.

'OK,' Leme said. 'I'm Detective Mario Leme. Who are you?'

'Oh, gosh,' the woman said. 'Is everything OK?'

'Senhora,' Leme said. 'Just tell me who you are.'

'I'm Ellie's boss, her editor at the magazine where she works. My name is Elizabeth Young.'

'Thank you. Now you said you need to talk to Ellie, that it's important. Can you tell me what it is you need to tell her?'

'I will, but I want to know where she is first, if you don't mind. I'm not used to strange men, detective or not, answering Ellie's phone.'

Leme sighed. 'I was with Ellie this morning,' he began. 'We went together to an address where she was supposed to meet someone, for a story, I think. She went into the address we'd been given and I waited. She didn't come back.'

'But you have her phone?'

'That's right.'

'But she's not there.'

'Yes.'

'Detective, are you telling me that she's gone missing?'

'We're not jumping to any conclusions,' Leme said. 'Are you expecting her at any point today?'

'That's what I was ringing to tell her,' Elizabeth said. 'Someone called the office last night and left a message for her, but no one spotted it on the machine until this morning.'

'What's the contact's name?'

'I don't know.'

'And the message?'

'What I'm trying to tell you. The message was … I'll read it exactly as my secretary wrote it down: "I'm worried about Fernando." That's it.' He heard the rustling of paper. 'That's all it says.'

'Who's Fernando? You have any idea?'

There was a pause. 'I don't think I do,' she said. 'Why? Do you?'

'What was the story? Know that?'

'That I do know.' There was more rustling. 'An investigative piece she's researching on social housing in Cracolândia. A land deal. Gentrification. That kind of thing.'

Leme nodded to himself. 'I think we'd better meet,' Leme said.

'OK. Can you come to me? Do you know where the office is?'

'I can. When's convenient?'

'Any time, actually. I'll be here all day. If there is anything I can do?'

'Call this phone if you hear anything relevant at all, OK?'

'Fine. Of course. Christ, this is terrifying. Should I be worried?'

Leme coughed. 'It's all a matter of routine at this point. Try not to.'

'OK. I'll try.'

'I'll be with you in the next couple of hours.'

'OK, great.'

Leme took the phone from his ear and was about to hang up when she spoke again, more loudly.

'Detective?'

'Still here,' he said.

'My secretary just passed me the name of the guy who left the message. He did leave a name apparently. Leandro.'

'Porra,' Leme whispered.

'What was that, detective?'

'Nothing. I'll be with you in twenty minutes.'

England, South Coast, Poole Harbour

Mid-afternoon, eighteen months earlier

A short time before she left England, Ellie and her mum went for a walk by the harbour.

They climbed the rocks where the old wooden groynes used to be.

'This is the right thing, you know,' her mum told her. She scratched at the boulder they sat on with a smaller rock. 'It's going to be a wonderful experience.'

'I know.'

She didn't look at Ellie, instead craned her neck towards the dinghies, shielded her eyes from the sun. She seemed to have forgotten her misgivings from several months before, Ellie thought.

'You can come back any time you want. I'll always be— '

'Mum, *please*.'

'OK, OK, I know. It's your adventure, but I do want to share in it. OK?'

Two small children paddled naked in the shallows. Knots of pink skin bulged at their ankles and knees. Giggling and screaming, they splashed each other and a rain hat fell down side-up, filled with water and sank.

She turned to Ellie, cradled her head in her hands. 'I'll miss you is all.'

The children squealed as they jumped the small waves, threw the hat back and forth. A mother looked on, unconcerned, eyes hungrily scanning a paperback as if she knew this moment of peace couldn't last and she'd soon be drying them off or comforting them, feeding them or dressing them. Attending to some need they didn't realise they had until it presented itself, and with the solution too, conveniently: her.

'You don't have to do this, Mum.'

'I'll never stop being your mum, Ellie.'

With her left hand she stroked Ellie's neck and with her right she threw the small rock into the harbour. It disappeared into the yellow-green sea, flashing white in the sun. Ellie imagined following it to the harbour floor, watching it nestle in the sand.

'If you take this job,' her mum said, 'there might be difficult decisions to make. I've heard it can be a dangerous place.'

'Mum.'

'I know. I'm allowed to worry.'

'It's a cultural magazine. I'm going to be an arts copy editor. They run listings for English speakers, restaurant reviews, that sort of thing. It's a start, is what it is.'

'So you're going to take it?'

'It's the only offer I've had. I've worked hard. It's an opportunity. Be happy for me. It's safe, it's *arranged*.' She paused and looked at her mother. 'I'm doing this on my own, Mum.'

Her mum smiled and wrapped her arms around her. Ellie squirmed a little, then let her. The children were by now eating ice-cream cones on the sand. Actually, what they were doing was smearing it over their faces and bodies. The mother hopped from one to the other with a tissue that was quickly disintegrating, the paperback abandoned.

There was an advantage to having a window seat as you approached São Paulo, Ellie realised, as she sat on the plane, *arriving*. You can see it from a long, long way away. It didn't seem possible when the map with the little plane on the screen told her that she was an hour from landing. It's already there, she thought, beneath you, creeping out.

Creeping up, it appeared.

She felt an odd contradiction; though she was heading towards the city of her own will, it felt somehow the reverse: that she was being drawn towards it, irresistibly.

The airport was to the north-east, but, in a holding pattern, they skirted the city and its size became quickly – no, *slowly* – apparent. São Paulo sprawled hotheaded and hungover, she imagined, throbbing under the cloud of pollution that gave off such thick warmth that she thought she could feel it despite the air conditioning – and the impossibility. Patches of green and threads of blue forced their way through the gaps between thrusting white towers and rust-coloured slums that leaked out from the centre, like a stain.

Before an uncomfortable, boozy, fitful sleep, Ellie had read that the city was a magnet. Post-slavery, immigrants arrived from Europe to work the fields around the city and then, later, from Japan and the Middle East. Hundreds of thousands trekked from Salvador and the countryside of the north-east coast to escape the droughts and the arid, hostile heat – and the ethnic mix is best reflected in the incredible array of eating opportunities.

That's what she'd heard.

You come to São Paulo to eat.

She pressed her nose against the window, convinced she could make out the line of skyscrapers that is Avenida Paulista. The highest point in the city, almost a million people commute here every day, so the guidebook told her. A similar number must go into central London, she thought. But you *know* that million. You're one of them. This is a million of unknowns.

She looked around the plane. Some of this million were sitting next to her in economy class, laid back, chiselled and comfortable, their children meerkat-ing about in the aisles. The man in the next seat noticed her looking out of the window.

'São Paulo is an island of heat,' he said, smiling at her. 'An island, like where you're from. It's the chemical reaction of concrete and CO_2, the exhaust from the seven million cars.' He laughed. 'I'm really selling it.'

Ellie smiled politely. She didn't like the sound of that very much.

The queues in arrivals were irregular jagged rhomboids determined by who was talking to whom rather than by where anyone was supposed to be. It was all flickering strip lighting, tired wood and plastic kebab-shop seating nailed to the floor. And the heat.

The heat.

Ellie sweating buckets; and watching, observing: a mass of Paulistanos moved with sexy, lazy economy, with their neatly combed, straightened hair, their clothes crisp and creased, ironed jeans and T-shirts, their roll-on luggage pulled like obedient dogs behind them, their dogs trotting at their sides like obedient children, their children playing tag on the baggage carousel, all of them jabbering at each other and into their mobile phones in a perverse-European, guttural hack – as foreign as the machine guns pointed floorward by the guards.

She was through quickly enough, no one stopping her, questions perfunctory, paperwork in place. But then what?

On the concourse, the heat all-enveloping, taxis jostled for position, beeping their horns and waving while wiry dark-skinned men in over-sized white uniforms bustled back and forth in the queue deciding, arbitrarily it seemed, whose car was whose.

The taxi driver was quiet, which was something of a relief.

Early days.

Ellie moved into a condominium, close to Paraisópolis. The condominium's towers blocked out the view of the favela, which was set low, in a crater, a settlement built in the hole of a great explosion, an apocalyptic, concrete and brick village, the rough houses pillboxes like machine gun posts.

Morumbi was new São Paulo she was told, again and again, by her neighbours. It wasn't like the traditional areas around Paulista Avenue with their neighbourhood bars, old-fashioned apartments and canteen restaurants. It was a place to move to and have children, or move to when your children have left home. It was dangerous outside the condominium gates, which is why she couldn't help but stare, fascinated, as she drove past Paraisópolis, at the harried faces and the slouch of rubbish and mess, at the half-naked favela children and the condensed, improvised houses, like an approximation of a home, at least in her narrow conception of one. The children stared back. Their parents ignored her.

From her balcony, through the gaps between other, smaller buildings, she could see a circular and impressive-looking tower block with helipad and gardens. At night, only a couple of the apartments were lit up. It was strange, Ellie thought. She asked around. A neighbour, Marcelo, laughed when she put it to him that they must be prohibitively expensive.

'Expensive?' he said. 'They're selling them at cut-price. Absorbing a huge loss.'

'So why are so few of the apartments occupied,' she asked.

Marcelo laughed again. 'They fucked up. There's been structural damage.'

'Really?'

'They were designed to have a swimming pool on every balcony, on every floor.'

Ellie raised her eyebrows. This seemed unusual even for Morumbi.

'Thing is,' Marcelo went on, 'they forgot to factor in the extra weight of the water. When they filled them all up, the fucking supporting pillars cracked! Idiots.'

It turned out only a few people will invest over a million reais in a dodgy structure.

Still. A few did. The city was like *this*.

Early days.

She never got accustomed to the smell in São Paulo. A sulphurous, acrid odour, pockets of fresh air leaden with pollution. Tasted like stale cigars scratching at the back of her throat.

Ellie was walking to the supermarket, and the air left her thirsty, and then hungry, at a waft of grilled meat on a roadside barbecue. The close boom of a truck's horn startled her. A small dog barked at the noise and its elderly owner tried in vain to calm it down. Men selling mobile phone accessories and cheap candy accosted drivers at the front of the queues at the lights, shouting out prices, feigning friendship – 'For you, mate, nothing more than a few reais.' They glanced in her direction. A gringa, alone, dressed in a short skirt and tank top.

The supermarket's air conditioning cooled the sweat on her arms. She picked up a basket and wandered around, still unused to the foreign packaging of goods that are commonplace in England. The colours of the fruit a touch garish, the vegetables brash. Even the ham had a pinker hue than she remembered in Sainsbury's. She made her selections, added a couple of bottles of Chilean red wine and waited patiently to pay, noticing a topless picture of a famous mother on the front cover of a gossip magazine.

The attendant rang up her goods, and asked Ellie three questions. 'Did you find everything you want?' ('Yes'). 'Do you need anything else?' ('No'). 'Do you have a reward points card?' ('Yes. But I've forgotten it.') They always ask these questions, Ellie had learned, though, confusingly, not always in the same order and when her Portuguese was even weaker, complications arose. The attendant might begin with 'do you need anything else?' and she would answer 'yes' expecting a different question, and then they'd have a discussion on what she might need from all the possible items in the shop, with lots of hand-waving and miming, which she could never follow. More than once she ended up in the utility goods aisle with an enthusiastic young man who wouldn't let her leave without a saucepan or dustpan and brush or, memorably, with an Octodog Hot Dog Shaper, which turned frankfurters into octopuses as they cook.

She left the supermarket and decided to go for lunch in a simple restaurant. She ordered filet mignon with rice and salad and a glass of beer. Groups of office workers talked noisily on pavement tables, but she was able to switch off and let the conversations wash over her. One of the office workers – a man in a suit with sunglasses, a purple tie and a confident smile – looked openly at her several times. He stood up and Ellie thought he was coming over to her table. She looked up expectantly – a knowing smile – but he passed by with no comment. His loss.

She swiped her phone and looked at her profile on the dating site, Single Gringa – it still made her laugh – that she'd been using, thanks to her boss's recommendation. She'd been out with some guys, but they only really seemed interested in her as a novelty, an English girl, a gringa. She'd been getting quite a lot of traffic, and one day she saw a message from a name she thought she recognised. It was a cute message, funny, a reply to something she'd sent some time ago, with all sorts of compliments about her photo, and suggestions that they had a lot in common. But she couldn't place the name, decided that she was confused, and agreed to go out with him. He suggested a bar that was close to her apartment. It wasn't until she was seated in the bar waiting that she remembered where she had seen the name. She'd been out with him about three months earlier to the very same bar. He was charismatic, attractive, and she'd invited him back to her place. Clearly, he'd completely forgotten about her, seen her profile again, thinking it was for the first time. He must have gone through the entire list once already. Ellie laughed at the memory. Men, eh?

Early days. They wouldn't last.

São Paulo, Jardim Paulistano

15 October, later in the morning

Ellie's office was based off Avenida Gabriel Monteiro da Silva in Jardim Paulistano. It was down among the one- and two-storey mansions and the private security. Low-rise housing meaning: *cash-rich*.

Leme watched the Lycra-clad, personally-trained, dog-walking housewives –

They strode along the middle of the spacious roads –

They looked affronted when drivers expected *them* to give way rather than the other way round.

Porra, Leme thought.

São Paulo has a lot of that: sharp reminders of what you don't have.

He'd left Lisboa to supervise the crime scene and track down Fernando. Work out the clip plan.

The traffic was lighter but the sun hotter. The car bonnet scorched. Tyres bare, squealing on the throbbing tarmac as Leme pulled onto Gabriel. Exhaust fog shimmered in the heat, hazy, like a waterhole mirage above the desert.

He'd been to Ellie's office once before. Not to see her. He did see her though, of course he did. She'd caught him on his way out, thrust a card into his shirt pocket, her finger pressed into his chest.

'You might need this,' she said.

'What for? English lessons?'

She pulled a face and withdrew her hand with the card still in it.

'Ah, vai, play nice, detective. I'm just offering my services in like, you know, an exchange? A – what's the phrase – quid pro quo? You know what that means, I'm going to assume.'

'I'll take the card.'

He reached for it and she pulled her hand back. 'Tsk-tsk, detective,' she said, shaking her head. 'You'll have to promise me something now. Make up for your rudeness.'

He smiled and looked at his watch. 'Fancy a beer?'

'Drinking on the job? Yes, please.'

They walked a hundred yards or so to a neighbourhood boteco. She ordered a bottle of Serra Malte and two glasses. Leme raised his eyebrows in appreciation.

'What?' she said.

'Nothing,' he smiled. 'Don't see many gringos drinking Serra Malte, that's all.' He nodded at a couple of businessmen in suits also drinking it. 'Sign of taste, you see.'

'So what shall we talk about?' she said.

They'd talked about what she wanted to do at the magazine. They'd talked about how her ambitions went beyond arts copy. They'd talked about how what she really wanted was to write about politics and crime. That politics *was* crime.

In terms of reporting, in terms of *genre*.

That was the word she'd used, genre. He hadn't thought of it like that before. But she was right, crime informed politics and politics informed crime. How else to examine society other than through the lens of those doing wrong – and those trying to do right?

Leme had been impressed; she'd not been in São Paulo long and seemed to have sussed it out.

Or at least sussed out her role in the place.

Everything else is detail, once you've figured out your role. Leme remembered Renata saying that when they first met. That was something they had in common: they both made their work their purpose, and when they discovered each other, all they had to do was realign their priorities a little. It had been easy, fluid, empathic.

It still felt like it could be.

Leme turned off Gabriel and parked in front of a private security booth.

He rapped on the window, waking the guard who was slumped back in his chair. 'Vamos, garanhão!' he called out. The old man looked confused.

Leme walked away towards the magazine's offices.

But he hadn't been able to help Ellie that much in the end. He'd wanted to. He let her pester him, answered her questions, shared information that fell just on the right side of legal, ethical. He'd even suggested a couple of ideas for stories that seemed the kind of thing she wanted to interrogate, ideas she might have developed.

One had been about a series of robberies of dentists' surgeries, and the other a spate of apparently random acid attacks on rich executives. But her editor – this Elizabeth Young, he assumed – had never green-lit her pitches. That must have changed: when she called the night before she was explicit that it had an important connection to a story she was working on. She may have lied about the body – and he didn't really feel like thinking about that right now – but she would not, he was sure, have lied about working on something.

She was an elegant redhead in her mid-forties, this Elizabeth Young. She sat across from Leme and weighed him up, seemed to have assessed him in their first exchanges. Her Portuguese was efficient, but marked by an abrasive, European accent. Unlike Ellie – and this Elizabeth Young had been in São Paulo for over ten years – she did not seem very Brazilian.

'I'm worried, detective,' Young said. 'Ellie is a brave and impetuous girl, but she is also very sensible. She doesn't just go missing.'

Leme nodded. 'We'll do everything we can. At this stage, though, we have to assume that she will be in touch with one of us and that there is a simple explanation, a misunderstanding. Technically speaking, enough time hasn't yet elapsed for her to be classified as missing.'

Leme heard his own voice and the officious platitudes sickened him. If he could be honest, he might get somewhere quicker, but he didn't want to raise suspicions or concerns, which might be unhelpful. Especially with someone working in the media.

'You certainly got here quickly,' Elizabeth Young said.

Was she implying something? Ignore it. 'On the way to my next appointment,' Leme said. He tried to hide the fact that he was worried. He was hiding it, he realised, from himself, too.

'OK.'

She leant back.

Antonia would describe her as 'womanly'. This was faint praise. Antonia rarely said anything that wasn't inflected with irony or some sort of agenda. She chose words with precision, marshalled them, sent them out to please or do damage in exactly the way she wanted. And she didn't often miss.

'This message,' Leme said. 'What's the piece Ellie's working on?' He was careful to use the present tense.

'Social housing, the enforced removal of residents from under-privileged areas.'

'This is the first piece like this that she's done?'

'Yes, I suppose it is. She's pitched stuff before, but we've never had the context to publish.'

'But that's changed?'

'The World Cup. The Olympics. Anything connected to that gets the go-ahead now.'

'And how is this connected?'

She smiled. 'I think you can answer that yourself.'

Leme nodded. 'Fair enough. I'll read the article when it's out. It's got political implications then?'

'I don't know. Perhaps. We do tend to try and avoid too political an angle though. We're a cultural magazine, ostensibly.'

'Does anyone else know about this?'

'About Ellie?'

'About any of it. Ellie. The story.'

'I don't think so. She hasn't been working on it long. Came to me with the idea and said she has a contact. This Leandro, I'm guessing. Usual policy when someone is on an investigative thing like this is to get on with it. Journalists don't like to share. They don't want anyone stealing their angles.'

'And what's her angle on this?'

'Cracolândia.'

'Cracolândia?'

'Ellie says it's being flattened, and that the residents, if you can call them that, are disappearing. Moved on, but no one knows where to. She claims there are people who live there who aren't drug addicts – families. I find that hard to believe.'

'Difficult to keep a piece like that apolitical, I should think.'

'That was my condition.'

'Go on.'

'It had to be human interest. Follow one of these families, highlight their plight, see if, in fact, they *were* moving somewhere better. It's early stages. She's finding her way in.'

'Sounds vague.'

She sighed. 'I suppose it is a bit.'

'So why did you approve it? Forget context or whatnot.'

'Her contact. Leandro.'

'What about him?'

'Apparently he works for the law firm that's overseeing the sale of the land. And is also supposed to be ensuring the rights of those displaced.'

Leme nodded. 'So, verifiable.'

'Exactly.'

'Ellie tell you the name of the firm?'

Leme knew this was in Leandro's Carteira. Problem was, the names of firms are often different to those recorded in official documentation. Brazilian bureaucracy.

'She did. Zarzur Cabral, I think.'

Leme had been poised to write it down. He didn't bother.

'Thank you,' he said. He gave her his card. 'Make sure you call me the moment you hear from her.'

'You do the same, if you don't mind,' she said, handing him her own card.

Leme sat in the car and read the message Lisboa had sent him. He was needed at the delegacia. The forensics had an idea about how many people had been through the house in the last few days, though no possibility, this quickly, of any concrete identification. No recognisable prints – at least that didn't match, pronto. They'd been given the case, officially now, so there was a report to write and Leme had to justify why he was there this morning, figure out how to explain Ellie's role in all this. Superintendent Lagnado was on the rag and he needed convincing. Lisboa told him to think very carefully about this before he arrived. If she was a suspect, or she was in fact missing, they couldn't afford to be accused of negligence. Not now. Leme knew what this meant: Lisboa wanted everything done by the book. Nothing should threaten his position, and the security of his family, his kids. He didn't need to spell it out. 'Think very carefully' was enough. He was telling Leme, again, that he owed him. OK, Leme thought. That's fine. I understand. You're right. I sacrificed the right to be selfish long ago, Leme thought. And the right to claim that work was ever more important than family. Problem was when you were helping other people's families by doing your job.

None of this had much of an impact on him though.

It was expected, he was prepared for it. He'd been trained.

The morning had gone very differently to how he'd imagined it would, but at each juncture his experience had told him what to do next, what would *happen* next, even. Following Ellie's taxi; watching her meet this Fernando character; driving to Paraíso; finding Leandro's body; and then weighing up the possibilities of what the hell has happened to Ellie, where the fuck she's got to.

But really, none of these things surprised him as much as finding out that Leandro Bastos worked at the same law firm as Antonia, his girlfriend. Antonia, his soon to be live-in girlfriend, a woman he had been with for over a year now. A woman he'd told he loved, not three months ago.

And this all meant, of course, that there was a good chance Antonia knew the lovely Fernando.

And he didn't like the closeness of this connection one bit.

Leaked Document Record: Land deal – Cracolândia
Recipients: Carneiro; Lagnado; Aguiar; Lemos; Amaral-Gurgel; Machado
Subject: Facilitator duties

On completion of the meeting dated May 2013, it is agreed that the duties of the 'facilitator' [Leandro, office clerk, Zarzur Carbral] are laid out henceforth:

1. That the facilitator will ensure that the residents of the neighbourhood under consideration are happy with all terms of the project and further assure said residents that they will be relocated under circumstances that benefit them, and, above all, that he will guarantee compliance from said residents
2. That the land deal itself is promoted as such in the press and international media to ensure that any public knowledge of said land deal is favourable to the project and therefore will not in any way create negative feeling to impact on the hosting of any state, national, or international events, or perceived capability to undertake such hosting
3. That the facilitator shall remain in place until said land deal is completed and development is started in order to reassure any remaining residents – awaiting relocation – that the terms of the relocation that the facilitator has outlined shall be adhered to
4. That the facilitator will use his influence with the leading members of the neighbourhood under consideration to enable a smooth transition
5. That Sr. Lagnado and Sr. Amaral-Gurgel await instruction before applying any measures that may be deemed fit to ensure this transition; i.e. the facilitator will be given due process to effect said transition without outside aid
6. That Zarzur Cabral will ensure that the owner of the

land is both briefed on and satisfied with the conditions of the sale and that the owner will agree to any previously unforeseen involvement effected, potentially, by Srs. Lagnado and Amaral-Gurgel

7. That the facilitator [Leandro] will be debriefed and detached from the project once his duties have been satisfactorily carried out

Signed: The recipients.

Offices of Zarzur Cabral

Five months and three weeks earlier

Leandro sat on a hard-backed chair outside the meeting room, waiting to be called in. He looked over the notes he had been given – a memo, a file that detailed his appointment and tasks, a list of contacts. He turned the new mobile phone over in his hands, examined it. It was pre-loaded with contact numbers and the bills paid for by Zarzur Cabral. His knees shook – nervous anticipation; he had never met anyone as high up in the company before, and he'd been told there would be some important players in the room with them today. He wondered – and not for the first time – quite why he was here.

'Mate, it's simple,' Fernando had told him. 'They just want to put a face to a name, entendeu? What you're doing is important, you know? No fucking way any of them would do it, so they just want to know who you are. Relaxa, eh, veado.'

Leandro had nodded. It made sense. 'Yeah, but—'

'Cara, it's foodchain shit, sabe? And you're the bottom. They're having a look, like a … like a fucking exhibit is what you are: the kid that can get them into the jungle. Ha, ha.'

Leandro had laughed, but it wasn't funny. 'Então,' he said. 'What you're telling me is that I'm the insider here, ne?'

Fernando looked up at him – sharply. 'Dude, you're just the fucking black-kid go-between,' he said, without malice. 'Ain't anyone else we know we can send into Cracolândia.' He smiled, rubbed his fingers together. 'Enjoy it, mate. You'll be richly rewarded.'

Leandro wanted to believe that was true.

So here he was, waiting outside Carneiro's personal meeting room: the meeting room of the senior partner of Zarzur Cabral. With him, at least according to that folgado Fernando, would be:

1. Victor Lagnado, Superintendent in the Polícia Civil
2. Danillo Aguiar, Secretario de Obras, the politician responsible for all construction in the city

3. Clayton Lemos, owner and director of CASA, the largest construction/development company in the country
4. Pedro Amaral-Gurgel, commanding officer of ROTA, key unit in the military police
5. Sergio Machado, State Governor

It's no wonder I'm nervous, he thought.

'Querido, ta boa?'

He looked up. One of Carneiro's secretaries, Moira, smiling, checking he was OK, handed him a coffee. 'Sim, Senhora, obrigado,' he said. His hand shook as he sipped at the plastic cup. He smiled.

She snorted and laughed. 'They're going to eat you up, garoto,' she said. She paused and, turning away, briefly placed a hand on his shoulder. 'You'll be fine.'

The door opened. Leandro was ushered in.

An oval table dominated the room and Carneiro sat at its head on the far side. There were pads of paper, blotters, expensive pens dotted about in front of the six men; elegant china coffee cups sat empty and a plate of empanadas and a fruit centrepiece were largely untouched. The men all wore navy suits, striped shirts with gold cufflinks, an array of colourful ties. Two of them had red braces. All of them had their hair slicked back, were freshly shaved, and reeked of ugly scent. They eyed Leandro.

Leandro thought of vampires, vultures. Lizards.

Carneiro opened his arms to welcome him. 'Leandro,' he said. 'Take a seat.'

He pointed at a chair set a little back from the table. Leandro sat. He tried hard not to bow his head deferentially.

'So I've been explaining to our colleagues your role in all this,' Carneiro began. *Our* colleagues. Leandro noted that. Carneiro went on, 'They were keen to meet you. Only a formality. Face-to-a-name situation, entendeu?' He grinned.

'Sim, Senhor,' Leandro said. He remembered what Fernando had said to him. OK, he thought. He knows his way around this world better than I do. Vamos lá.

Carneiro leaned back in his chair. 'We've all got the same documents you have that detail what you'll be doing for the company, for us. It's an important job. You'll be on the ground and facilitating important changes. You'll be as important to the residents as you are to us. Faz sentido?'

'Sim, Senhor,' Leandro said, again. He tried to smile. It was harder than he imagined it should be.

'I just wanted to reassure our colleagues' – and here Carneiro gestured around the table – 'that we've chosen you to do this for a very good reason. Obviously – *obviously* – your professional skills and suitability for this are the main reasons. But we do have a couple of questions.' Carneiro leaned forward, flashing white teeth, gold fillings that matched his cufflinks. 'If that's OK, of course?'

'Sim, Senhor,' Leandro said. 'Claro. Thank you.'

A couple of the men around the table exchanged a look that Leandro didn't much like. He didn't know who they were. It didn't matter.

The man closest to Carneiro spoke. 'Ricardo, if I may?' Carneiro nodded. He continued, 'Leandro, isn't it?' Leandro nodded. 'We're thrilled you're on board. As Senhor Carneiro was saying, it's an important role. To reassure the residents that they will be looked after, that they'll be relocated for the best possible reasons, that they'll *benefit*. This is of singular importance.'

The man paused. Leandro examined the files in his lap. 'Obrigado, Senhor,' he said. 'I understand. Of course.'

The man nodded – pensive. He looked around at the others, for permission, Leandro thought. There were gestures, looks that said *go on*.

He said, 'You have friends, contacts down there, don't you? People you know, who trust you?'

'In Cracolândia?' Leandro said.

The man smiled – thin. 'You have friends … where our project is taking place. Não e?'

'Sim, Senhor,' Leandro said.

'And these … *friends*, they're influential in the area? Is that right?'

'Sim. Acredito que sim.'

More nodding.

'This is a land deal, as simple as that,' the same man continued. The others seemed happy to let him do all the talking. Leandro wondered who this man was. 'There are myriad legal complications with the way this land has been used, built on, *lived* on for the past, oh, God knows how many years, you understand?'

Leandro nodded.

'The key thing,' he said, 'is that the residents – the *legal* residents, entendeu? – those that actually live there, and not just—' And here he smiled – knowingly. 'Not just … those who *use* there, the important thing is they feel they will benefit. Which they will.'

Leandro nodded. 'Sim, Senhor,' he said.

The men looked at each other.

Carneiro made to wrap it up. He stood. Leandro did too.

'Study the documents carefully,' Carneiro said. He smiled. 'And now then, lad, you get on your bike. Take the rest of the day off. Enjoy yourself, certo?'

'Sim, Senhor,' Leandro said, and left the room, closing the door carefully behind him.

Moira gave him a warm smile as he passed.

'Told you you'd survive,' she said, winking at him.

Leandro blushed, flooded with something like pride.

He decided to walk home.

It wasn't often he got to be in the city during the day, during the week. It'd been a long time since he'd had that privilege, though, of course, when he did have it, it was nothing of the sort: unemployment was not something to aspire to in São Paulo. He didn't really know what he *was* aspiring to, but he knew what he didn't want: the life he'd had in the north. And this job, and the small amount of money he'd inherited, meant something, he knew that now. And this vote of confidence at work, this opportunity to be involved in a major piece of business, was exciting, in its way. He knew why he had been chosen; he wasn't under any illusions about that. But, hell, why couldn't a favela kid accept a lift? Not as if our status counts for much, most of the time. *Any* of the time.

The heat beat down. He walked up Juscelino. The temperature thirty-six, according to the boards that flipped adverts on rotation, though he'd been told they conduct heat too, so they're sometimes something of an overstatement. It felt thirty-six degrees, and more so in his polyester threads, his scratchy trousers and stiff shirt rolled to the elbows, which dripped in sweat. That's one thing he'd do when he could cash in after this project: buy cotton. There, there's an aspiration for you, he thought. He smiled. And *cash in*? Hardly. But yes, he could buy some new shirts.

Juscelino was teeming, cars shunting slowly, motorbikes zipping in between them, workers moving fast from office to restaurant or café or bar, sticking to the rare patches of shade. The heat from the stationary car engines *shimmered.* He angled towards Ibirapuera park, and the streets narrowed, trees cooled, and the noise of the main road subsided a touch. He would walk across it, he decided. Have a gander at what a life of leisure might look like.

There was nothing for Leandro in the north-east, certainly no father – he never knew him – no job, no future. He lived in a simple house on the outskirts of Recife and his mother scraped a living working as a maid. His sister, when she was old enough, left school to help. He left school young – well, he simply stopped going – and spent days lounging around the house, kicking his heels on the dusty streets of the neighbourhood, keeping out of trouble, sheltering from the sun.

The light in Recife was intense white; it glinted on darkened skin. In São Paulo it was filtered through the smog: streaky lines of faint yellow paint.

He ambled towards the park. To his left he could see the Hotel Unique, with its boat-based design, its portholes as bedroom windows, its exclusive bar on the roof where Fernando had once taken him, where they'd bought drinks that cost more than Leandro earned in a day, and he'd slunk off, quietly, but happy, when Fernando's playboy friends turned up. Fernando was good to him, on the whole. He'd ask him round for a drink to celebrate this little work success, at some point. He'd have to clear up a bit first, he realised. Fernando had a chip though, and Leandro wasn't sure what it was. He knew he was living with his parents again – which Leandro wasn't, of course – but it wasn't clear why. He could be a little aggressive about money, that was true, but Leandro had never really known this privileged crowd, so put it down to playboy banter. Fernando was good to him, yes, and he had been this morning, before the meeting, in his way. The views from Unique were spectacular, Leandro remembered. The pool bathed in purple and orange light, the hill rising up towards Leandro's own house, the skyscrapers glowing golden as the sun slipped out of sight.

This had been something to enjoy, to aspire to, he thought now as he entered the park, and he could do it again.

Doing nothing in Recife was a stubborn position: it would have been easier for Leandro to get into something stupid. Down on the beaches to the north of the city centre, there were always plenty of tourists to fleece. Pale Europeans and flabby Americans spending their money on trinkets fashioned in the favela, a genuine piece of Afro-Brazilian culture. Sometimes more if they met the right michê, hustler. Better not to get involved, but hard when everyone he knew was doing it.

'You need to decide what you want to do,' his mother would say. 'Se Deus quiser, God willing, you'll find something. But you'll find nothing while you don't look.'

'But, Mãe, there is nothing to do. Why look?'

And she'd shake her head and tut. 'You're handsome and strong and intelligent. You could find work doing anything you want. Look at your sister: she works. This rice and beans don't come for free, you know.'

He dreamed of escape, not spending his life working all hours for a pittance and living in a hovel. But escape to what, to do what?

One day, he got his chance.

'Your grandmother in São Paulo has written to us,' his mother told him. 'She says you can go and stay with her until you find work.' She was sweeping the kitchen floor and didn't look up. 'I think you should go. You'll be whatever God makes you.'

São Paulo represented a vague possibility for Leandro: yet it was exactly what he was looking for. He was sixteen.

He never saw his mother again. He never *heard* from his sister again, until an envelope arrived with a cheque made out to him with her name on it. The proceeds from his mother's estate, he guessed. There was no note. It was her way of saying, he knew, ciao and good luck, you've made your choice. He moved out from his grandmother's house after that and found a small place in Paraíso. It wasn't much, no, but, hey, acknowledge it, why not, it was *his*, for now. It wasn't even strictly legal; the landlord had turned one small house into three much smaller houses, three corridors, really, each with three small rooms. But the rent wasn't too bad, and the landlord a decent enough bloke; he hadn't got the hang of exploitation, clearly,

Leandro thought. The whole point about cramming tenants into inadequate space was to charge them extortionate rent; he didn't have the heart for that, though, and his tenants respected him for it.

During those early nights in São Paulo, he wandered the streets around Avenida Paulista, searching out little corners from where he could watch the lights and people and follow the lines of traffic up the hills and winding down to Frei Caneca where he met other boys who'd buy him a drink.

It turned out there were ambitious boys like him from São Paulo, from the favelas down there, where he lived with his grandmother, Paraisópolis. She worked at the mosteiro, teaching young women how to be seamstresses. There were other classes too, on accounting, basic legal theory, which Leandro took. If you were prepared to do a boring job, for little money, there were opportunities. It was a question of hearing about them, which companies wanted to swell their diversity ranks a little, get a real-life favela assistant. He was prepared to do these things.

Like his mother said: he'd be whatever God made him.

The park was beautiful, serene. He crossed the lake at the bridge and stopped, leaned over to look at the fish that gathered beneath it. The no-fishing signs were clear on that, but he'd often wondered about who might pop back at night and pull a couple out. It couldn't be too hard, he thought, the fuckers were huge, and *stationary*. One way of feeding a family.

And there were plenty of families by the lake, feeding ducks, riding bikes, while rollerbladers and runners lapped them, muscled men with their tops off and Arnie-style Terminator shades, gym bunny women in tiny Lycra bending into yoga moves on the grass, teenage boys playing football, pretending not to look. The trees by the lake were low, their reach wide. Solitary men and women lay in their shade reading, one or two couples sat talking, one or two others lay toying with each other, one or two others underwent difficult conversations, it seemed to Leandro. He didn't have much experience in those areas, though, and he found himself looking a little too intently, as if he might learn something, as if he might have the experience himself one day if he did learn, and he had to check himself.

He knew the creepers and doggers wouldn't be there until after dark, and he didn't want anyone to think he'd arrived early.

The patchy green-brown of the grass seemed to skim the lake, continue into it, and the lake glistened in the sun, while the algae and mud sat thick, just below the water's surface. Leandro sat for a moment and the colour stretched out ahead of him, as far as he could see: ground, water, shrubbery, the trees on the far side, impenetrable, deep. He breathed it all in. He couldn't remember ever seeing so much of the same colour, so much green. And the quiet. The voices, the sport-chatter, the planes above, the water spurting from the fountains from the lake on the other side of the park, splashing heavily; all these were sounds you didn't normally hear in the city. They were there, of course they were, but they didn't exist in isolation, they blurred into one intense pitch of urban concentration. These noises, he realised as he let himself focus on one or another, emphasised the tranquillity of this place, of this *moment*.

He sat there for a long time, letting himself enjoy the minor success of the day, feeling *settled*. As the afternoon drew itself in, and the light and the green smudged in the thinning sun, he got up and headed home, mind closed off from the bustle of the main road at Brigadeiro for the fifteen minutes or so it took to get there.

Leandro's flat was untidy; he had been neglecting it. The meeting that day seemed to call for a new start or something, and he thought about what Fernando would think if he saw it like *this*. He looked at the kitchen, smiled and set about it as his grandmother had taught him.

Plates were stacked up, used pans black with fat on top of the stove. To get to the taps he had to empty the sink. He put the plates together, one on top of the other in descending size, and piled the pans on the other side of the sink. In the bottom of one, charred beans. He ran in some cold water and detergent until the smell subsided. He left it to soak. The plates had not been rinsed and food had hardened on them. He had to scrub a dirty, smudged rainbow left by eggs, beans and barbecue sauce clean with a wire brush. He placed the plates on the rack to the right of the sink to dry and worked his way through the pans. He boiled water to help shift the more stubborn stains, and scoured them clean. They used to be non-stick, but misuse had left them scratched, lines of silver marked out rough diagonal patterns in black. The glasses were next. He rinsed them and lathered up a cloth in detergent and ran it inside and outside the glasses. He rinsed them again and placed them on a tea towel to the side of the drying rack. The cutlery was last. Smeared with stains, he used the scouring brush to wipe them clean, but had to pick off with his fingernails the bits of food that the brush wouldn't shift. He left them standing in a plastic cup to dry.

He found another towel and dried the clean plates, pans and cutlery. He placed them neatly back in cupboards above and below the sink. A sense of normality returned, of order and cleanliness. He looked down at the lino floor. It was scuffed through overuse and there were dark patches of dirt that could never be cleaned. He went into the service area and found his cleaning products and a bucket and mop. He mixed detergent with water and poured a little of it onto the floor, the lighter marks vanishing at the touch of the mop, washed away like footprints in the sand. He pushed it back and forth from left to right, bending into each pass, stretching the tired muscles in his back. After two circuits of the floor, it was as clean as he could get it and he tipped the water down the sink.

He looked around him and smiled at his work, at his day.

Delegacia

15 October, late morning

Leme and Lisboa slouched in broken chairs in their dingy, shit-can office. The window was thick with dust. The light bulb was naked. The cables from their computer wound in clumps to the floor between them. They wore mid-price suits and drank filtered coffee from plastic cups.

Lisboa scratched at his chin and pulled at his crotch.

'Kid Leandro's been dead twenty-four hours tops, they reckon,' he said. 'Bread knife. Blunt, probably. Lacerations fit the type. Find one in any home.'

'Except his.'

'Yeah. True. No sign of it.'

'Family?'

'Strange one. The house is in the same name as his. Well, as in his Carteira, so we assume family home, right? But we can't find a record of anyone. Being checked downstairs in admin right now. They could be dead. They could have dropped off the system. Either way, looks like he was there alone. At least until twenty-four hours ago.'

'Explains the fucking state of it.'

'Maybe. Kid's supposed to be good though, sabe, responsible. One of those who took things seriously, tried to make something from nothing, entendeu?'

'How d'you know that?'

'Employer. We spoke to his boss, informed him. There was no one else to tell.'

'You let on it's suspicious?'

Lisboa gave Leme a pointed look. Leme had seen it before and smiled. 'I told him there'd been an accident and this was routine. I asked about him out of politeness. To make fucking conversation, entendeu? You know.'

Leme smirked. He did know.

Lisboa went on. 'He'd been there eight months. A clerk. Office boy. Running errands. Like I said, good kid.'

'How'd they take it?'

'Pretty fucking well, actually. Not like the kid was mates with any of them. You see him out drinking with those cunts in Itaim on a Friday night? Not fucking likely. You saw the Carteira. He was a cheap maid in a cheaper suit.'

'What's your point?'

'They'll pull another mixed-race boy out of poverty in a second. Filling quotas or some shit. *Doing good*, right?'

Leme knew about this. Renata had worked pro bono in the favela, legal aid helping the disenfranchised.

The big firms employed a couple of underprivileged kids to fetch coffee and do some photocopying to keep pressure groups sweet.

The kid probably helped out twenty or more lawyers on a daily basis, and Leme bet not one of them would be able to pick him out of a line.

He hoped Antonia didn't know him. More than that, he hoped the kid had never helped her so she'd have a reason not to recognise him.

'What about fingerprints?'

'Coming soon. Guy said there are definitely several sets, but no immediate matches.'

Leme nodded. 'And Fernando?'

'Addresses at his office and home. I was waiting for you.'

'Good.'

They sat in silence and swivelled on their broken chairs. Leme dumped half his coffee in the bin.

Leme was pleased Lisboa popped the social injustice angle.

'Ellie's editor said that Leandro was her contact for a story and that he was verifiable. It doesn't really sound like it though. Fetching coffee. Unless…'

'Unless he was doing something he shouldn't. Or rubbernecking like a good favela boy, trying to do the right thing.'

'Então.'

'And Ellie?'

'Nothing yet. Remember, she's not a suspect. I'm going to her place now. You sit tight and wait for anything they dig up downstairs.'

'Suits me.'

'We'll talk to Fernando together, maybe tonight, certo?'

'Terrific,' Lisboa said. 'I can't wait.'

Leme was out the door, keying Antonia's number into his phone. He'd worked out a way to ask her if she knew this Fernando without giving anything away. He was glad he'd thought it through. She was too smart not to spot something was up.

He'd made that mistake before.

Morumbi

Three months earlier

'You're doing very well so far.'

'It's not my first time.'

Ellie smiled at Fernando and pushed her knee against his under the table. They were in a restaurant in Morumbi, the Casa da Fazenda, close to where Fernando lived. It was his idea. He picked her up from her apartment in Pinheiros. She'd not been in São Paulo long. And an invitation to the Casa da Fazenda, Fernando had told her, was quite something.

'Tonight, I'm taking you out of this awful place,' he said into the intercom when he came to pick her up.

'Cheeky bastard,' Ellie replied. 'You should think yourself lucky if you ever get invited inside, young man.'

She didn't buzz him in. Instead, she cut off Fernando's laughter by slamming down the intercom phone. She checked her appearance in the lift mirror. In heels, her dress came down to just above her knees. There was a split that showed off her thighs. She hoped it would be worth it.

Pulling into the restaurant car park, the air seemed thinner, fresher. Thick vegetation blocked the view of the traffic jam they had just escaped, grinding its way down towards the river one way and the Paraisópolis favela the other. They walked hand in hand, which felt grown-up, somehow appropriate given the way Fernando had opened the passenger door for her and nodded his thanks to the valet, leaving the keys in the ignition. Walking hand in hand seemed the done thing, Ellie thought, as if your treatment at the restaurant depended on your being in a couple, that the requisite attention at a high-end place like this would not be lavished on you if you were just friends. If a man takes you to the Casa da Fazenda, the atmosphere seemed to say, then you'd better make sure you do him proud, that you, as his guest, match up. She smiled at the receptionist. Receptionist? She laughed. In a *restaurant*?

The dining room was all colonial elegance and high wooden-slatted ceilings. The maitre d' invited them to take a quick turn around the gardens. The air, Ellie realised, really *was* fresher: slap bang in the middle of the Morumbi maze. The favela not far below. The restaurant was on top of the hill; Fernando had pointed out the markings on the stone pillars on the road a little before they arrived that marked the entrance to the old farmhouse. It had certainly changed, she could see that. Gentrification makes everything the same, she thought, the world over. There's a clever line she could use one day.

'Twenty, twenty-five years ago, this was all greenery,' he told her. 'Before you were born,' he smiled – flirtatious.

Ellie raised her eyebrows, mock-stern. 'I'm twenty-*three*, Fernando.'

He ignored her. 'And this was the farmhouse, hence Casa da Fazenda. It was all run from up here. Now though, it's all prime real estate. It's why I live down the road. For now, there's a bit more space. There won't be for much longer.'

Ellie listened politely. She felt like a guest, which, in a sense, she was, and it wasn't her scene. Ah, leave it, ne? The kid's a good kid; and I came, didn't I? What's the harm in learning something? she thought, with only a sliver of irony.

In the gardens there was a sort of cave with peculiarities and original memorabilia from the farm, an ox's yoke, dusty jars with faded labels, thick, ridged paintings of brightly coloured parrots. Candles flickered in the dusk and couples clung to each other. Not them though, not yet.

'Not your first time?' Fernando asked.

Oh, Ellie thought, was that a hint of jealousy? Jealousy or suspicion, though really what was the difference at this stage?

'Not the first time a man has tried to impress me,' she said.

Fernando smiled, gave a gentle, self-assured laugh that Ellie liked. 'Is it working?' he asked.

'I'll let you know after the main course.'

After two months in São Paulo Ellie had decided to take matters into her own hands. Until then her social life had involved drinking with her colleagues in neighbourhood bars and being hit on by Brazilian men who seemed to think that foreign women ought to be grateful for their advances, and were indignant and rude if rebuffed.

Apparently, sending a waiter over with their phone number written on a napkin was on its own enough to invite first a drink and conversation, then kissing, and then sex, often in one of the expensive motels in the centre, as the men, though arrogant and entitled, normally lived with their parents, on the assumption that it made little sense to sacrifice their mothers' attention and their maids' cooking and cleaning until they had found themselves a satisfactory wife to take over.

Ellie quickly became notorious in a number of the magazine staffs' local bars for rudeness and causing indignation.

She decided to talk to her editor, Elizabeth. Elizabeth, with her bosom and her bum, her long red hair, her pale freckled skin, her porcelain, dappled thighs that peeked out now and then when she crossed her legs, dressed in her pencil skirts; Ellie reckoned she must have some idea about how to negotiate this depressing scene. A woman who looked like that was a novelty; and Ellie found out very fast that novelties were in demand. For short-term use, at least.

They went for a drink in a bar where Ellie was sure some prick cocksman in a pastel-coloured polo shirt and shiny shoes would send over his number. And one did. And he really *was* a prick, flicking his hand in the air and tutting in distaste when Ellie sipped the drink he sent over but sent *him* away.

She took her chance. 'How do you ever learn to deal with this?' she asked.

Elizabeth thinned her lips into a smile, and narrowed her eyes. 'There are ways.' She paused. 'Depends on what you're looking for, I suppose. What are you looking for?'

'Some respect, I think. But some fun, too. I'm here to work, of course. But I do like going out with men. An invigorating social life is important to me. Nothing wrong with that, is there?'

'Nothing at all.'

'But I don't like being *approached*, especially.'

Elizabeth nodded. 'Not an easy balance. You'll either have to start going to much more expensive places than this.' She let the sentence hang as the waiter dumped fresh glasses of chopp in front of them.

'Or?'

Elizabeth smiled. 'I can let you in on a secret.'

And that was how Ellie learned about Single Gringa. 'Really?' she said. 'Single Gringa? Fuck me, that doesn't sound very classy. Not something,' she added, 'I would associate with you, Elizabeth.'

'Here.' Elizabeth pushed a card across the table. 'Trust me.'

It was a members only website, access to which was secured only after a consultation – based on the mandatory recommendation from a current member, Elizabeth – and then the payment of a monthly subscription of several hundred reais. The website was designed to arrange meetings for sophisticated individuals, and to cater principally to foreign women. It was not, however, a form of escorting; profiles were readily accessible and arrangements were made via private messages on a mutual and reciprocal basis. The difference between this and other dating websites was that the woman always initiated the in-person meeting, the men couldn't ask you out. Ellie liked this.

'Don't tell anyone I recommended you,' Elizabeth had said to her once her consultation was arranged. 'In fact, don't tell anyone, even the men you meet. It always runs much smoother if the whole apparatus appears invisible, like a trapeze artist's safety wires. The illusion of spontaneity is a powerful one,' she mused.

The waiter at the Casa da Fazenda simpered and smiled.

Fernando made a big show of letting Ellie choose the wine.

'What a feminist,' she said to the waiter, who laughed.

She picked something reassuringly expensive.

'Chin-chin,' she said to Fernando when the wine arrived and she didn't bother to taste it.

But Ellie hadn't told Elizabeth everything. She'd signed up to a host of dating websites already – it was just that she wasn't using them solely for dates. She didn't want to meet just any guy; she wanted to meet someone who could help her get access to the sorts of stories she wanted to write. Two months of fannying about with the arts listings and doing endless and tiresome copy editing of the Brazilian writers' English was quite enough. She hadn't been pretending when she'd told Elizabeth in her interview on Skype that she wanted to be an investigative journalist. And within weeks of arriving in São Paulo she understood that contacts were essential if she wanted to learn anything about how this city worked. And then she met Fernando on Single Gringa. He was a lawyer – hotshot, he made out, cash and suits, fine wine, et cetera. She'd made all the jokes: another lawyer? Oh thank *God* – but she wanted to go out with him to find out quite what he did.

And he was attractive. And eager to please, he *liked* her. And she had fun with him. And he'd started to tell her about this business in Cracolândia, and it was interesting, and she found his interest in it interesting. This is why she was here: to engage in the place. It was a lot more fun than sitting in her condominium.

'How was your main course?' Fernando asked, as they drank excellent coffee and disgusting brandy, which Ellie found she could barely swallow.

'Impressive,' she said.

Fernando smiled and signalled for the bill.

Later, Fernando found himself lucky enough to be invited into Ellie's apartment. She let him spend the night, sleep next to her, afterwards. She had surprised herself, a little, by doing that. It wasn't often she'd allow that intimacy; there had been times, in the past, when she'd pretended she had to get home to change her contact lenses. There'd never been anything wrong with her eyes. The next morning he put her in touch with a young intern at Zarzur Cabral called Leandro Bastos. Not long after, Leandro received an email from Ellie. They would meet; he would be her contact. He would, at some point soon, take her into Cracolândia.

Out for dinner with Fernando a month or so after the Casa da Fazenda, Ellie reflected that this, this arrangement, this *understanding* she had secured, was, in her experience, always so much easier with men.

Itaim Bibi, Offices of Zarzur Cabral

15 October, lunchtime

It happened when Leme least expected it. Her voice. It would start like a detuned radio coming into focus. Then it was unmistakeably Renata. His wife, Renata.

Normally some pearl of fucking wisdom or other.

The kind of half-baked, clever-clever bullshit that used to drive him crazy.

Quietly, but it did drive him fucking mad.

But these pearls of wisdom, these little moments of theory, of *analysis*, made sense now.

What a fucking surprise: course they did.

And now here was her voice as he sat in his car outside Fernando's office.

She was saying. 'Patience. Something you've never had. So wound up about nothing problems, imagine what you'd be like with a *real* problem. Ne? Imagine. There *are* no problems.'

Yeah, Leme thought. He was finding that out now she was gone.

As he'd left his office he'd keyed in the number for Antonia's office. Antonia didn't often take personal calls on her mobile at work. Antonia didn't like to have the natural lines of work and home blurred. She was very particular about that.

But as Leme stepped into the lift at the delegacia and a receptionist answered 'Zarzur Cabral?', on an impulse he'd asked to speak to Fernando Melo.

As he was patched through, he hung up.

He called back.

'Sorry, the line dropped. Fernando Melo. Is he in?'

'Yes, sorry. He is. I'll try again.'

Again Leme hung up. He made a decision. He drove across town to the office where his girlfriend worked with the only lead he had in a murder investigation and possibly a missing person. He didn't feel too good about this.

He sat in his car over the road from the office. He looked up at the glass-fronted building, a corporate behemoth, a sculpture, like an offering to some capitalist god.

'The glass is the only transparent thing in there,' Antonia had said to him once.

He dialled the number for reception again. 'Fernando Melo, por favor.'

'Ah, he's actually just on his way out of the office for a meeting,' the receptionist said.

Leme said, 'Thanks,' and hung up.

Result, maybe. Leme sat tight – gambled.

He saw Fernando leave the office by the front door and climb into a white taxi. The taxi pulled out and headed down the road towards the Itaim end of Juscelino Kubitschek. Leme followed. The taxi driver's window was open and his arm hung out of it. He was dawdling, little urgency. Easy work, Leme thought.

They went down the avenue and turned right onto Faria Lima. It was mid-morning, almost lunch, and the roads were heating up, busy.

Leme stayed three or four cars back. Not that he was worried about Fernando making him.

And the taxista clearly didn't give a fuck.

They crawled past the Sports Clube de Pinheiros and then Shopping Iguatemi. Twin reminders. *Again*. What you don't have:

An exclusive membership and money to spend on luxury goods.

The taxi turned right onto Gabriel, then left, almost immediately. Leme let him get slightly ahead. He wriggled through the backstreets, crossed Rebouças, and out onto Rua dos Pinheiros. The cab turned right, went up towards Paulista for a hundred yards and then indicated left.

Leme sat. He let it marinate a moment.

And that's when he realised where Fernando was going.

Leme was parked on the other side of the road from Ellie's condominium building. He watched as Fernando waved at the porteiro. The porteiro let him in. The porteiro came out from his booth. The porteiro slapped hands with Fernando. Playboy bullshit. Fernando a playboy then? No, Leme thought. False-friendly charm. Make the staff feel wanted. They chatted for a short time. They slapped hands again and Fernando headed off towards the lifts. Leme opened his door and walked across the road.

The porteiro didn't come out from his booth when Leme buzzed.

'Yeah?' he said.

'I can't hear you,' Leme said into the intercom – quietly.

'What?'

'I can't hear you.'

There was tinny radio music in the background.

'What? Who is this?'

'Just fucking come outside.'

'Why should I?'

Leme turned to the camera.

He made a face that said: drug dealer or cop.

Leme heard the radio being switched off.

The porteiro stepped out from the booth.

'Então?' he said.

Leme nodded towards the lifts. 'That guy live here?'

The porteiro smiled. 'Why should I tell you?'

Leme gave him the look again. It said: there's an easier way, cocksucker.

'OK,' the porteiro said. 'I know you know he doesn't live here. What do you need to know?'

'You seem friendly with him.'

'Então?'

Leme smiled, looked away. 'What is it with you fucking guys?' he said. 'This cunt paying you? No. Think his fucking girlfriend gives a fuck about you?'

He shook his head.

Another look: make it easier.

'You a cop?'

Leme raised his eyebrows. 'Settle down. And talk. I'm guessing he'll be back pretty soon.'

'OK, OK. Relaxa, ne? Nem vem, cara.'

Leme eyebrow-raised him. He shot him a look: patience is limited.

The porteiro took a deep breath. 'He doesn't live here, which you know. He's dating an English chick who does. Been here a bunch of times. Nice guy. Her name's Ellie. Journalist or something. Very nice girl.'

'She here?'

'No. Staying with Fernando, that's his name, for a few days. He's just picking up a few things for her. That enough?'

Leme nodded. He turned and walked back to his car. The porteiro clicked his tongue against his teeth and muttered something Leme didn't catch.

He started the car and drove quickly around the block. He hung back a little so that the porteiro wouldn't see him. He waited for Fernando to leave the building.

He could grab him now, bring him in, but on what cause? The cunt was a lawyer, and he had nothing. Yet. Best see where the little fuck goes next.

Fernando went through the two gates with barely a look at the porteiro. He was carrying a small sports bag. He turned left onto Rua dos Pinheiros.

Leme eased the car forward. Fernando hailed a cab and Leme followed.

The cab headed up Pinheiros and looped back onto Rebouças.

Leme followed.

They wriggled again through Jardim Paulistano and back onto Faria Lima.

Leme followed. He lit a cigarette.

He hung four cars back. Easy again.

Another lazy taxista.

They drove past Shopping Iguatemi and Clube Pinheiros.

Leme laughed:

He knew where they were going.

Leme parked in the same spot he'd been in earlier:

Outside the offices of Zarzur Cabral.

Fernando took his phone from his pocket and made a call. He turned a couple of circles as he spoke. Leme remembered Ellie's phone in his bag. No sound came from it. Fernando wasn't calling her.

Fernando holstered the mobile phone and waited outside.

Leme watched.

Fernando looked over his shoulder.

Leme sank back into his seat.

The front door of the office revolved. A woman came out. She was hidden by a pillar, and then by Fernando.

Fernando handed her the sports bag and they talked briefly.

Fernando jerked his thumb towards where Leme was parked –

Leme sank further back.

Fernando went inside.

Leme's view of the woman was unobstructed –

She leaned towards where Leme was parked.

The woman frowned. She turned and went back inside.

Fuck, Leme thought.

The woman? Antonia –

Had she seen him?

He sat tight. Ran it: bringing in Fernando now…

A minute or two later his phone buzzed, beeped –

Hey. How are you? xx

Antonia. She'd seen him.

Fuck.

Leme ducked further down. Did she see him? Box it. Doesn't matter a fuck now.

Fernando slouched away, middle-class rudeboy limp, hands swinging low.

Prick.

Antonia waved a large security guy over. He got into Fernando's taxi – passenger seat. She got in the back.

The taxi moved off. Headed towards the river, then pulled round right, threaded its way into Itaim, and then left onto Faria Lima towards Clube Pinheiros and Shopping Iguatemi. If he knew Antonia, he knew where she was going on a lunch break.

The taxi skipped two lanes, beeping, one hand on the wheel and the other out the window, directing.

Flat palm means: stop. Index-finger wag means: oh no you don't, son.

Arrowed up the ramp entrance of the Shopping, tyres squealing round the tight bends.

Show off, Leme thought.

He was more circumspect, kept a little distance. He figured where they'd park; didn't take Sherlock Holmes to unpuzzle that particular headscratcher. Valet. For some, if it don't have valet parking, it don't exist. Antonia had her moments of that creed, Leme sure knew. Some kid opens your door for you and you're Jackie fucking Onassis.

This was the second time he'd been to Shopping Iguatemi in a couple of years. The posh Shopping. A year before he'd witnessed that Rolezinho fad – an invading swarm of hundreds of kids, all over the mall, scaring the customers with an anarchic glee. Leme had spent a few minutes, head spinning, stomach churning, in a sportswear shop, assistants looking at him like he was some alien life form, an old man gasping for air, while disenfranchised teenagers briefly ran riot, dancing and singing and chucking beer cans about the pristine monument to high-level consumerism that was this mall. With hindsight, he was glad he'd witnessed it, actually. There was something liberating, satisfying, about low-level protest. It was mischievous and yet had a serious point: these kids were literally being excluded from parts of their own city, based on how they looked. Oh, don't be soft: based on their skin colour.

What other response was there?

The rich women tottering about on heels, in tight $1,000 jeans from Miami, unbalanced by Botox and tit jobs, were worth more – *literally*, in terms of investment in their physique, what they wore – than these kids' families earned in a year.

Yep, Leme admired the fad, understood it.

But it was over now, basically. The malls upped security; military police outside some of them. Those machine guns quite a deterrent to low-level protest, the kids found out. Way outside remit, but it didn't take much to work out how the militars were persuaded to help. Swaggering back to work with wet palms and bulging back pockets: textbook.

Leme hung back while Antonia and her cão de guarda got out of the cab and headed to the lift. They split the lifts here, Leme remembered: ground floor one side and minus one the other. They went minus one. Easy. There's a nail salon down there.

Makes sense: when you live with a bird, you get to know her manicure habits.

Leme parked up quiet, away from the valet area, and jumped the lift.

He went slow: turning circles, window-shopping. It would have appeared dead on, he thought, to your casual observer. Except he never checked what was in the fucking window until he was right up against it. Then again, he always had an excuse to be looking at a gold bracelet, matching luggage, string-thin underwear, sorry, *lingerie*.

And his excuse was right *there*.

There she was. Nail salon. Boom.

Leme hung back.

Sports bag, yes. Does she have it? What's in it?

He found a spot in the lower-level food court. He had a view of the salon and was hidden behind an impressively large, fake plant. Antonia was stretched out in the classic entitled manicure/pedicure pose: left arm bent at the elbow, hand at her ear, speaking on the phone; right arm lazily extended, hand tended to by a diligent nail technician who said nothing.

Just got on with her tending.

Legs draped, shoes off, bare feet, two other technicians, tending.
Hair hanging back behind her chair: swinging, lustrous.
Clearly laughing with whoever she was talking to.
She was gorgeous.
Looked like fun.
No sign of the bodyguard. Maybe getting his hair done.
Leme chewed his nails. His own technician.
This wasn't right. Not funny any more –
Not right.
He loved Antonia. He should leave this –
Go home.
He had to clear his head.
He was meeting Antonia at her apartment that evening –
Arranged: not some bullshit suspicion-impulse.

Leaked Document Record: Land deal – Cracolândia
Recipient: Carneiro
Subject: Transition of residents in Cracolândia

From the office of the Secretario de Obras

1. Confirmation that with each satisfactory resident transition a percentage of the legal fees ['the compensation'] will be transferred to Zarzur Cabral, as a bonus, reliant on numbers-based success
2. That the office of the Secretario de Obras will demonstrate through its accounts the legality of 'the compensation'
3. That Zarzur Cabral will ensure that said compensation is in line with the legal fees agreed, as well as the final sum as confirmed with the landowner as represented by Zarzur Cabral

Signed: The recipient.

Itaim Bibi, Offices of Zarzur Cabral

Two months earlier

Antonia sat at her desk and wondered how the hell the city got into this whole land/home ownership palaver. How did a couple of foreign investors become key to this whole absurd land deal? Jesus – Brazilians and Europeans: what a sham. The rich Brasileiros are so fucking deferential to old world style – even the fucking teenage old world of fucking Miami – and yet they then slag off any patronising that the old world *rightly* hands back. Ah, Brasil, how quaint you are with your money and technology and your cute little slums that house the staff who work in your homes, at your bidding, of course, as you're giving jobs to the disenfranchised, yes, how cute and quaint your third world ideas about philanthropy are, meus queridos … Porra, she thought, and laughed – grimly.

She looked at the legal documents that outlined the land ownership details of the area now known as Cracolândia. It was a straightforward sort of capitalist history.

A bunch of British – well, Scottish, to be, you know, *fair*; Antonia knows how precious these Brits, *Scottish*, can be – came over to build the railways in the late nineteenth century. She knew the story, she'd learnt all this at the British school, that some *chap* called James – Jock, ha! – Brownlees had brought expertise and materials to put together some bullshit transport scheme that hadn't exactly survived in the modern Brasil. And there were two paths for those who stayed: buy up a bit of land, fuck off home and then let the natives build on it and secure a tidy, clean little profit as the city and state grew and grew, or stay and hang out, found that ridiculous Clube das Inglesas, SPAC, and live an easy life. She'd been there: you can play – what was the name of those childish, idiotic pursuits? *Bowls*? – that was it, *bowls*, and fucking croquet. And take tea at three in the afternoon. Gosh. How civilised. Thanks, Old World. Thank you so much for bringing us that.

She looked at the names of the English families they represented at Zarzur Cabral. No, she thought, they're not – *he's* not – key to this deal: he just wants it done. Which means her boss does. Which means she does. Which means young Leandro and playboy Fernando need to get their work done.

She'd make sure they fucking did, she thought.

Fernando's House

Four months earlier

Fernando studied the computer. This whole business was costing him more money that he would have liked, and one thing he didn't have was money. He hoped it'd be worth it, he needed something positive in his life, a distraction. He felt he was getting older, and things were getting away from him, and that time was like money, in the sense that it was running out.

When he had gone for the interview, the lady who sat across from him – assessing him, checking his particulars – had been surprised.

'You don't look like the sort of man who needs to use a dating service,' she said.

He'd enjoyed that, that brief victory. 'I gather what you offer is a little more than that.'

The woman smiled, pleased with his answer, as if she had been testing him. She looked at the papers on her desk. 'Very well. Ta tudo em ordem. You can be up and running in a few hours. Go live, as it were.' She smiled again.

'Ótimo.' Fernando stood. 'Muito obrigado.'

They shook hands. As Fernando moved to the door, the woman said, 'Discretion is the only rule we have. Very important though, entendeu?'

Fernando nodded. 'Of course.'

He'd looked for a week before he found someone, someone he liked the look of.

He examined her profile. She was the right age, she worked in journalism. She appeared to be just the right mix of serious and fun. Fernando was convinced that she would be looking for something more than a few dates; she wanted to get ahead. And Fernando approved of her photo, which was important. Approved? She was pretty hot. She might be a gringa, but, Fernando reasoned, if she were as elegant and discerning as she seemed, then that would be exciting, *and* a novelty. He was getting ahead of himself, he knew that, but he needed this excitement. Everything else was too serious, too frightening, really. The magazine she worked for had an international audience Fernando was keen to hear more about. That was interesting.

He followed the Single Gringa playbook. He indicated interest – all that's allowed – and sat tight. His profile: heavy-hitting cuntman, the kind of guy he *appeared* to be, at least. In no time she sent him a message. He waited two days and replied, and they arranged to meet.

Textbook.

The key, Fernando told himself again and again, was not to get carried away. Easy come, easy go, as his friends told him, often enough, was what got the girl.

Fernando's House

15 October, early afternoon

Leme didn't dwell on what he'd seen. He put it to one side. He was going round to Antonia's later that evening. He hoped the bag might be there. That was all he would think about.

He was getting better at this:

Compartmentalisation.

It was something he had worked on since Renata. It would have been impossible to do anything if he hadn't developed the capacity for it.

He rang Lisboa.

'I need Fernando's home address.'

'You going there now?'

'Yeah. I'm sparing you that, at least. Send it over.'

'Certo. Ta no caminho.'

Leme's phone beeped with the address.

Lisboa said, 'I'm going back to the scene. Forensics are finishing up for the day. See if there's anything new.'

'OK.'

'Don't forget, Mario, this is the priority, porra. For now. *Not* the girl, entendeu?'

'OK.'

'I'm serious. She's not missing yet, sabe? Not until there's a notification.'

'OK.'

'I'll call you later.'

'OK.'

Leme sat in his car outside Fernando's house.

It was a house, not an apartment. This surprised Leme. Then he realised that Fernando lived with his parents.

It was early afternoon, siesta time. Maid outside watering the plants. Gardener digging up earth around the gates. Mother on the sofa with a wet flannel on her forehead, no doubt. Lunch hangover.

The house was low-rise but spread wide. Big enough for Ellie to be in there unnoticed. Leme needed to get inside. Leme needed a cover story. It was hot and still and oppressive outside. Too hot to be too suspicious of anyone –

No one tries it on, on an afternoon like this. Leme dug around in his glove compartment. He found the badge for a private security company that looked after rich people's houses. He found the court order legalisation document that showed he was legitimate. He found the business card with his own mobile phone number on it. He got out of the car and walked a little way down the road. He stopped close to a security booth. The old man inside was fast asleep, slumped against the desk, the radio on. The radio on – loud.

Leme took out his phone and filmed the scene for thirty seconds.

He rapped against the window. The old man came to with a start. He rubbed his eyes and looked at Leme.

'Fuck do you want?' he said, voice thick with sleep.

Leme pressed play. He pushed his phone against the glass.

The old man nodded. 'Like I said,' he said.

Leme said, 'What's the name of the company you work for?'

'Name of the guy that owns it: Resende Security.'

'OK. You're going to come with me to the house down the road, number thirty-two. A kid lives there called Fernando Melo. Know him?'

The old man glared. He shook his head.

Leme rapped on the window, harder this time. He said, 'I'm shylocking this, cocksucker, entendeu? We're going to knock on the door and you're going to tell the maid that I'm from a company that works with yours.' Leme showed him the badge and documents. 'Then you're going to tell the maid to get the lady of the house so that we can have a few words with her.'

Leme took his Polícia Civil badge from his back pocket. He showed it to the old man.

'Then you're going to stand there and say nothing. And if you do say anything – today, or whenever – you'll lose your job and never get another one. Entendeu?'

The old man nodded.

'Então, porra. Vamos,' Leme said.

Fernando's mother offered them both coffee. Leme said, why not? Fernando's maid brought them two small cups. They drank them standing up around the kitchen table.

Fernando's mother said, 'So, Sr. Leme, what would you like to see exactly?'

'This is just routine,' Leme said. He waved his hand. 'We're just getting to know the area properly. We like to see inside the houses, just to know the layout. Gives us an edge should anything happen, you know?'

Leme gave Fernando's mother a reassuring smile.

'No problem,' she smiled back. 'It's good to know, actually.'

They walked through to the main living room.

There was a set of sliding doors that opened onto a deck area, just beyond which was a small swimming pool. At the far end of the garden, a barbecue had been dug into the brick wall. Leme feigned interest.

'Be useful to see the perimeter of the property,' he said, indicating outside.

'Of course.'

They walked alongside the pool.

Leme looked up.

A helicopter buzzed overhead. It flickered in and out of cloud thickened by pollution. It landed, wobbling, like a boat anchored in rough seas, on a building on Faria Lima.

'Who else lives here?' Leme asked.

'My husband and I, our son Fernando, and the maid, Dona Elena. There are two spare bedrooms.' She pointed at the back of the house. 'I'll show them to you when we get back inside.'

Leme looked at the old security guard. He was implacable.

'Anyone staying with you at the moment?'

'No.' Fernando's mother smiled. 'Just the family. It's nice. Fernando was living with a friend, but … well, he had to come home for a bit.'

Leme nodded. Leme made an educated guess. 'Expensive renting in São Paulo, nowadays, ne?'

Fernando's mother flashed him a nervous smile. 'Yes, that's very true.'

Bingo, Leme thought.

Fernando's mother said, 'Much harder for this generation, you know, in a way.'

Leme coughed in agreement.

Fernando's mother continued, 'Even with a good job it's hard. But, you know, it's lovely to have him around. He'll be back on his feet soon enough.'

Leme smiled. 'Of course he will.'

So Fernando needs money, Leme thought. OK.

'Can we see the rooms inside?' he asked.

They went through every room in the house. Ellie wasn't there. There was no sign of her. Leme made sure to examine all of the en suite bathrooms, nosed around in Fernando's bedroom.

Nothing.

He thanked Fernando's mother and left with the old security guard.

They walked back to the booth.

'You ever see a young English woman go into the house?' Leme asked.

The guard shook his head.

Leme said, 'I guess that doesn't mean much though.'

The guard opened the door to the booth. He looked defeated.

'Don't worry,' Leme told him. 'This is between you and me.' He closed the door firmly. 'Right?'

The guard nodded.

Leme went back to his car. Fernando had lied to Ellie's porteiro. Fernando needed money. Fernando had led Ellie – and Leme – to a dead body. The dead body was a colleague of Fernando's. Ellie was using Fernando to get information for a story on Cracolândia. Ellie was missing.

Porra.

Leme figured some odds. He needed more on who might have been to Leandro's house in the last few days. He needed more on what exactly Leandro had been doing for Ellie.

He called Lisboa.

'Nothing doing until the morning,' Lisboa told him. 'There'll be a briefing first thing. Make sure you're at it, certo?'

Leme hung up.

He checked the time.

Couple hours before meeting Antonia.

There was just about enough time to try Ellie at one more place.

Leme first played tennis as a boy. He didn't take it seriously until he was in his late-twenties. His attraction to it wasn't surprising. Repetition. Routines. Calmness and aggression. An idea of improvement. No tangible aim. Just get better. A goal that's impossible to measure. Hopeless, really. It was the perfect sport.

'Shit or get out of the woods.' That was what Leme's coach always told him.

'You've got all the shots, Mario,' he'd say. 'You're just too indecisive. No killer instinct.'

Leme had started the coaching after Renata. Leme was sick of playing weekends with the men in his condominium. Passive-aggressive doubles with men who were never sure when to encourage him. When to chastise him. It was awkward. And Leme was sick of the awkwardness. Let them say what they want, he thought. But they never did. Too busy checking for when the clock hit midday so they could start on the beers. Leme didn't need that. Leme had enough influences.

He had the shots in the tank –

He could goose a sliced backhand, fishtail a clever angle at the net.

Leme needed discipline. Not a rigged game. That was why he went to the club.

It was a swank club, for public courts. Full of young, king-in-the-belly cunts who dressed right in Nike and Adidas and holstered three racquets each.

Peacocking about with their caps turned back on their heads.

The odd fat ex-pro lumbering about the court with a fag on, dinking and swerving and chipping and laughing at the executive finance guy dressed to the Lycra nines running about after the ball, never too close to it. The executive squaring things afterwards over a drink and a sharp reminder of who was developing the high-rise towers creeping up either side of the diamond-wire meshing. What sort of cash the ex-pro was taking off him. Where it came from. Banter. Enchendo saco. Keep the old soak former champion in check.

Leme loved the atmosphere there. Known, but not known.

Bit of peace, bit of rest.

Thirty, forty cross-court, down-the-line forehands –
Thirty, forty top-spin second serves kicked out wide –
Thirty, forty split-feet volleys.

Repetition. Routines. Calmness and aggression. Three times a week.

Leme doodled on a pad at the desk waiting for the manager. Drawing ever-decreasing circles. Putting a line through them.

'E ai, meu,' the manager said. 'Tudo bem?'

'Ah, you know, it is what it is, all good, ne?'

'Uh-huh. Can I do for you?'

Leme scrunched the paper. Leme pushed the pen across the desk. 'My friend, the English girl. I play with her time to time.'

'Yeah, I know her.'

'She here today?'

The manager shook his head, waggled his finger and clicked his tongue against his teeth, twice. 'Nuh-uh.'

'When she last in?'

'Few days. You playing today? Looked good last week, porra.'

Leme smiled but ignored this. 'She doesn't have a lesson today? We sometimes have a hit after.'

It was Leme that had introduced Ellie to the place.

'I need to do some, like, exercise?' she'd said. 'But, you know, something befitting a classy girl like me. Entendeu? Running is boring. Gym bunnies make me want to scratch their eyes out. Swimming is for wet fish.'

Leme laughed. 'Tennis?'

'You imagining me in a tank top and a short white skirt?' she said. 'Pervert.'

Leme smiled. 'I know just the place.'

He set her up with his coach. 'It's like circuit training for discerning types,' Leme said, with a hint of irony. 'Right-thinking, entendeu?'

It turned out Ellie was pretty fucking good. Ex-county, whatever the fuck that meant, and went for it, really stuck her foot in the breadfruit.

Ellie jumped down the throat of anything short. Ellie worked up a good sweat at least twice a week. She was there for the same reasons he was.

When you lose your wife you have to keep doing. It doesn't matter what, just keep doing.

The manager checked the schedule. 'She moved the lesson to yesterday, actually.'

Leme nodded. 'You see her?'

'Funny thing,' the manager said. 'A young, good-looking guy took her lesson. She called in to sort it couple hours before.'

'He been here before?'

'No.' The manager paused. He smiled, raised his eyebrows. 'You jealous or something?'

Leme feigned embarrassment. Gave him a look that said: *dude*.

'No, never seen him before. He was just starting out,' he said. 'Friend of Ellie's. She'd taken pity on him apparently.'

'He any good?'

'Nope.' The manager laughed. 'You've got nothing to worry about.'

Leme laughed, acted cool. 'Get his name?'

'Yeah, think so. Wait, it's here.'

He flipped the page in the ledger. 'Fernando Melo,' he said.

Leme nodded. He played like a cuckolded lover. He smiled. 'That little cunt!'

The manager laughed. 'He's taking her next lesson too. Couple days' time. Apparently she's away with work or something. Keep an eye on him, entendeu?' He laughed again.

Bingo.

Leme winked. 'Ah, vai se foder, eh cara.'

They slapped hands and Leme left.

Ellie's Apartment

Two months earlier

Ellie scrolled and clicked. She was looking for articles – proper, journalistic pieces – about social cleansing in São Paulo. She was surprised to see there were a few. She found two, both written by a guy called Something Silva – he only went by his surname. What style.

The articles were about nine years apart. The older one was all about death squads marauding the streets killing the homeless – sort of vigilante shit, like, we'll take responsibility to make this city what it should be. Terrifying. All about hatred, not money. *That* was what was terrifying. Money here made things simple, easy to quantify. Gangs of do-gooding murderers were beyond even her conception of Latin American justice. Jesus.

The second was recent, just a few months ago. And guess fucking what? The tagline: World Cup, Olympics. Gentrification and cleaning up – limpeza – through crime. Avoid any petty crime for when the gringos come calling, no mugging and whatnot, keep them safe and spending their dollars by committing what wasn't a million miles away from genocide. The National Centre for the Defence of Human Rights called it 'euphemistic sanitisation'. What a phrase. Though for the people who had disappeared – nearly two hundred in a little under two years – the phrase might as well be *euthanistic* sanitisation. Clever girl, Ellie.

This second article seemed to suggest this limpeza was state-sponsored, state-approved and carried out by the military police. It was easy to disguise disappearances under a banner of drug gang purges.

So where did this Cracolândia business fit in?

Ellie clicked and scrolled. There was nothing definitive.

But she guessed the second, more recent article was more likely the template.

But who owned the land that made all this hideousness so desirable? Where did the money end up?

Follow the fucking money. OK, I will.

She thought about what Fernando had told her. She didn't think it was especially confidential, but she probably shouldn't have shared quite so much. It was flattering, really; cute guy trying to impress her by being engaged with her work. Well, the work she *wanted* to do.

He'd said that the Cracolândia deal was all about the sale of the land, the area around Luz. She knew it was riddled with drug users and dealers and the destitute, and it was being sold, he'd said, to a conglomerate led by a construction and development company called CASA for gentrification, before the World Cup and Olympics. A sort of clean-up-the-centre-for-tourist-buck scheme. Problem was that the *land* is privately owned, and therefore can only be sold to CASA and the conglomerate. Ellie hadn't understood this at first.

'Look,' Fernando had said, 'the land is one thing, simple actually. It's there and it always has been. The issue is the houses, sabe, the shacks that were illegally built on this privately owned land. Technically, though, these dwellings are legally owned by the residents who built them. Understand?' He paused. 'It's a classic favela ownership issue. Who owns what and where to put the favelados who are getting the fuck in the way.'

'Is it alright you're telling me this?' Ellie had asked.

'I'm not telling you anything that isn't basically common knowledge.' He paused. 'Perhaps don't quote me,' he said, smiling. 'I don't know any more, really, too junior.'

Ellie wasn't sure about that, but she didn't press him on it. She'd have to figure out what it meant herself. Follow the money.

So:

There has to be state and city government intervention to 'relocate' these residents to facilitate the private sale, which means contracts, which means a potential fat wad of cash. So who'd benefit? She'd talked to Leandro plenty, and they'd visited the site. That was the illegal aspect, and pretty fucking clear. She'd done a bit of digging, a bit of dot-joining and came up with a list, which she looked at now. It seemed too implausible – or too bloody obvious. That's what she'd have to figure, she supposed.

She read her notes through again.

So who gains from the Cracolândia land deal?

LEGAL:
1) Landowner (whoever the fuck that is)
2) Danillo Aguiar: Secretario de Obras (City/State government – kickbacks)
3) Clayton Lemos, owner/director of CASA: State-sponsored materials/post-development profit potential: Large kickbacks
4) Ricardo Carneiro, head of Zarzur Cabral, Law firm facilitating legal relocation. Agency percentage: Large
5) Fernando, Zarzur Cabral, organises legal aspects of resident sale
6) Leandro, Zarzur Cabral, on-site facilitator for resident relocation

ILLEGAL:
1) Military Police Chief
2) 3 Military Police goons: Low-level – drug money
3) 'Prince' Felipe, Cracolândia drug dealer

It was quite a list. And she was connected to two of the people on it.

She could go back to Cracolândia, try and score, even, snoop around. But that was a pretty terrifying idea.

Or she could talk to Leme – he might be able to put two and two together and not get Ellie in over her five.

Ellie's independent attempts at investigative journalism began in June 2013. She, quite simply, decided to take the initiative. It was about time. She'd been in São Paulo a little more than six months by then, and still hadn't got used to it. It wasn't hard to see why. Even moving to a bigger condominium hadn't helped; if anything it had made it all a touch harder – she was further away. Isolation with a swimming pool, a gym, a restaurant, tennis courts and so on, was still isolation. She'd enjoyed the first few months there, lying around in the sun at weekends, getting to know the other residents, but sliding into a routine where she barely left the condominium was not how she had seen her life in Latin America panning out.

She told herself: I am here for a reason; I have a higher purpose than *this*, this life of lager and sun, nice as it is. And she worked out the critical overlap: she had to *experience* the city if she were going to write about it; investigative journalism as a by-product of an investigative life.

And it was *all* kicking off in June 2013. Even with her shaky grip on the language, she got it. And she got the key point: it wasn't about the thirty-cent bus fare hike. And it was something that her mother didn't understand. 'Thirty cents?' she'd emailed, incredulous, a link to the BBC report on the story. 'We should be so lucky!'

Ellie had rolled her eyes at that, but laughed, too.

'The point is, Mum,' she'd replied, 'the key social issue here is crystallising around the cost of public transport. It's not about the fares; it's about the haves and the have-nots. And there are a lot more of the have-nots.'

And, of course, she was beginning to realise, it wasn't just the have-nots that were angry. She was spending more and more time talking to a colleague, Lis, about how her city was changing. Lis was almost ten years older than Ellie, had worked at the magazine for nearly eight, and was done, it seemed, with filing arts copy, and wanted an adventure. She was soon off on one, and seemed determined to impart as much wisdom to Ellie as she could before she was gone. A mentor, a guide; Ellie liked having both.

'I'm proud of São Paulo, its size, its importance,' she once said. 'But I feel that pride from a distance now. That's my saudade. You understand? I had a very happy childhood in this town, you know.'

'Really?' Ellie said. 'Seems it would be a hard place to grow up.'

'Nem fodendo, amiga, no fucking way! Avenida Anacé. Our house was ordinary, on a street of identical, ordinary houses and I spent a lot of time playing football with boys, swapping food with our neighbours. This is like twenty years ago, and there weren't as many condominiums creeping down the Morumbi hill as there are now.'

Ellie nodded. She was living in one, after all.

'The wasteland was to the north, sabe, and the favela skirted the edges of low, rust-roofed houses in which we lived, wedged between the two main roads, Estrado do Campo Limpo and Avenida Giovanni Gronchi. It was different then, is what I'm saying.'

'Yeah, I can't imagine that kind of freedom now,' Ellie said. 'I barely leave mine if not by taxi or a lift.'

'I don't know,' Lis said. 'Sometimes I feel it's me who has changed, that the city's stayed the same. When you're an adult, you need different things. The problem is the people. We don't grow; we prefer the jeitinho Brasilieiro, the shortcut, than to work for what we want. But, of course, not everyone's like that. There are twenty something million of us, for fuck's sake.'

'And that's why you're leaving?' Ellie asked, saddened that she was.

'Like I said, I've outgrown São Paulo. But it hurts to leave, and the saudades are strong!'

They laughed. Lis continued. 'But it hurts even more when I think about staying.'

Ellie was beginning to understand the difference between the condominium life of those with a little money – or a lot – and the rest of the city. It wasn't so much a noted contrast, as purely the reality of São Paulo. The fact that this was unremarkable was, well, sort of remarkable.

The condominium was like a club: a huge swimming pool and deck, tennis court, sauna, squash court, barbecuing area, bar, snooker tables, even a disco. The balconies curved like guitars with Niemeyer elegance – Ellie had done some homework – and each of the eight towers was marked by a single stripe of different colour. A sort of art deco utopia. With security guards.

And Ellie was learning that this lifestyle meant that the default São Paulo setting was distance, it felt. You lived in your cars and shopping malls, blocking out the realities of the city with tinted windows, avoiding mundane, everyday routines by paying someone else to do them, taking sensory pleasure in the artificial – mood lighting, air conditioning.

And then bureaucracy! Ellie needed to visit a notary on Avenida Brasil, and Lis went with her to translate, make sure she wasn't fucked over, forced into buying any unscrupulous official a cafézinho, a little coffee, a bribe.

'Every small town,' Lis was saying as they walked down it, 'has an Avenida Brasil.'

Ellie studied the street. Avenida Brasil was modest. Functional. It felt too ordered, not a true reflection of the city. The buildings were detached and single or two-storey, pastel-fronted and lined with cars with blacked-out windows. The road was wide, but the traffic felt sedate. Palm trees swayed elegantly, politely. Boards announcing the temperature throbbed and shimmered in the sun and smog. What was this São Paulo, Ellie thought?

Surely with a name like Avenida Brasil, it should be the most important street in the city? Ellie asked Lis.

'Well, OK, but it's not, ne? It divides Jardins, ne, connects Praça Portugal with Ibirapuera park, entendeu?' Lis had stopped them and was pointing out the cross section of the road. 'Also, look you've got Itaim, all chic, ne, sophisticated over there, and then Avenida Rebouças, the traffic, the ugliness. Also the artistic communities of Vila Madalena, and the plastic surgeons of Jardim America.' She turned Ellie round. 'And look across the road: a fucking Ferrari dealership next to the city's most famous church. São Paulo, ne?'

Ellie nodded again.

'Ah,' Lis says. 'And look at the side streets.'

Ellie did. There was a maze of minor roads, curving away from the main drag, lined with neo-colonial houses, and she noted their names as they walked: Inglaterra, Estados Unidos, Uruguai, Nicaragua, Venezuela, Mexico, Portugal, Alemanha, Cuba, Argentina, França.

'You see,' Lis grinned, giving Ellie a look that said: you should know how clever I am by now.

'Avenida Brasil is at the centre of the world.'

And Ellie was beginning to understand that, too, the energy of the place, the feeling of importance the city seemed to confer on you, the politicisation: São Paulo made London feel like a village.

After the first rush of the city, the first novelty of chaos, she'd retreated, she knew that, embraced the condo lifestyle, this distance she'd identified. She'd been affected by it all, but, the truth was, she hadn't really understood what had happened. It felt like it was the city that had done it, and she was able to compartmentalise. If anything, it had made her more determined to find her purpose in work. She'd tried to put an article together on it all with that journalist fella Francisco Silva, but nothing came of it. And now Lis was leaving the office, and the city, and another connection, another contact seemed to be slipping off. But before Lis did leave, she had a plan for Ellie.

'Think of it as my legacy for you,' she'd said, laughing over beers in a bar in Itaim. 'I've introduced you to the heart of the Brasilian contradiction. Alegría – we are joyful, we celebrate alegría as we live in a country that is so recognisably unjust, and, deep down, despite this outward appearance of joy, with the sex, the dancing and whatnot, we are lamentably sad.'

Ellie laughed. 'You're funny.'

'The question is: are we happy despite our fate or because of it?'

'Very profound.'

'The true, inexorable sadness of life, dear Ellie, is knowing that it will end.' Ellie rolled her eyes, made a face: yuh-huh, it said. Lis continued. 'Perhaps Brazilians have it right? We have to fill our lives with alegría while we have the chance. Which is why I'm getting the hell out of this town. The essence of alegría is to understand where – or with who – you find it, entendeu? Because like much in Brazil, it's physical, sensual. Breathe it in. Go on.' They both took exaggerated breaths. Lis said, 'Feel it expand. Let it settle.' She laughed. 'There it is.' She touched her chest. 'Right there: *Alegría*.'

'Very good.'

Lis swallowed down the last of her beer and signalled for another. 'Ah, I'm a philosopher,' she laughed, 'faz o que, ne? What you gonna do?'

'And what exactly is this legacy then?'

Lis looked her in the eye, serious. 'I'll take you to the protest. You can write about it. My final act as a patron of journalism.'

The beer arrived and they clinked glasses.

'I'll certainly drink to that,' Ellie said.

And a couple of days later, there they were.

They joined the march at Vinte Três de Maio and shuffled towards the Centro. Lis manoeuvred them over to the right-hand side of the road. It was a vast freeway, a *Bladerunner* sweep to it, free-standing, low, buildings rearing up, flanking it either side, from which flags and banners were draped, most of which stated: 'Tarifa Zero Paga Pelos Ricos.' Crowds cheered on the marchers like it was a victory parade, chanting the same message printed on the banners and flags: 'Free Public Transport Paid For By The Rich.'

'Not quite so catchy in English, ne?' Ellie said to Lis, who laughed.

'Well, protesting is becoming something of a national pastime, querida. They're running out of tunes.'

The noise was extraordinary. A low rumble, rolling down the road, like some animal's angry growl, punctuated by horns and drums, but this was no celebration, Ellie realised, no *Carnaval*, this was hostility and rage, fear and desperation, a whole wedge of society understanding that, yes, fuck it, chega, we've had enough.

Ellie examined the crowd. A real hotchpotch. And there was a thrilling, visceral edge to being a part of it, it was tangible, she could feel it coursing through her. But *what* exactly? She wasn't sure, but it was there, inside her, this *feeling*. Like energy, a jolt, like jumpstarting your engine. This crowd, this day, jumpstarted Ellie, again. She could feel it.

'Take it in, menina,' Lis said. 'This is just the start, trust.'

Ellie had never been to this part of the city on foot. She'd been told not to. It was still known as the Centro, and while the concert hall, the Sala São Paulo, the Pinocateca museum, the Estação da Luz and a whole lot of other attractions were down there, it was a pretty lawless place, a seemingly permanent stand-off between ferocious-looking military police and ravaged addicts and low-level dealers, muggers and perverts. It was in stark contrast to the almost colonial elegance of the buildings, the older ones, municipal headquarters, most of them, Ellie thought. Though even these buildings were ribboned with graffiti, layers and layers of it, so that it became a sort of art of its own, so much of it, it was reduced, somehow – a great concrete drip painting, several kilometres long. Clever girl, Ellie, she thought. Too clever for the sort of article you're trying to write, perhaps, which goes to show quite how clever you are. It's exhausting, she thought to herself and smiled.

Ellie felt another surge as the chanting intensified. She shivered. It was almost sexual. She laughed: getting off on the violence of politics, how very Ballard.

'Having fun?' Lis asked, cocking an eyebrow.

'It's exhilarating, ne? Like electricity.' Or a line of decent chop, of course, she thought.

Lis nodded. 'Just remember why we're here, gringa.' She smiled. 'I know you're not a tourist, but this ain't Capoeira, entendeu? This is a real fight and blows will land.'

Ellie nodded, knew that Lis was talking sense, didn't especially like the *slightly* patronising, earnest tone of the educated third worlder teaching the first world ingénue how it is, but it made her feel a touch superior herself so, you know, let it slide, chalk it up to their passionate and serious friendship or whatever.

The crowd and the noise rumbled on. Ellie thought of surfing, that was what this felt like a little, the push to connect, the wave's crashing embrace, that panicky oblivion when you're knocked, winded, under. And Ellie had only been surfing a couple of times, down at Camburi, so she knew all about that tunnel, that shock, that suspended fear.

They reached the intersection, just past the Metro at Tiradentes, where the road split and became Praça Armênia and Avenida Santos Dumont, way down town. The crowd divided, the majority were funnelling left down Santos Dumont, but a tighter, compact group were moving quickly, urgently, off to the right, down Armênia, towards the large metro and bus station by the Marginal freeway and the Tamanduateí part of the river that ran alongside.

Lis nodded at the smaller group. 'There's your story,' she said. 'Let's follow them.'

'Why?' Ellie asked, but Lis didn't hear her as she was pushing through the mass of bodies and Ellie had no choice but to follow *her*. She reached out for Lis's back, and Lis felt her hand there, and then grabbed Ellie's fingers with her own hand, and flashed her a smile over her shoulder, and wriggled on, squirming through gaps like a grass snake through thick sand-dune heather.

Ellie sensed a shift in mood. It wasn't clear quite what this shift was, but it was discernable. That fizz of energy inside her had a transgressive vibe, suddenly. Ellie thought of the word 'outlaw'. The crowd was much thinner down here, but was moving with real purpose, it felt, and shouts were bouncing back and forth, plans being made, Ellie thought, though she didn't catch the Portuguese. Another jolt, and Ellie noticed bags being passed around, and then realised that she could no longer see many faces, that bandanas were being drawn around faces, balaclavas pulled down over faces, and then Lis was in her ear, her hand on her arm, and she was saying, 'hang back, hang back,' so they slowed down a touch and about a hundred or so people surged past, straight towards the bus station.

Then Ellie saw things being thrown, heard glass breaking, violent, nasty, edgy cheering as it did. Flares were lit and thrown, firecrackers smacked and popped against walls and buildings, and Ellie saw streetlights being smashed now, and it was darker, forbidding down these roads and she was scared. The station's entrance was gated and locked, but several pairs of wire cutters were produced, and a combination of these and the protestors clambering up the railings, pulling and kicking at the grill, brought it all crashing down pretty sharpish.

Ellie and Lis hung back.

'What's going on?' Ellie asked.

'They're making a point. Look, ' Lis pointed at the station. 'Bus fares rise, fuck up the bus station. They're destroying the ticket machines.'

Ellie could see that, and they were using anything they could get their hands on to do it: rubbish bins, bricks, fire extinguishers, seats ripped up from the floor. They were really going for it. Stubborn buggers, though, Ellie thought, these ticket machines: harder to smash the fuck out of one of them than you might think.

'Cash points, too,' Lis said. 'It's all largely symbolic. We should fuck off though,' she added, eyes darting around her. 'The militars won't be far away, and they'll be in head-breaking mode, I'll wager. This way.'

Lis pointed back the way they'd come. 'Quickly, Black Blocs, this mob. Proper anarchists, entendeu? Seriously, vamos.'

They broke into a run as dozens of black-hooded tops poured past them, running, it seemed to Ellie, to a pre-arranged plan, organised.

Moments later, an explosion, loud, a bang that frightened Ellie to the core, literally shook her. She shrieked, gathered herself, and turned to where the noise seemed to come from.

'Fuck me,' she said.

A bus, turned onto its side, was in flames, dense smoke pouring and swirling from it, a gasoline stench. It had been rolled next to a row of shops selling electrical goods, and then their windows were cracked and kicked through, and Ellie caught sight of her first ever live looting.

'Jesus,' she said.

Lis grabbed her arm. 'Come the fuck on, Ellie,' she said, pulling her further down the road. 'We need to get up to Paulista before they shut all this down. You can watch it on the fucking news.'

Ellie nodded. She wanted to get out of there, and while it was exhilarating, electric, she saw the fear in Lis's eyes, and this set her teeth on edge, and she was scared. As they walked-ran through the centre, away from the crowds, and then up Rua Augusta, past the strip clubs and cheap neon hotel-brothels, and the student botecos and padarias, tables covered in empty beer bottles, youthful activists and troublemakers boasting and tall-taling, Ellie started to relax, her breathing subsided a little, shallowed, and she began to process what she had just witnessed.

They hit Paulista and found a taxi rank. There was only one taxi, though.

'You take this,' Lis said. They embraced. 'We'll talk.'

Back at home, Ellie watched the news reports, flicking between several channels. The incident at the bus station was getting a lot of coverage. And there were others. What looked like a full-scale, pitched battle between Black Bloc groups and military police was still going on outside the municipal courthouse. At least two other buses had been hijacked and burned. Branches of Banco do Brasil and Banco Bradesco had been attacked, windows caved in, cash machines staved in.

It's the fucking Wild West, Ellie thought.

How was she supposed to write about it, to *contribute*?

It was a start though. She felt *alive*.

Antonia's Apartment

15 October, evening

'Querido, are you planning on unpacking any of these boxes any time soon?'

Antonia's head was in the fridge. Leme ignored her. He took his beer out onto the balcony.

His balcony too, now. Bit nicer than his –

This one with its built-in electric churrasco, its swing seat, and the faux beach-stone floor.

'Helluva fuck pad,' Lisboa said the first time he'd been up.

Leme liked his own white plastic table and chairs stained by red wine and cigarettes.

They weren't coming with him.

The first time he and Antonia slept together, she bit his finger so hard he yelped in pain. He liked the way she made him pin her arms on the mattress way up above her head and twanged his whole body with hers.

'Good bed for bonking, this,' Antonia said. 'Excellent coverage.'

It was a new bed. They were both very happy with it.

Leme wasn't sure he'd done any *bonking* before.

It was simple with Antonia.

She'd known Renata. They complemented each other, sort of. What was it Ellie called her earlier? Corporate hussy. Wasn't far off and Antonia wouldn't mind. Renata was all pro bono, social action and responsibility.

It was uncomplicated with Antonia.

She'd brought him out of his shell when it had felt like he might have curled up and rotted in it.

It was fun with Antonia.

He made her laugh, something he hadn't done for anyone in a long time. They sat by the condo pool together on Saturdays and drank cans of lager and ate cheese pastel with molho da pimenta.

Sun-gazing with the nipped and tucked and the hairy-backed fat boys with their young families.

It was exciting with Antonia.

They'd go upstairs and he'd taste the chlorine and the tanning lotion on her and his heartbeat zoomed.

And now a year on they were moving in together.

But there was something unbearable about parting with the things he and Renata had bought together, even when seeing them reminded him of arguments. 'Building a life together is about accepting the objects, the books, the furniture your partner brings with her,' Renata once said. 'It's not about feeling different or inadequate because they're not yours. Because you would never have thought to get them. They're all ours now, anyway.'

Now they were all his –

And someone else would use them.

Some other couple –

Some other family.

Now, when he lay behind Antonia at night and felt her push against his stomach, the knots he felt dissolved.

He liked how she reached her hand over her shoulder for his as he fidgeted and nuzzled her neck before she woke up.

He liked how she pulled the covers over their heads when they fucked in the mornings.

And how, afterwards, he always ended up scratching around on the floor, looking for her earrings.

After a month or so he'd asked her to stop biting his finger. He wasn't sure if it had been a mistake.

Antonia spoke, snapping him out of his reverie. 'It's just that they're taking up space and you do have to *actually live here* in two days when your tenants move in.'

Leme nodded. 'I know,' he said.

But he was thinking about what he'd seen earlier that day, at Antonia's office. He left the kitchen, went outside.

He was moving in so they could make some money. They lived in the same condominium. They could wave at each other if they got the angles right from his utility room and her back bedroom.

But rents were fucking skyrockets and they both owned and they figured, let's throw in and see where we are.

Two days.

Leme looked out from the balcony across the street.

Electricity crackled at eye-level. Warm orange lights glowed in windows like embers in a gas fire. Voices floated up from the garage bar next door. Leme had stepped in once to buy cigarettes on a Saturday.

A three-piece Samba band played for old men and favela cooze.

'Oh, here you are,' Antonia said.

Leme smiled as if to say, 'Yes, that's right, I'm here. *I* am *here*.'

Antonia drank a glass of white wine. She didn't sit. She leant against the balcony rail and looked down.

She turned and looked at Leme.

She said, 'If it doesn't rain, it drips.'

Leme coughed on his beer.

'Expression my dad used to use,' Antonia said. 'About the city, sabe? Means: even when there is nothing happening, something is happening.'

'Very profound.'

'You'd be surprised.'

Leme said nothing. Leme was thinking about the bag that Fernando had given Antonia. Leme was thinking that if Antonia *had* seen him earlier then she had better fucking say something about it. Leme was thinking that maybe *he* should say something.

Leme said, 'Oh yeah?'

'Just work.'

Leme sat up. They were moving in together. 'Go on,' he said.

'It's this project.' Antonia sat down. 'It's complicated, not something we usually deal with.' She lit a cigarette and offered Leme one. Leme took it. He leaned forward and lit his cigarette from the lighter she held across the table. She went on, 'You know I'm cynical about a lot of what we do? Well, that's the problem. This project is with a social housing organisation. An organisation that is doing some good.'

'So what's the problem?' Leme asked.

Antonia made a face. A face that said: you know.

'Seriously,' Leme said. 'That sounds like a good thing.'

Antonia snorted. 'It is, obviously. The *problem* is that we have to apply all these corporate, lawyerly principles to it. Loses its charm, its innocence.'

Leme laughed. 'A good problem is innocent.'

'I know.' Antonia smiled. 'I thought you'd like that.'

'So tell me about it,' Leme said. She was usually so poised. This was unsettling.

'It's about ownership,' Antonia said. 'Ownership of property, ownership of land. And, perhaps unsurprisingly, the complicated nature of this relationship.'

Leme raised his eyebrows. Very her:

Define the problem on a theoretical level first.

Leme wasn't too bothered about the theoretical level. Leme just wanted to hear where this project was, and what fucking pineapple it was they had to peel.

Leme futzed with his cigarette.

'So, land and property,' he said.

'Yes. The issue is who owns what. And it's far from clear.'

'Why?'

'The land is owned by one person, well, one company. And by land, I mean the *actual land*.'

'Thanks. I'm aware of the concept.'

Antonia smiled. 'Point is the land was owned by the state, but it's been sold on. And I think the state government has done that for a reason. A pretty clever one.'

'Explain.'

'If I tell you where this land is, you might figure it out.'

Antonia toyed with her wine glass. Antonia nailed the last mouthful. She waved the empty glass at Leme. 'Just a sec.' She levered herself off her seat and went inside.

Leme reckoned he knew what the problem was. Didn't hurt for her to spell it out though. Or they could double-team it, get there together. That might be better, considering.

Antonia sat back down. She snagged a cigarette from Leme's soft pack of Marlboro. 'Cracolândia,' she said.

'Oh.'

A smile played on Antonia's lips. She said nothing for a minute. Leme peeled the label on his beer. Another minute passed. Antonia said, 'So. Figured it out, detective?'

Leme took the bait. 'Illegal housing. Dwelling rights. Something like that?'

Antonia applauded. 'Very good, detective. It's exactly something like that.'

'Go on.'

'The land has been sold to a developer. Gentrification and whatnot. Thing is, the residents built their own houses. Shacks or whatever, doesn't matter, legally speaking, they have rights. The developers can't simply move them on.'

'So while the land is theirs, the buildings aren't?'

'Exactamente.'

Leme played the ingénue. 'So they buy the buildings then?'

'Theoretically, that would work,' Antonia said. 'But there are hundreds of them and each one needs deeds and paperwork and negotiation. Not time-efficient, entendeu?'

'And everyone wants to be greased at every stage, I'm guessing.'

Antonia opened her arms. 'Makes the world go round.'

Leme snorted. 'So what's the reason the state sold the land then?' He knew the answer to this.

'Because it's no longer their problem. That's the reason. Simple as that.'

'What's your role in all this?'

'What we're doing is trying to make a unified sale of the properties to a social housing organisation at a philanthropic cut price to resolve it all quickly and get the residents somewhere else, somewhere better. And that's created another problem.'

'Half the fuckers are drug addicts.'

Antonia nodded. 'Not the easiest people to do business with. Shall we eat? Food's about ready.'

After dinner they finished off the bottle of wine and then went to bed. The sex was punishing. Leme found that his anxiety about Antonia made it harder for him to come. Leme tried harder. Antonia bit his finger for the first time in a long time. Leme felt present. This, too, for the first time in a long time. After they finished, Antonia fell asleep.

Leme lay awake for half an hour. He got up and went into the bathroom. He opened the cupboard under the sink. It was empty. He went back into Antonia's bedroom. *His* bedroom in two days. He slid her wardrobe door open. He felt behind the hanging dresses and under the rack of shoes. Nothing. He went out into the corridor. He weighed it up. Spare room was too obvious. He would certainly be in the kitchen, so that was out. There were two rooms that he might not go into on a normal evening with Antonia, the second bathroom and the TV room. He went into the kitchen and got a glass of water from the cooler. The second bathroom had nothing in it apart from a hand towel and a hand-soap dispenser. He tried the cupboard under the sink. It was empty.

He went into the TV room.

There was only one place: the unit under the TV itself.

He edged the glass door open –

Three shelves with DVD player, stereo, Blue Ray, whatever the fuck that was.

A loose panel at the back.

He reached behind.

Bingo.

He wheeled the unit away from the wall.

Inside the bag he had seen Fernando give Antonia earlier that afternoon, the bag that Fernando had picked up from Ellie's apartment, was a computer. Nothing else.

He went back to the door. He sipped at the glass of water and stepped towards the bedroom. Antonia hadn't stirred.

He went back to the TV room.

He opened the computer –

It was password protected.

The username: Ellie1.

Antonia: Leme thought back. Leme thought back to where it all started. Leme didn't know what to believe any more –

How did they meet? Condominium life was a funny thing. You know everyone; everyone knows you. But do you, really? Antonia and Renata had known each other at college. They were like roads not taken to each other, running roughly parallel lives but with a fat wedge of cash in the middle, separating them. A fat wedge that belonged to Antonia. Leme had always liked her, liked her frankness, her distance, her amusement at the world. She made life look a little like a game, but played it with a style that suggested it wasn't. Renata used to talk about hidden depths being a contradiction in terms; Antonia seemed to prove that thesis a false one.

And one day they'd sat together in the condominium bar and shared a few drinks, ate some deep-fried cheese, that sort of thing.

Her lips pursed into wry approval, her eyes sliding off the Saturday activity that circled them: teenagers flirting, middle-aged men roaring, nailing their lagers, maids and nannies chasing toddlers, the parents at a large table wolfing their feijoada, the low thrum of gym machines, the thwack of tennis balls.

And she'd said something: 'You're not cheating on her memory. *Yet*.'

But she'd said it with a smile, teasing him.

She'd known exactly what it was that he'd needed, he realised now. Before it had even *occurred* to him.

And he was stirred by the comment, by the sarong knotted around her neck, clinging to her body, damp from an earlier swim, moistened by tanning oil.

He'd needed to get laid, he realised now. More than that, he'd needed the comfortable intimacy of doing it with someone he liked.

He remembered something else she'd said, during that first drink they'd had, jerking her chin at a group of teenagers. 'They've got it all to look forward to.'

'What's that then?'

'This,' she'd said, waving her cigarette between the two of them.

'And what is *this*?'

'This is everything,' she'd said. 'The human condition, you know … life.'

She'd smiled. And he'd thought: she might be right. Why not?

That acknowledgement: that was the start.

Antonia –

What to believe now?

Leaked Document Record: Land deal – Cracolândia
Recipients: Carneiro; Lagnado; Aguiar; Lemos; Amaral-Gurgel; Machado
Subject: Military police involvement in resident relocation

To run in parallel with the legal facilitation of the resident relocation:

1. That the Militar/ROTA troop with jurisdiction over Cracolândia shall ensure compliance at all stages in terms of residents and noias/criminal element
2. That the Militar/ROTA troop have autonomy in activities which may assist in this compliance
3. That the Militar/ROTA troop shall eliminate criminal activity including, but not limited to, the supplying of narcotics, the dealing of narcotics, and the purchase for use of narcotics
4. That the Militar/ROTA troop members chosen for this task be briefed on the importance of discretion and that other members of the troop learn of these activities on a strictly need to know basis

Signed: The recipients.

Taxi Heading into the Centro

Two months earlier

Leandro, Ellie thought as she looked at him in the taxi, so this is you. I wonder if we know quite what we're doing here.

'Leandro's going to take you tomorrow,' Fernando had told her the night before. 'He knows people down there, certo? His type, if you know what I mean.'

Ellie made a face.

'Ah, vai,' Fernando said. 'It is what it is. He's from that type of people.' He smiled and tugged at her finger. She shrugged. São Paulo, she thought. You only had to look at the lines by the bus stops and the faces driving the cars to know on what race lines the place was drawn.

She was pleased that things were progressing. Having her own contact in Leandro was a step forward. And Fernando seemed to be leading her to a story, and helpfully, she realised, and without getting too involved in it, passing on a little information and letting her get on with it. She was pleased, and it made her like him more.

Leandro turned around from the front seat. 'About five minutes?' he said.

'Great.' Ellie gave him a warm smile.

'It's not a very nice place, Dona Ellie, so be prepared, entendeu?'

Ellie nodded. Dona Ellie. That was funny. Nice kid this Leandro – deferential, though she wasn't exactly sure why.

Cracolândia. Ellie was excited, actually. These sorts of things rarely scared her. She had convinced herself that she was chameleonic, with a sort of grizzled experience as traveller and truthseeker, and knew how to win people over in alien situations. Luck too, she thought. She thought of herself as lucky. That scene at the protests over the bus fares had been a sharpener and she was well up for it now, now that she knew a bit more about the place, a bit more of the language, felt a bit more at home.

They climbed out of the taxi just off a busy road close to the Pinacoteca museum. Ellie had been there several times but hadn't known it was close to Cracolândia. No wonder they want to clean it up, she thought. Before the graffiti and the smoke and pollution damage, this area was beautiful. Post-colonial elegance ruined by the reality of the mega-city.

'We're not going in too far,' Leandro said. 'Just on the edge, really. But best to go on foot, entendeu?'

He was nodding earnestly and eager to please. He led her across the Parque da Luz. The station clock reared up above, like a small St Pancras.

'He's a good kid,' Fernando had told her. 'And, like I said, he knows people and is known. He's liked. There's nothing to be scared of.'

'There's never anything to be scared of, Fernandinho,' Ellie said.

They circled round a square. Ellie noted the name: Praça Julio Prestes. It smelled of urine that had been baked in the heat. There were palm trees that swayed drunk in the light breeze. Small groups of dark, defeated faces scurried about them, occasionally words escaping their toothless mouths, either an offer or a request. Leandro stuck close to Ellie.

'It's just past this corner,' Leandro said. 'The house we're going to see is owned by a couple who were friends with my mother. They've lived here for over a decade. They're good people and they trust Zarzur Cabral to do right by them as the company sends people like me to reassure them. So it's a big responsibility. There are a couple of other liaison officers, as we call them, from similar backgrounds. We're working to help them make the right decisions for themselves, so that they can see that moving to new properties is a very good thing.'

Ellie gave him a tight smile. It felt dense, lawless in this place. And yet she knew the Sala de São Paulo, where she had seen the national orchestra perform, was only moments away.

'The place we're going is at the top end of Rua Helvetia,' Leandro was saying. 'Very close to the train tracks and not far from Sesc Bom Retiro.'

Sesc? Ellie thought. She visited one of the Sesc complexes quite regularly, for the theatre, sometimes to swim. She was amazed there was one here.

Leandro smiled. 'You see it's an oddity, this place. No one's sure why it became what it has. And you can understand why there is such interest in the land. If you look up rather than keep your eyes at street level, you could be in Europe.'

Ellie looked up and saw his point. That was a good line. She'd remember it. It might be a good one to start the article with, whatever the article turned out to be about.

It was pretty bleak, Ellie thought. A group of swollen-bellied, dirty-faced women sat on the road, cackling. Two extremely ugly, disgusting men – extremely ugly and disgusting even by the standards of very poor Brazilians, Ellie thought – were wrapped in dirty blankets and passed out on each other on a sofa underneath a street light, the stuffing of which pushed through the covering, bulging, as if trying to escape from these ugly and disgusting people. A couple in rags shuffled back and across the road, arm in arm, muttering. Ellie tried these sentences out in her head. A squat woman in a beanie hat called out, 'Quem quer crack? Quem quer crack?' Interesting sales technique, Ellie thought. She didn't dare pull out her phone or a notebook. A shifty-looking twenty-something boy called out, 'Quem tem maconha? Who has dope?' He was a little better dressed than the others. But, Ellie thought, it was a pretty desperate place to come to score a little weed. Each person they passed glanced at them and quickly looked away. Leandro had a confident but humble air and Ellie felt safe. Fernando was right about that.

They approached a crossroads.

'We'll turn right here,' Leandro said. He pointed diagonally. 'Train tracks are just there, running parallel to Alameda Cleveland. The houses we're going to look at were put up basically across the road. They're a cluster, like stone shacks.'

'So they're illegal?'

Leandro smiled. 'Technically there was no planning permission when they were put up, which is the case in the favelas too. But the occupants have rights once they have been in place for a specific amount of time. So while the homes are there, the dwellers have rights.'

'While the homes are there?'

'Yes, exactly. Which is why we're going to have a look at one, meet the family.'

At the corner the scene was no more wholesome. It was mid-morning and Ellie scanned faces, trying to work out if they were coming up or coming down. She didn't know much about crack addiction, but apparently up and down were quite alike; just a nasty madness embedded in their eyes and expressions.

It took her a moment to realise that Leandro had stopped and she had walked half a dozen yards on. She turned and stepped quickly back to him.

'Weird,' he said. 'I mean, really fucking weird.'

Ellie was surprised by his tone, his language. He had been so polite up to now.

'What?' Ellie said.

'This is fucked up.' He stood scratching his head, turning half-circles, making what looked like measurements with his arms.

'What?' Ellie said again.

'I don't know … I don't…'

Ellie caught sight of movement from between two buildings that backed onto the train lines.

'Leandro,' she said.

'I…'

Ellie tensed. The movement was three people and they moved towards them with purpose. The addicts, the noias that were sitting close by, moved slowly but deliberately away, dragging themselves down the road deeper into Cracolândia. There were a few strangled shouts. They weren't exactly evacuating with any urgency, but Ellie caught a sense that it wasn't wise to stick around this particular street corner. The three people – men, carrying guns Ellie could now see – were fifty metres away.

Leandro continued to murmur and shake his head in confusion.

'Leandro,' Ellie tugged his sleeve. She pointed up the road. The men were yards away. 'I think we should leave.'

'Puta que pariu,' Leandro whispered. He breathed out and looked at Ellie. 'No, best we stay, relax, it's fine.'

He took her hand and gave it a squeeze. This had the opposite effect of that intended. She fingered the wad of cash she kept loose in her purse for exactly these kinds of situations. She slipped her phone and wallet under the flap at the bottom of the bag, hopeful no one would think to search too carefully. She knew that if she ever were mugged, they'd simply take the bag, but it felt reassuring to do it. Equally, if they didn't find cash or a credit card, they wouldn't bother kidnapping her and bleeding her account over a week or so. This was supposed to be a comfort.

And then Ellie saw the vests that the three men wore: military police. This was either a good thing, or a very, very bad thing. Leandro played nonchalant, but he wasn't kidding anyone.

The three militars spread out to confront them. They chewed gum. Two of them had automatic weapons and the third had unbuttoned the holster on his revolver. Ellie kept a neutral expression; she examined the three men quickly and carefully and tried to work out the best card to play.

'The fuck are you doing here?' The militar without the automatic weapon spat the question at Leandro.

'Visiting friends.'

'Friends? You have friends that live here?' The militar looked at Ellie. 'This *gringa bitch* has friends here?'

'She's a journalist,' Leandro said. 'She wanted to interview my friends.'

'This true?'

Ellie nodded. 'Yes, absolutely, and perhaps afterwards I could talk to you? It would be a fascinating…'

'Where do your friends live?'

Leandro glanced at Ellie and a look of panic flashed across his eyes. Oh, fuck, she thought.

'Here,' he said.

'What do you mean here?'

'I mean that. They lived *here*. This stretch of road. There were a number of concrete shacks that ran from just by the train tracks down to about here. I don't understand.'

The three militars looked at each other. Ellie tried to process what Leandro was saying.

Leandro went on, 'I work for the law firm that is helping the residents find new addresses as the land is to be sold. I've been liaising with some of them for months. The friends I came to visit were close to my parents. I don't understand. I've heard nothing of this.'

Ellie didn't especially like Leandro's honesty. He was blundering into something that she didn't want to be a part of.

'Interesting,' the militar said. 'You come to score dope for this whore and then make up a story about disappearing houses when you get caught. Vagabundo, filho da puta. You think it's a good idea to be fucking a crack whore gringa cunt? You're travelling, malandro. Muito stupid, sabe? Muito careless bringing a pale, Euro cooze down here. Muito … naive. If she wasn't an AIDS-dosed junkie we might have anchored her right over there in the back.'

'I'll call my friends,' Leandro said. 'They can vouch for me.'

'You think I'm a patsy faggot?'

'No, no, of course not.'

Ellie watched the other two militars.

'Wait,' the militar said. He beckoned the other two to step a few yards away.

'Move,' he said to Ellie, pointing at Leandro, 'and we'll fucking shoot him.'

He looked at Leandro. 'Speak, and we'll shoot *her*, entendeu?'

They spoke quickly.

There was some nodding that looked like reassurance.

They laughed and nodded some more.

One of them pursed his lips and rubbed forefinger and thumb together.

Ellie knew what that meant.

Another slapped the back of his hand into the palm of the other.

Ellie knew what *that* meant.

The one who had spoken shook his head. He flicked his fingers several times.

Ellie knew what that meant too.

Which was it to be?

'Vem ca,' he said. *Come here.* Ominous, she thought.

Ellie and Leandro walked over to them.

The militars searched them and took all their cash but left everything else.

'Now fuck off, embora,' the militar said, flicking his fingers. 'Don't worry about your friends.'

Ellie and Leandro turned and walked very quickly back the way they came.

Antonia's Apartment

16 October, very early morning

Leme couldn't sleep. He fidgeted. He tweaked the duvet. He fidgeted. He re-tweaked the duvet. He speared his right leg with his left foot. It was five a.m.

Antonia hissed, 'Stay. *Still.*'

When was it, *exactly*, he thought, that your girlfriend turns into your fucking mother?

But Leme *couldn't* sleep. He had to be awake and up before Antonia. He futzed the pillow. He sighed. He leaned over to Antonia. Antonia brushed him away. He breathed hard, annoyed.

Antonia hissed, 'Que porra essa?'

He rolled onto his back. He steamed. Ten minutes. Ten minutes would do it.

Ten minutes passed. He got up.

'I'll let you sleep,' he grunted.

It was five-fifteen a.m.

He went into the kitchen. He rubbed the tiredness from his eyes. He wiped the drool from his mouth. He turned on the coffee machine. So many *things* in this apartment. *His* apartment in two days. Sleek lines.

The coffee machine gurgled its brouhaha. He leaned over the sideboard. He spritzed the coffee with a drop of milk.

He had about ninety minutes, maybe fewer.

He settled down in the TV room and cranked the TV.

The bag was undisturbed.

'Hey.' Antonia stood by the door. She'd showered and perfumed. Her hair was in a towel. She wore only underwear. Leme stirred. He coughed himself awake. He looked at Antonia.

'Steady there, garanhão,' Antonia said. 'Nothing you haven't seen before.' She smiled. She was apologising. 'You want some breakfast?'

Leme grunted yes. Renata used to do the same, make him breakfast. He liked women who were fierce and independent. He prided himself on that. The same women liked to make him breakfast. This worked, Leme thought.

He checked behind the TV. Nothing had moved. Neither should he.

'Pão na chapa OK?' Antonia called.

'Yeah, I'm watching the news,' Leme called back. 'Have it in here with me.'

'Yessir.'

Antonia hummed a tune. A Seu Jorge song.

Leme smiled. His head throbbed with fatigue. His mouth scraped.

The newscasters jabbered –

Leme killed the sound and listened to Antonia.

He didn't like this. Renata had died two years ago. Antonia was a second chance. He didn't think he'd ever get a second chance. He didn't think he'd ever want a second chance. He thought about the bag. In about twenty minutes he'd know a little more.

'Here.'

Antonia handed Leme a plate. No razzle-dazzle, just a wedge of bread fried light in butter.

'Hang on.'

Antonia nipped back into the kitchen and brought two cups of coffee.

'So,' she said. 'What's the news?'

Leme unmuted the TV. Leme shifted left. Leme made space on the sofa for Antonia. He chewed. He sipped.

'You know,' he said.

Antonia was dressed and made up. Leme was dressing-gown slumped. They ate and drank.

'What time you off?' Antonia asked him.

Leme weighed his answer. 'Late-ish start,' he said. 'Meeting at ten, sabe?'

Antonia nodded, pensive.

'You?' Leme asked.

'Off soon. Straight after this,' she said, lifting her plate.

Leme nodded. Right.

The newscasters joked. Silly season.

'You OK?' Antonia asked.

Leme started. She rarely asked.

'I just…' Antonia said. 'I didn't mean to pirouette earlier. You know?'

Leme knew. Leme knew his fidgeting was annoying, sometimes. It had been charming. It still was charming, at weekends. When they could disappear under the bedclothes and play.

'I'm sorry,' Leme said. 'You know how it gets.'

Antonia knew. That was the thing, Leme thought, when you reached a certain stage. *You knew.*

Leme was mind-fucked tired. He had to hold on, though. He needed to stay in this room. Just a few more minutes.

Antonia took the plates back into the kitchen. He sat tight.

A few minutes passed. Antonia appeared in the doorway. 'Time to go,' she sang, smiling. 'See you tonight.'

He kissed her on the mouth. She left.

He waited five minutes. He fished the bag out from behind the TV. He opened the bag. He took the computer out from inside the bag. He opened the computer. The same password protection on the screen. He looked at it. He scoped the options. There weren't any.

He took his phone from his dressing-gown pocket and dialled the admin department at the delegacia.

'Sr. Mario,' the guy said. 'Bit early for you, ne?'

Leme snorted. 'Settle down. Need a favour. You busy?'

'Not for you.'

'I've got a computer.'

'Finally you're accepting the twenty-first century. Parabens, eh.'

Leme ignored this. 'It's password protected. Think you can get into it?'

'More than likely. What is it?'

'A computer.'

The admin guy laughed. 'You being a twat on purpose?'

Leme said nothing.

'What make is it?'

Leme looked at the computer. 'Says MacBook Pro. Mean anything to you?'

'Shouldn't be an issue. Bring it in.'

'That's the problem. It needs to stay where it is, entendeu?'

'OK.' The admin guy shouted something to a colleague that Leme couldn't hear. He said, 'Take a photo of the computer closed, both sides, and one of the screen. Send them to me. I'll bike over something identical and you bring yours in. A bait and switch, entendeu? I'll set up the replacement so it's impossible to get into it. That work?'

'That works. How long?'

'Where are you?'

'My girlfriend's flat.'

'Fuck me,' the admin guy said.

'Yeah, alright,' Leme said. 'I'll send the address with the pictures. It's Morumbi, Giovanni Gronchi.'

'OK. About an hour, certo?'

'Ótimo.'

Leme hung up. He took the photos and sent them with the address. A minute later he got a response: **Well done.** Leme didn't reply.

Nothing to do but wait. He stood to take a shower. He sat back down. Antonia might come back. Only a slim chance, but not worth the risk. He killed the sound on the TV again and leaned back into the sofa.

Leme had a thought. He jumped up and fetched his bag from the kitchen. He rifled inside. He snagged Ellie's phone which was in a thin plastic bag. He hit the power button through the bag. The phone lurched and groaned into life. He looked at it and waited. There was a text message. Only one.

It said:

Hello gorgeous xx

He clocked the time. It was sent the night before.

He clocked the name: Fernando.

Last night. Quite late last night. Fernando didn't know that Ellie was AWOL. Or he did and this was bait. He was either innocent, or he was working Leme. Leme swiped right – passcode protected. Fuck. Either way, admin will sort that – quick.

Fernando wouldn't be swerving him much longer.

Antonia: Leme thought back. This is how it started. Like this –

The day after they first slept together – the first day they woke up together – was a Sunday. They'd tiptoed around each other in the morning, drinking coffee on Antonia's balcony, reading her papers, eating papaya and bread and butter. Leme felt like a much younger man acting out a role: this is how adults behave. It wasn't that he didn't enjoy it – it was a surprising relief not to be alone – but he knew very well how relationships are essentially hours and hours of learning how to co-exist in a confined area. The knowledge of when to speak, when to be silent, when to step out from your individual space and encroach on your partner's; this knowledge was earned, hard-earned, after years of trial and error.

Renata, inevitably, he realised with a smile, put it more succinctly: 'To live together is a choice; to make it work is also a choice.' It's you that's responsible for your choices, no one else, Leme believed that, certainly. But living together could feel like a submission. 'It's no good relying on someone else for your own happiness,' Renata would say, when she'd pissed him off and he'd sulk on the balcony, drinking until the small hours. That was a hard one: as independent and self-contained as he'd always been, how couldn't he rely on her when she'd provided what looked like the first bit of real meaning he'd ever experienced? And yet if he *did* rely on her, did submit, did let her identity define them both, he might end up losing her.

'It's a pickle,' Lisboa said when Leme had tentatively voiced these fears once. 'Birds, mate, what are you gonna do?' he'd added.

That'd put an end to the conversation.

It was that first morning with Antonia that he came close to understanding: you've just got to choose, and then choose to put the hours in.

At lunchtime, they went down to the pool and lay in the sun, reading, drinking the odd beer, not saying much, feeling each other out a little, Leme thought. His mates had spotted him, and eyebrows were raised – and lagers, in a none too discreet toast. At least they weren't yelling profane encouragement. Being a widower meant he was spared that. When a man from the condominium separated from a wife, a girlfriend, a lover, the principal cheerleader, Big Nelson, would raise his lager and bellow, 'Congratulations, comrade! Liberdade! Fraternidade! But there is no igualdade, no equality, son!' in a proclamation far cleverer than anyone would give him credit for, but exactly as coarse as expected.

In the evening they went out to an Italian canteen, not far from their building. Classic Paulistano tradition: Sunday evening pizza. Were they there already? Leme thought on the drive over. And then: does it even matter?

It was a family-run place, not wildly expensive by São Paulo standards, but prohibitively so, keep out the riff-raff, entendeu? Or, as the euphemism of their advertising stated: Italian for discerning types. 'Discerning?' Renata said the first time they saw it. She snorted. 'I've got a friend who works in advertising. They won the contract for some flash car company, and he came over to discuss strategy. They had all sorts of ideas of how to appeal to the right demographic blah blah blah. My friend just said, "Make it in black, tint the windows, and make it fucking expensive. It'll sell a shit tonne that way." He was right. Discerning. Fucksake. Tell people with money in this city that something is expensive and they'll think they have to have it, it must be the best. Easiest fucking marketing strategy in the world.'

Leme remembered this little riff of hers as he and Antonia pulled into the car park. He wanted to mention it, talk about it, talk about her – it was funny after all – but he held back. There, in that moment, lay the crux of all this. The fact that he knew it, he recognised as a good thing.

'So,' Antonia said, leaning back, examining Leme. 'You've been here before, then?'

'Yes, yes I have. I suppose you have too?'

'Oh, yes.'

It was busy, but Antonia had that presence that attracts waiters effortlessly. Two or three of them seemed to be on hand – or at least keeping an eye on their table – at all times.

'Wine?' Antonia asked.

Leme nodded. 'Red, ne?'

'Oh, well done.'

'You choose,' Leme said, smiling.

'And well-played.'

They sat across from each other, grinning, eyes dancing, straining to contain what felt to Leme something very much like excitement. Had it just been that? Sex? Was it that simple?

The waiter showed the label of the bottle to Leme. 'Quer provar?' he asked. 'A taste first?'

Leme grinned some more. 'I think she should, mate,' he said, pointing across the table.

Antonia bowed her head and clapped quietly in mock applause. 'Just pour,' she said to the waiter, looking all the time at Leme.

They drank. They studied the menu.

'You have a usual here?' Antonia asked.

Leme smiled. 'Well, it's that fucking sharing-dish thing I can't stand, entendeu? I mean, what if I want veal or something, and you want straight up pasta? It's just—'

He paused, noticed Antonia's expression, which had changed slightly, less amused, like she was working something out.

'Sorry,' Leme said. 'I … I sound like a cunt.'

'Only a tiny bit.' She reached across and touched his hand. 'I forgive you.'

'It sounded better in my head, you know, funny. But, well, I just sound … sem graça, ne?'

'Yep.'

'It's clearly not a routine I can pull off.'

'It's OK, Mario,' Antonia said. 'I understand.'

'What do you mean?'

'Renata was funny, she had, as you say, *routines*. That sounded like it might be one of them.'

Leme nodded, looked down, felt ashamed, stupid.

Antonia gripped his hand. 'We can work on yours, don't worry. And in the meantime, how about we share the veal?'

He kissed the hand that held his and they smiled at each other. Less febrile, but more necessary.

Yes, Antonia really did know better than he did, about what he needed.

And he was beginning to see that that was something that he wanted.

The day before he followed Ellie, and found Leandro, and lost Ellie, and all this started, was something like a simpler time, Leme reflected – rueful. He'd been standing outside the condominium, morning fresh, waiting for Lisboa, when he'd eyed him ambling over, racquet in hand.

'Fuck me, mate,' Leme said. 'That's a pair of shorts.'

'Alright, settle down, McEnroe,' Lisboa grunted, rearranging himself. 'Been a while, entendeu?'

'Tight fit?' Leme smirked. 'Come on, you big bugger. This'll be fun.'

Leme popped the borrowed car. They gunned it up Giovanni, past the swank American school on the left – all gates and barbed wire, cameras, dangerous-looking black men in good suits and shades – Blockbuster video and pharmacy opposite.

It was early and the bus queues were forming. Tired-looking black men and women in work clothes, or cheap shirts, shiny polyester trousers, faces set at neutral, empty, waited – passive. Labourers swaggered low under the weight of their helmets, their tools, orange overalls knotted around their waists, topless, calling out to each other in dialect, faces lined and dirty, hands like tar, bodies hard like coal.

They made a right into the padaria car park, where Leme's old mate Luis worked. Top of Paraisópolis: the favela ran away from them down the hill below and up the other side, like an oil spill.

'We'll have lunch here after, ne?' Leme said.

Lisboa said nothing.

They snaked down the track and through the entrance – gated and locked. Play Tennis, Morumbi. Same chain that ran the club in Itaim where Leme sometimes played, got coaching. Same deal here too – not private, as such, but fucking expensive. The rabble stayed well away. And military police ate at the padaria, pretty much 24/7, so no wide boys ever chanced their arm at the till.

Leme was mates with the guy who ran the pizzeria at the top end of the club. The guy could wheedle discount courts when they knew it would be quiet. Leme nodded at the kid behind the counter.

'Usual, eh, cara?' Leme asked.

'Isso.' The kid winked. 'Until midday, certo?'

'Beleza,' Leme said. He looked at Lisboa. 'Vamos lá?'

Lisboa shuffled forward. 'Vamos.'

They got into a clay court rhythm – quick hands, slow feet.

Lisboa was a bulky fuck, but he moved with economy and had an eye on him.

An ugly lefty spank to his forehand and a snide sliced backhand. His shorts strained heroically.

'Like you've never been away, son,' Leme said as they chugged water.

Lisboa sweating bullets: 'Porra, ne?'

'Age, mate. Faz o que, ne?'

Lisboa nodding: 'Ah, well, you don't lose some things.'

'That style of yours for a start – unique.'

Lisboa laughing, choking on his water: 'Se fodeu.' He picked up his racquet. 'Let's go again, bonitão.'

Hitting was therapy –

Metronomic. Thwack. Move. Thwack. Move. Thwack. Move.

Leme all effortless precision – textbook: legs bend, hips pivot, arms circle in a slow, open-hand slap. The ball – travelling. Serious throttle on it.

Lisboa moved like a crab, two steps either side, no more. Fat strapping on his right knee and left elbow. A comedy sweatband round his widening forehead.

'I ain't balding,' he once said. 'My brain's getting bigger.'

They hit and slid on the clay, slid and hit, hit and slid. Move. Thwack. Move.

Therapy.

Lisboa framed a couple *hiiiiigh* over the fence. Favela-bound.

Leme hit deep, deep, deep: Lisboa flicking balls off his feet, racquet like using a spade.

'Puta, Mario,' he yelled as another dud flew *waaaay* long.

They stopped every fifteen minutes and gulped at bottles of water.

'Mate, you wanna drop it short every now and again? You're killing me,' Lisboa said, gulping-gasping.

Leme winked. 'Good little workout.'

Next rally, Lisboa stepped in, aggressive. Leme dropped one short. *Waaaay* short, well-disguised.

Lisboa slipped, fell. Mouthful of clay.

'Puta que pariu,' he shouted. 'That's bang out, mate, a drop shot when we're hitting up. You know that. Caralho.'

Leme smiled. Shouted back: 'You asked me to drop it short.'

Lisboa stalked back to the baseline. Lisboa looked at his watch. 'Ten minutes more, certo?'

They drank chopp in frosted glasses in the padaria. They wolfed pastel and bolinho de queijo. Lisboa ordered more drinks, a side of fries. He noticed Leme's raised eyebrow.

'Ah, vai,' he said, mock-indignant. 'This is recuperative, entendeu? It's like part of the exercise, you know, like a … like… '

'Like an ice bath,' Leme said.

Lisboa laughed. 'Yeah, exactly.' He raised his frosted glass. 'A proper little ice bath this. Anyway,' he paused, swallowed more deep-fried cheese, 'as if the athlete's diet you're on is any better.'

'I'm just enjoying an entirely unjustified feeling that I might actually be healthier than you, porra.'

Lisboa laughed. 'Don't conflate talent and stamina, son. It's not sex, after all.'

Leme laughed. 'You're lucky to conflate anything in that department, querido.'

'I'm not sure you know what conflate means, mate.'

They chomped their fries, necked their lagers.

'Antonia alright?' Lisboa asked.

Leme weighed the question. He thought that she probably *was* alright. It was how *he* felt that was causing him doubt. Lisboa's eyes narrowed – suspicious. Leme shrugged, smiled. 'Ah, you know,' he said. 'Women.'

Lisboa chewed thoughtfully, considered this, eyed Leme. He took another slug of his beer. Then he said, 'Amen.'

They got good and lunch-drunk. At home, Leme napped in his sweaty kit.

When he woke up, he checked his phone.

Message from Ellie, the gringa journalist.

He studied it –

She wanted him to follow her, something about a lead.

Fucksake. He smiled. Tomorrow might be interesting after all.

São Paulo, Delegacia

16 October, morning

'You about ready to do some work?'

Leme squinted up at Lisboa. Leme said nothing.

Her voice, a detuned radio. Her voice, murmuring. Renata.

'You missed the meeting.'

Leme nodded.

Her voice saying, 'Don't be afraid.'

Her voice saying, 'Don't stop.'

'Reports.' Lisboa lugged files across their broom-cupboard office. 'Look, don't flip me off, Mario. Read them, OK?'

Lisboa left. As he closed the door, silence.

Leme flicked through the documents. Lisboa had smudged his signature, Leme noticed. Good lad. Makes some things a little easier. Reports were factual, key information on the victim, early forensic reports, time of death and whatnot. It all chimed with what Leme knew, with what Leme saw. End of it all though, he realised, they knew next to jackshit nothing.

Lisboa shouldered the door, ambled in and handed Leme a doubled-up plastic cup of steaming black filth. He offered Leme a croissant.

'A croissant?' Leme asked.

Lisboa smiled. He patted his stomach. 'My wife doesn't seem to understand that breakfast is the most important meal of the day.'

Leme raised his eyebrows.

Lisboa said, 'Woman logic – don't eat, lose weight.'

'And that's wrong, is it?'

'Fuck yeah. Don't eat, get hungry, *eat*. You know how to not get hungry? Eat breakfast, that's how.'

'Right.'

'Most important meal of the day.'

Leme pointed at the croissant. 'That a meal, is it?'

'Well, when you factor in yours too, it is.'

Lisboa reached across and took a bite of the second croissant.

He sat down heavily. The chair creaked. His shirt opened in between the buttons where a thatch of hair was pushed through by a roll of flesh. He yawned and scratched at his jowls.

'Diet going well then?' Leme said.

'Ah, vai tomar no cú, eh.'

Leme smirked. 'You always struck me as such a disciplined man, Ricardo.'

Lisboa sprawled on his chair. Lisboa *hogged* the space.

He said, 'How's the *move* going, Mario?'

'Why don't you tell me what happened in the meeting?'

Lisboa straightened. 'There isn't much to tell. The victim's been identified, firstly by the Carteira, and then by a colleague. We couldn't find any family. The house is registered in his parents' name, as you know, but it seems he lived alone. Forensics reckon there had been some movement in there in the few days before, but that's fucking obvious, right? There are traces of footprints, fingerprints. They're running them, but no matches so far, which suggests there weren't any convicts in there, or they used gloves. They're still going over the scene, looking for fabric, that kind of thing, anything that might have blood or spit or fucking semen on it. They *loooove* that shit.'

'What about the neighbours?'

'A couple of uniforms interviewed the lot. I talked to them last night.'

'And?'

'Nada.'

'Nada?'

'Ah, there's nothing no fucker's going to say. For them it's "menos um", ne, one less? Some poor cunt – and by *poor* I mean *cash*-poor, sabe? – gets sliced and it's nobody's business but theirs.'

'So no one saw anything?'

'What was there to see? Someone going into a house? The uniforms said it's done, sem dúvida, it is what it is, they weren't hoodwinked, entendeu? There was nothing to see, because no one was looking.'

'Very profound,' Leme said.

'I have my moments.'

'Know anything about his private life?'

'A topsy-turvy cluck. Kept to himself, entendeu?'

'What the colleagues say?'

'He ran, liked running. Skinny fuck. Bone-thin. That was it. I only spoke to a couple of them.'

'Yeah? An athlete?'

Lisboa shrugged. 'Oh, and one guy said he'd been knocking about with your English girl.'

'Yeah?'

'But you knew that.'

'Então.' *So?*

'Guy implied, you know, they might have been boning. You know anything about that?'

Leme shook his head. 'What was the name of the colleague?'

'You know. You told me to find him.'

'Fernando Melo?'

'Fernando Melo.'

'Tricky cunt.' Leme muttered. 'Misdirection,' he said. 'Melo was sleeping with Ellie. No way she was with Leandro. I'm sure of that.'

Lisboa raised his eyebrows and nodded.

Leme wondered when to tell Lisboa about following Fernando, about the bag. It would mean telling him about Antonia. He wasn't ready for that. The admin guy had the computer right now and was examining it. And a Macbook Pro fortress sat behind the TV at … at home.

'Said something else, too, this Sr. Melo.'

'That he knows where Ellie is?' Leme asked hopefully.

'That he *doesn't* know where she is. Throwaway line, like "Yeah, Leandro was with her a bit and now she doesn't take my calls", entendeu?'

'Lying prick. He saw her yesterday.'

'I know,' Lisboa said, mock-patient. 'Which makes the other thing he said even more interesting.'

'None of this is in the report, though. Thanks for making me read that.'

'He said he thought Leandro was a noia.'

'Maconha?'

'No, crack. Discreet, but a user, sabe?'

'Autopsy'll tell us that.'

'Fernando said Leandro may have introduced Ellie to it, that he'd heard they'd been into Cracolândia to score. Sound likely?'

Cracolândia. Bingo.

'No,' Leme said. 'Not a chance. She's too smart to use and too sharp to get dosed.'

Lisboa nodded. 'What I thought.'

'Fernando offer all this?'

'We got the few people that worked closest with Leandro. He was one of them. And by *work with* Leandro, I mean order the skivvy black punk around. Their words, sabe?'

Leme weighed this. It must have happened in the afternoon while he scoped Fernando's house schmoozing with his mum, looking for Ellie.

They had nothing. He and Ellie in a botched contact meet. Fernando never saw Leme, that was clear. One dead kid and no Ellie.

The phone rang. Leme and Lisboa looked at each other. The phone never rang.

Leme answered, formal. 'Pois não?'

'Detective Leme? It's Elizabeth Young here.'

'What can I do for you?'

'It's Ellie. I want to report her missing. She didn't come into work again today and she's not at home. I'm worried, detective.'

'OK,' Leme said. He needed to think. He needed some time. 'Can you come to the delegacia to file an official notification?'

'Yes, of course. In one hour?'

Perfect. 'Perfect,' Leme said.

Just enough time to talk to admin and have a look at this computer.

Bus from the Offices of Zarzur Cabral to Paraisópolis

Morning, five months earlier

One thing that hadn't changed, Leandro thought, was the time it takes to get home. Home. Perhaps not, any more.

Leandro coughed and a middle-aged woman glared at him. He shot her a sheepish apology, but she closed her window anyway.

The bus was half empty: going the wrong way, heading out. The driver talked to a woman who leaned forward to listen. He's telling her that these days the traffic is the same all day, every day, Rodizio car regulations or not.

The woman nodded. 'E isso, ne?'

'What we need,' the driver explained, 'is another site for this fucking city! Sabe? Move a few people out.'

The woman continued to nod enthusiastically. 'Exactamente!' she said. 'Too many folgados and ladroês. We're best rid of them.'

Leandro sat stoic – fantasy is pretty fucking pointless, he thought. And he knew exactly which people *were* going to be moved out, moved on, relocated. He knew, because he was a part of it, facilitating. His grandmother was not going to be impressed. Her incantation: 'I thank God every day, Leandro. You're so blessed. And that's *my* blessing.'

The bus swept around the stadium and up. Cheap Tricolor São Paulo flags and football shirts hung from lines like washing.

Up and up Giovanni Gronchi, the bus driver battling with the gears. The closer he got to home, the sharper that sense of anticipation. Time and distance created meaning; there hadn't been enough of either yet.

Leandro got off the bus and stepped down into the labyrinth of Paraisópolis. He stared into the glare of traffic at the top end of the favela, a snaking line of polished black and silver reflecting the sun. It was a way to avoid the endless, shuffling queue on the main road Giovanni Gronchi – the most direct and busiest route to the centre – but the potholes slowed everyone down. That and the buses doing three-point turns in a space boxed in by carrossos laden with rubbish, boys rolling tyres down the hill, men unloading cases of fruit and cans of beans from rusty, double-parked vans. Beeping and shouting as more people joined the queue, with little regard to what was road and what was pavement. Schoolchildren meandered right in the middle, slapping the bonnets of the better cars and waving into the darkened windows, not going to school exactly, but not *not* going, in that classic Brazilian style, jeito.

Leandro smiled: been there.

'What I do is provide a means to earn a living,' his grandmother used to say. He would watch her turn fabric in her hands, mark creases with chalk, pins lined up between her lips. 'This is a trade. With hard work and faith, you can make a life from this skill.'

He turned up the alley, towards home. What once was home. The ground was concrete now and a thin groove ran through it as a makeshift drain. Wooden palettes were stacked either side of the narrow entrance. The buildings rose up and leaned over, embracing. Satellite dishes with Sky written across them in orange matched the exposed brick. The houses had no uniformity, no smoothness, built on impulses not plans. Plastic drains, lopsided brick and concrete jutted out at awkward angles. He rubbed shoulders with washing hanging from empty window frames, ducked under power cables that sagged in the space between homes, stepped over rib-thin, sleeping dogs. Pillars marked the start of one more space for yet another family. Through the gap where the living area will be, Leandro saw the hill rise up, but there was no grass there any more, only a few trees stretching their branches like limbs between the red-orange pillbox houses. Brick by brick, this will all be filled, he thought. He panted in the concrete heat, this third-world weather. Two boys pushed a cart laden with junk up the hill, swerving under the weight.

But when he arrived, Leandro's grandmother was not home. There was a note on the door:

Querido. At school

Of course she was. And there was no way to get in and wait for her here. She took his key when he left. She said that way there'd be no chance of him losing it and someone working out which house it opened. Leandro shook his head. He thought: I'm all that's left, and she seems to want to keep me out.

He reached the Mosteiro where his grandmother taught. The militars were relaxed in the street outside, a hangover from Operação Saturação when they filled the place and declared war on the PCC gang's dealers. Here, though, was safe enough. Lean dogs licked at their paws, limbs entwined in a scruffy circle, tails flicking up at flies. Leandro bent down and patted one on its head. 'Coitado, eh?' he said. Poor thing. It looked up at him as if to ask: 'How would you know? Don't judge, dude. And would it kill you to bring me something to eat?' It settled again, scratched at its underside, shrugging off its disappointment.

'Oi, querido.' One of Leandro's grandmother's colleagues waved him through the door. 'Como vai?'

She embraced him. 'I'm fine,' he said, kissing her on both cheeks. 'You?'

'Ah, you know. Everything well. Graças a deus.' She paused and winked. 'She's expecting you.'

She pointed down the hall. He passed classrooms with small children reciting the alphabet, saw teachers in animated poses directing them. The school was part-education, part-childcare for parents who couldn't afford it, couldn't sacrifice their small paychecks to look after their children themselves. A room where toddlers lay napping on mats on the floor hummed with faulty ceiling fans straining against the heat. Further down the corridor, teenagers were listening to a lecture on Brazilian history, a story of displaced migrants and marginal gains.

The hallway wound to the right and the technical classrooms where she taught. Leandro stopped in the doorway and watched. He saw her circle the room, giving instructions. She was a costureira, a dressmaker, a seamstress, like a good number of honest, favelada women, and a group of young women and a couple of men stitched and cut patterns from a long piece of cloth that flapped in the breeze from the fans. She placed her hand on the back of one girl, whispered something in her ear and they both laughed. She paused, as if aware that something had shifted in the atmosphere of the room, and turned to the door, waving Leandro in.

'Everyone,' she said, 'this is Leandro, my grandson. Say hello.'

The class smiled and greeted him as one.

She looked down at her watch. 'Time to pack up. You know the routine.'

The class busied themselves with boxes and scissors and gathered loose fabric from the floor. Leandro's grandmother angled her way among them, picking up bits and pieces until she reached him.

'Querido,' she said, simply. And sighed.

'Vó, it's nice to see you.'

She folded him into her, pulled his head down to her neck. The smell was a sharp reminder of home.

'Come.'

She guided him back into the corridor and they stepped through the fire escape and out into the little recreation yard. They sat at a rusty table on chairs that wobbled and whose thin bars pinched at Leandro's thighs. She picked at a loose thread caught on her overalls.

'Tell me.'

'I went home. You weren't there.'

'I was here. I left a note.' She paused. 'Not your home any more. Not for some time.'

'I know that.'

'Well then.'

'You could give me a key.'

She shrugged. 'You don't need one.'

'Vó, let's not do this, ne?'

She smiled. 'Embora, ne?' she said. 'We'll talk at home.'

From the mosteiro, they walked back through the favela. At home, on the walls, the plaster was ridged and swollen; the cloth that separated her bed, threadbare and miserly.

Beans stewed on the hot plate; a swamp of the cheap meat, smelling of Leandro's childhood.

He said, 'There is something I want to talk to you about.'

'Ah. Claro, ne? Of course there is.'

Leandro sighed. 'It's about your friends. The ones that live in Cracolândia.'

'Então. What about them?'

'It's to do with work.' Leandro paused. His grandmother

crossed her arms. 'It's simple really. A land deal is happening. Their neighbourhood—'

She snorted. 'Neighbourhood? Cracolândia? Deus me livre.'

'Their *neighbourhood* is going to change. They'll be relocated. It's all above board, legal, entendeu?'

'And what's it got to do with you?'

'I'm … liaising. I wanted their number, their address, so I can talk to them personally.'

'This is what you do now?'

'Vó.'

'Ah, I just mean that after your parents passed, after you got your … *casa* – if you can call it that – in Bela Vista, with their money, after you got your *job*, this is how you live? Helping? Is that what you call it?'

'Vó, favor, eh?'

She took a piece of paper and scribbled down a number and an address. She pushed the paper across the table towards him. 'Aqui, ó.'

'Obrigado. It's for the best, believe me.'

She flashed him a false smile. 'I need to go. Church meeting, entendeu? Remember your faith? I hope you do. You'll need it, Leandrinho.'

He nodded. He took the dirty plates to the sink and ran the tap.

'Leave it, querido,' his grandmother said.

Leandro bowed his head.

'Ate mais, ne, Vó.' See you later.

He left the house and headed back towards the bus stop.

In two hours, if he were lucky, he'd be back at work.

'O Cara' (The Dude) – Society Drug Dealer

What you say your name was again? Fernando? Right, yeah. Mate of that tricky fuck Alex, ne? Ha. Motherfucker's a piece of work, sending you to meet me. What, you his cão de guarda or little bitch? I'm kidding, caralho, relaxa.

Tell me what you need.

That's doable. You probably thought I'd be some favelado rude boy, ne? You did? Mate – ingénue, entendeu? I ain't selling no yellowing, sulphur-based ten-reais bag of speedy bullshit, ta ligado? This stuff's proper. Which is why I'm going to have to come back. Give me an address. Don't worry, you can tell Alex that I'm coming – it's all good. I've been to his. It's my job, porra, and I don't cross the road for less than what you're buying, certo?

And that's why you're paying what you're paying. This is pure grade, Amazon, factory-made chisel, my friend. Serious racket. I can do you a vial for a grand from which one hit will keep you up for fucking *daaaaayyyys*, ta ligado? Don't balk, playboy, I'm the go-to guy for rich fucks like you. Be surprised how many of your folks' friends are doing a vial on a weekend dinner party up in Jardins or fucking wherever. It is what it is and it is a desirable motherfucker, entendeu?

What, you want provenance? Ha. Look, there's me, connected beyond the fucking hoodlums of the PCC, none of that fast, loose tiro-teiro fear that you get in the favela, I'm a mid-chain man, sabe? You don't need to know nothing more than that this shit is what you pay for and I am well fucking away from that boca de fuma playboy scoring weed in the dark from a kid in flip-flops in the entrance to Paraisópolis, certo? For the likes of you, you're paying for more than just the pó, porra: you're paying for security. You don't like that, then fuck off down to Cracolândia or take your chances in the favela. You'll have a lot less fun and be a lot more scared, playboy, viu?

And you want some MD? Two prices, certo. Me, I'd go big. Your amigo Alex will be all over that like a militar in a cheap bordel. OK? We clear?

Nice one, cara. I'll see you in a day or two. And you remember one thing: something doesn't pan out, you got this shit in a boca in Paraisópolis, viu? Viu?

This is a *careeeeer*, my friend, and not one no playboy fuckhead like you or your cunty friend is going to ruin. Haha, mate, relax, I'm filling your sack a little. It's us, it's good, certo?

I'll call –

Now do one.

A Nightclub in Itaim

Six months earlier, late

Fernando looked across the dance floor. The room swelled. BOOM. There it was. A light switched on in his head. An electric crunch. Eyes widened. His snide friend Alex loomed over him, tongue wet in his ear. Fernando could smell the cough-syrupy energy drink he'd mixed with Scotch as he breathed over him. 'Pegou, cara?' He was asking if the drugs had kicked in. They had. They'd been dabbing at a bag of MDMA and Fernando's vision was strobing and face tingling, soft to the touch. Went well with the coke, if you got the ratio right. Alex was saying something Fernando couldn't hear, and anyway, a tanned pair of legs in a white denim skirt snagged his attention and she was pulling him towards her, a fish on a line.

Fernando was out with a whole gang of them, mob-handed. Friends from school, the expensive British one in Jardins. Rich and privileged, all of them, and used to getting their own way. Snide Alex had asked him to sort out some coke and had given him a number. 'You do it. Guy's giving me shit over a freebie he threw my way. I just don't need the grief. OK? He delivers. No biggie. I'll do the other stuff.'

So Fernando sorted it out. It *was* easy. The guy was friendly and helpful. *The Dude* was his nickname. Fernando felt good about doing his friends a favour. Everyone was grateful. It was a hoot this night, proper deranged fun.

They were in a balada full of girls. Alex lorded it. They got a private area and bottles of vodka. It got pretty messy, pretty quickly.

Fernando was enjoying himself. It was good coke. He was in the bathroom *a lot.* He'd palmed a fifty into the attendant's hand. It was all good.

The noise was pulsing through the room now and Fernando was caught in it, swaying with it like a submissive dance partner dominated by someone with more jeito. 'Here. Toma.' Alex handed him a shot of something foul-smelling and he tipped it back.

'Vamos, eh?' he said and they were back in the toilets and Alex palmed another fifty into the hand of the attendant who smirked and watched them go into the cubicle together. Alex sprayed powder about on their wrists like it didn't mean shit. One. Two. Three. And they were wiping their faces and in the neon mirror Fernando saw hollow eyes and clenched jaw and then was back through the door and BOOM. There it was again, though this time a little less intense, but some deep house fucking anthem or whatever had just dropped and there was a euphoric swelling. Alex moved smoothly in front and smiled at the barmaid. 'Problem with trying to fuck barmaids,' he was saying, loudly so she could hear, 'is that they're invariably sober and bored. They'll smile for any filho da puta, any son of a bitch. Not a level playing field. Trick is finding one who'll put up with you.' He winked and she giggled. Fuck this, Fernando thought, and headed back to the bathroom.

On the way, he got chatting to some guy, basically his age, though clearly not of the same social class, or whatever. The guy was asking about the VIP area, about the girls.

Then White Skirt wandered past again and Fernando ignored his new friend and tried to smile but felt his mouth widen into a drug-gurn. She lingered for a moment then headed over to her girls, a group standing around a table sipping at … champagne? They didn't look like they'd have the money for that. Not in there. Bem brega, tacky all of them. But White Skirt's legs bent and hips rolled. Alex saw Fernando looking over at her. 'Shooting pussy in a barrel, baby,' he shouted. Fernando winked at his new friend.

His new friend smiled – wolfish, expectant, hopeful.

Fernando took pity on him. 'Ah, beleza cara. I'll take you up there. But first…' and he led him to the bathroom.

They shouldered a cubicle door. He pulled out his coke and the guy smiled, but not in a good way.

He pushed Fernando back against the wall of the cubicle.

'This is going to get real,' he said. He pulled a badge.

Holy fuck.

The guy smiled. 'Off-duty, but still. You fuckers are bang out of line.'

Fernando froze, heart raced, blood rushed from his head. He thought he might faint.

The cop laid it out for him. 'Call your guy. Get him to bring ten more of these pacotinhos to the club. For that sort of money, he'll shit. You're going to meet him a little down the road. Across from that hamburger joint, you know it?'

Fernando nodded.

'He deliver by car?'

Fernando nodded again.

'OK. Make the call.'

Fernando did as he was told and it was on. The Dude would be there in twenty minutes. The cop made a call of his own. He turned to Fernando. 'You think of doing anything stupid, you and your friends will be in some serious trouble. Entendeu? This is not an option. I'm talking *serious*. The kind of thing you playboys wouldn't dream of. Got that?'

Fernando was terrified. The cop was genuine and it was terrifying.

The cop strongarmed him to a cashpoint. Between the cash in Fernando's pocket, the amount he could take out, and a couple of hundred from the cop himself, they got the money together. 'It's important the money changes hands,' the cop said.

Fernando was sobering up. His teeth locked in a coke chatter. His bones in a drug rattle. His phone beeped. The guy was just down the road. The cop winked. 'Just go and do it.'

Fernando leaned into the window, made the exchange. As he did, two cars boxed the guy in and the cop was badge and gun out and pushing Fernando to the ground. Fernando sloped off – fucking *crawled* off, it felt – and watched from a distance. It was odd. The Dude got out of his car, opened the boot, handed the cop a bag and then simply drove off.

Fernando was dazed, he didn't know what to do so he waved down a cab and went home and buried himself under his covers: shamefaced, surreal, frightened, some sense of relief. 'Like wanking on a comedown,' was how Alex always described that feeling. It was much, much worse.

The next day the Dude called him. They met in a café in Pinheiros. The Dude was very reasonable, considering. He knew exactly what had happened and he told Fernando how it was going to play out.

'So I gave them fifty grand of what we call "arrest-cash". Everyone's happy. Cops get theirs and I don't go to jail. Thing is, I'm fifty grand out. And that's your fault.'

Fernando didn't know what to do. The Dude knew where he lived and he could hardly go to the police. He couldn't tell his parents and he didn't trust his friends.

He nodded. 'OK,' he said. 'I know. I'm sorry.'

The Dude smiled. 'I'm a reasonable man,' he told him. 'We'll set up an instalment plan. But you will make the payments, *without fail.* Got that? I'm not going to hurt you, really I'm not. Not my style. But you don't make the payments, I will ruin you, you gash-lapping homo playboy fuck. I will *ruin your life.* Certo? Understood? Think of it as paying back a bank loan, that's all. Certo? Beleza, então.'

Fernando went home, shaking.

Delegacia

16 October, mid-morning

Admin department was all fucking euphemism. Assorted geeks and fuckheads. They sat in the dark. They squinted at screens. They growled in-jokes that their visitors didn't get. Uppity fucks, the lot of them. What did they do? Find stuff out about people and use it against them. Illegal, most of what they did. But no one was going to arrest *them*. And no one was going to complain.

No one even knew they'd done what they did. It was always too late.

If they ever did find out, it usually meant they were in jail.

Leme went down. Leme stalled on the stairs. He hadn't figured what he wanted to find. Sometimes, the best thing a detective can know is what he wants to find.

Leme dawdled. He joined the dots:

Ellie goes missing. Fernando takes her computer. Why? Something incriminating. Fernando gives the computer to Antonia. Leme left that. Something incriminating.

Leme bounced.

The admin guy looked like shit. Leme had got a fuckhead not a geek. He smiled at Leme. 'We're in,' he said.

'Isso,' Leme said. 'Let's have it then.'

He sat down next to the fuckhead. 'What are we looking for?' he said.

'Just show me what's on it. I'll know when I see it.'

The fuckhead muttered something uncomplimentary.

He opened the documents folder. 'Start with this, shall we?' he said.

A number of folders. Names like "Key Admin", "Camera Uploads", "Art", "Tax", "Writing".

'Open that one called writing,' Leme said.

The fuckhead tap-tapped. More folders. Names like "Contemporary Short Stories", "Dissertation", "Misc.", "Work".

'That one, work,' Leme said. There were eight documents, all with dates for titles. 'Open the most recent one,' Leme said.

The computer yawned and the document opened. It was in English. Leme scanned it.

'Hmm,' the fuckhead grunted.

'What? You didn't expect me to speak English? Porra.'

It wasn't a finished article. Notes, mainly. Things like:

We need each other, but we destroy each other.

This made Leme think of Renata. As did this:

I would rather be a failure at something I value than a success at something I don't.

The first line:

If you look up, you could be anywhere in a beautiful European city. Though most of the residents in Cracolândia don't spend much time looking up.

Leme scanned more.

A line jumped out.

...Militars didn't seem concerned about the crime that was going on around them. The main guy spoke in vulgar slang, but it seemed put on, like he was playing a role. They took our cash and told us to fuck off out of it. It didn't feel right. How could a row of houses simply *disappear*?

The fuckhead said, 'I'll copy the lot, shall I?'

Leme nodded, distracted.

'Photos too?' The fuckhead winked.

Leme shook his head. He needed to call Carlos, his friend in the militars.

Fernando's House

One month earlier

When I touch myself, I think of you. That ok?? ;) xx

Fernando smiled. What a minx. He was enjoying this. Sexting. He'd never done it before.

I want your head between my legs. Ooh. There. I said it x

Yikes.

He tap-tapped his phone.

Shall I come over? xx

No. No good. Too needy. He deleted the text. He started again.

That sounds amazing.

He smiled and shook his head. I'm better at this, he thought. He hit delete, hammering with one finger. He looked at his open bedroom door. His phone beeped again.

I want to see you.

That's better.

He replied. **Me too. When?**

A moment. **Soon.**

He smiled. **Soon is good. When?**

I always want to see you.

MINX, he thought. **Now?**

Calm down dear. Soon.

He put his phone out of reach on his nightstand. He reached for it. I'll just … he thought. And then it beeped again.

Excellent.

I'm looking forward to seeing you xx

He smiled. Leave it at that. Keep the upper hand. But he couldn't resist.

Me too xx

And then.

Sure you don't want me to come over?

He hit send and regretted it immediately. He waited a moment.

Nothing. He stood up and paced his bedroom. Come on, he looked at his phone. *Come on.*

'Fernandinho!'

Shit. His mother was calling him. He went to the door. 'Oi?' he shouted. 'I'm in my room. What do you want?'

'Telefone!'

He hadn't heard the landline ring. 'I'll get it here!'

He picked up the hall extension. 'Quem fala?' he said.

'Quem fala? Not very polite, Fernando. It's Antonia. Don't you answer your mobile phone?'

Shit. 'I think it was on silent. Sorry.'

'That or you're sending dirty texts to your new girlfriend.'

'It's not like that.'

Antonia intimidated Fernando. She wasn't his boss *exactly* but she was his senior and she was *a* boss. But that wasn't why he found her intimidating. It was that she was older, more intelligent, more assured and seemed, in a withering glance, to be able to reduce him to the nervous adolescent he had been before discovering that having money really did mean you could behave pretty much as you wanted.

Though now he was discovering that *not* having money meant you had to behave pretty much as other people wanted.

'I'm just checking in, that's all,' she said in a tone that made it clear she wasn't just checking in. 'Making sure you're working hard.' Her tone lightened and she laughed. 'Progress report, entendeu?'

Fernando checked the hall for his parents. He could hear them in the kitchen. They were laughing, probably drinking wine, leaning against the counter and talking about their days in that easy way they had that used to make him feel warm and safe and now made him feel bitter, resentful and, frankly, astonished that such a relationship was possible.

'Please, Antonia.'

'Remember what you promised, that you'd do any extra work I ask you to, it's not much,' she said. 'And remember what you need – money. You told me that. I'm trying to be helpful, that's all.'

Fernando rested his head against the wall. He should never have told Antonia that he needed money. Rookie mistake. He was backed up into a corner now. The fucking *Dude*.

The payments meant he had to move back in with his parents.

The payments meant that he was looking for ways to make quick and easy money. All he wanted was to get this over with. A lump sum and it went away. And an off-the-books lump sum was what he was being promised. So long as *his* promises panned out.

'OK, Antonia, you know I remember. I need to go. That OK?'

'Claro, querido. We'll talk.'

She hung up.

Fernando's phone was flashing. He swiped. Ellie.

Not going to work tonight, garanhão. I'll let you know, but soon.

No kiss. Fucksake. He felt the air sucked from him.

Soon? What does soon mean?

He paced. He was at the beck and call of every fucker it felt. Even his girlfriend, if she even was his girlfriend. And he'd been helping her! Not fair!

He stalked. He looked at the time. She wasn't going to *reply*? She wasn't going to reply. He speared a message into his phone.

Ellie

His phone shook immediately. **Fernando**

He tap-tapped. **You're not going to answer?**

You pissed me off. I'll see you. SOON.

Fernando threw the phone across the room.

It hit his pillow and didn't break.

Jardim da Luz, near Cracolândia

Two months earlier

Ellie and Leandro sat at an outside table in the Pinacoteca Museum café. They both drank beer.

'Two chopps,' Ellie said to the waiter. 'And what do you want?' she asked Leandro.

He smiled. 'The same.'

It'd been a sensible decision. They nailed the first drink in two gulps, both of them still shaking. They'd crossed the main road by the Estacao da Luz and by some tacit agreement ended up in the café. For Ellie at least, it was reassuring to be surrounded by the trappings of culture and civilisation, by art and sculpture and nice food and polite waiters. So what if she could see the hookers working the park just metres from where they sat? There might as well have been a transparent screen. It was like a zoo. And the animals left you well alone: they interacted only with each other.

'So,' Ellie said. 'What just happened?'

Leandro shook his head. 'I don't know.'

As they scurried away from the militars, it had occurred to Ellie that perhaps Leandro was acting out some strategem that she didn't know about. Disappearing houses? Really? He had looked genuinely confused though. And there was something up with the way the militars dealt with them. They didn't seem bothered about the noias, addicts, and the lowlife dealers. So why were they there?

Ellie decided to test him. She wanted to know if he would try and brazen it out, or if he was telling the truth. She'd picked the right side of men a whole lot trickier than sweet young Leandro.

'Where exactly were you taking me, Leandro,' she asked, her tone sharper, though undercut by the softness of the alcohol. 'That was *not* an experience I appreciated.'

Leandro breathed in through his nose. He looked at the table and then looked Ellie in the eye. 'I was taking you to see the house of some family friends. The house wasn't there. The house isn't there. I'm sorry you had to go through it.'

Ellie narrowed her eyes.

'That's the truth.'

Ellie nodded. She was sure he was telling the truth. 'What now then?' she asked. 'Your friends got a phone number?'

'Wait.' Leandro fumbled in his pockets. He pulled out his wallet. 'There's a number.' He showed Ellie a receipt with a mobile phone number scrawled on it, as if he needed to prove he was telling the truth. He dug his phone out of his back pocket. He punched in the number.

Leandro shook his head. 'Weird,' he said again.

He took his phone from his ear and studied the display. He punched the number in again.

'No,' he said. 'It was right the first time. No dial tone, nothing. Just a repeated message that the number doesn't exist.'

'You've called them before, right?' Ellie asked.

Leandro nodded. 'I'm not sure how else I can get hold of them.'

Ellie's own phone buzzed. She flipped it over on the table. Fernando.

Hello. Saudades. F xx

She flipped the phone back face down.

'OK,' she said. 'Let's figure out where this leaves us.'

'I was telling the truth, what I told the militars. I'd not heard anything about this, this … change. I feel pretty sure that my friends would have called if they'd had any warning. I'm guessing it happened very quickly.'

'And the question is why you can't contact them now.'

'Yes. This is all very strange.'

Too fucking right, thought Ellie. Flattened houses, disappearing families. She signalled for another chopp. She watched as elderly Korean women pushed carts across the park, laden with knock-off tracksuits and other tat to sell around the corner on 25 de Maio. The phrase "underclass retail" popped into her head. She tapped it into her phone.

'Hang on,' Leandro said. 'I'm going to call the office.'

He stood up and wandered a few yards away, towards the park. Ellie pulled at her fresh beer. She felt a long, long way from Poole harbour. She felt a long, long way from her teenage self. But perhaps she wasn't. Hadn't she learned anything in the few years since? There are moments, she reminded herself, when you have to accept something negative in order to benefit in the long term. Her entire career was based on that.

She watched Leandro talk on the phone. He was shaking his head. He was rubbing at his eyes. He was gesticulating with his free hand. He looked over at her and grimaced an apology. She waved to him that it was fine, to keep on talking. She wondered if she should call Fernando. He might be able to help, or at least he might know something.

She watched Leandro weave between tables to rejoin her.

'Então?' she asked him.

Leandro shook his head. 'No one's telling me anything.'

'What do you mean?'

'Just that. Nothing.'

'What, they don't know?'

Leandro frowned. 'I don't know. I spoke to a couple of people, also involved. Both just said it's done, it's all taken care of. I asked them about the houses, the families. They just told me not to bother about it, that the bosses had dealt with it themselves. Not to worry.'

'Did you speak to Fernando?'

'No. He was in a meeting. And anyway,' Leandro sighed, 'I don't think he'd know. He seems completely uninterested in the whole project sometimes. Like he doesn't have a clue. Porra,' he said. 'This is fucked up.'

Ellie nodded. 'I think you might be wrong,' she said. 'He knows. We'll have to work on him together. Separately, entendeu, but in tandem, sabe?'

'OK. What do you suggest?'

Ellie smiled. 'Give me a couple of days and I'll be in touch.'

'Certo. What's your number?' Leandro asked. 'I don't have it. You've only got mine. Just in case, sabe, I find something out.'

'Of course,' Ellie said. 'Here, give me your phone. Be quicker this way.'

Leandro passed her his mobile phone. Ellie tapped her number into the contacts, careful to ensure that only one digit was wrong.

Best Leandro doesn't have it, for now at least, she reasoned. Best to

Fernando's House

Three weeks earlier

'That Ellie is fucking nasty. Girl likes some serious shit. Entendeu?'

Fernando was lying back on his couch wrapped in a blanket despite the heat. Bed-hair and body odour; dog-breath horny. He squirmed about, pulling the blanket up between his legs. Leandro sat awkwardly on the other side of the room. Fernando liked how uncomfortable he looked.

'I said she likes some serious shit. Independent woman, know what I mean? White, middle-class Beyoncé shit: "Question." Get me?'

Leandro, wary, confused, nodded.

Fernando continued in that way of his, deliberately appalling. 'It's really not our fault that all these young women want fingering, entendeu?'

He watched Leandro's response carefully. Leandro looked sheepish, unsure how to react.

'It's a selfless act, really. Feminist, in its way,' Fernando mused. He took an exaggerated breath through his nose. 'Take a shower. You stink,' he said.

He rubbed his crotch and watched as Leandro loped towards the bathroom. He slammed the door.

Fernando heard the water start up, sprung across the room and grabbed Leandro's phone. Messages: him, Antonia. Just arrangements. Scroll down. Ellie. An address he sent to her. And then:

What you told me is extremely important and you mustn't tell anyone else.

Fernando snapped the phone shut. He looked at the bathroom door, slightly ajar.

Ellie was foreign, respected, known. Their connection was personal and clear. It was recorded online. Discreetly, yes, but still recorded.

No one would believe Leandro. No one.

The running water stopped.

Delegacia

16 October, late morning

Leme jumped the stairs.

He shook his head. He muttered to himself: 'Admin guys got arseholes of iron, sat on a hard chair in front of a soft screen all day.'

Leme shuffled across the open-plan to his cupboard office. He heard Lisboa talking and a woman's laughter.

He cracked the door.

Lisboa was batendo papo, chit-chatting. He winked, grandstanded. Elizabeth Young was sitting on Leme's chair, legs crossed. She twirled her hair with a finger. Her white thighs peeked out. Lisboa goofed. Elizabeth Young mooned. She turned to Leme. Lisboa ogled and winked. The Big Man. That was his MO:

A pussycat, larger than life.

'I'll get us all some coffee,' Lisboa said. 'Que filezão, eh,' he whispered as he left.

Leme growled in distaste. Lisboa sounded like his condo mates. Not like him. Filezão: a tasty bit of aged steak. Jesus.

He and Elizabeth Young were alone. Leme closed the door and got straight to business.

He said, 'Então, no word from Ellie?'

'No. Nothing. That's why I'm here.'

Leme nodded. 'OK. Paperwork is fairly simple. We'll get to it in a minute. I've a few questions first though.'

'Of course.'

'You've tried Ellie's apartment?'

'Yes. Both in person and on the phone.'

'Did you speak to the porteiro?'

'Yes.'

'What did he say?'

'Only that she hadn't been home for a few days. That she was staying with a boyfriend.'

'He tell you the boyfriend's name?'

'No. He said he didn't know it, but that she'd told him she'd be gone for a little while.'

Leme nodded. Made sense. Porteiro doesn't want to give anything away. He'd talk to Leme, sure, but to a nosy gringa? Nem fodendo.

'And you don't have any other contact numbers for her?'

Elizabeth Young shook her head. 'Mobile phone and home, like you, detective. And you have her mobile phone, right?'

'I have it,' Leme said. 'We're looking at it.'

'And you know her,' Elizabeth Young said. 'I find that a little strange.'

Leme nodded. He needed to feed her something like the truth. 'I can understand that. We met at your offices actually, a while ago. I was there to meet a colleague of yours. She approached me. We swapped details. Then she helped me out with an investigation last year. I pointed her in the direction of a few stories. I don't think anything came of the ideas though.'

Elizabeth Young snorted. 'You *pointed her in the direction of a few stories*? What do you think it is she does at my magazine?'

Leme made nice. 'She talked about wanting to do some investigative journalism, crime, political stuff, entendeu? I gave her some ideas, that's all.'

'Investigative journalism? Yeah,' Elizabeth Young drawled, eyes wide, 'she's a fearless, hard-charging, righteous, crusading journalist, our Ellie.'

'Why do you say that?'

Leme thought of the conversations they'd had a year or so before, when she'd talked candidly about her ambitions as a journalist. Ellie had said this Elizabeth Young had been on board. Nothing had come of it, of course. Ellie played games.

Elizabeth Young said, 'She wrote arts copy. For the listings. Recommended restaurants and gigs, plays and events, sabe? She sometimes did some proofreading for our Brazilian writers.'

'What about this Cracolândia story you told me about?'

Elizabeth Young's eyes danced. 'I was humouring her. And when I told you about it, I was giving her the benefit of the doubt. Being nice, entendeu? This contact she claims to have? We know nothing about him. I don't think she ever met him. I was letting her play at being a serious journo. I care about her. She's a fucking kid though.'

Leme nodded. He thought about the notes the admin fuckhead had got from her laptop. It looked like she knew what she was doing. That analysis of who gets paid from this deal. Seemed legit. He said, 'What about that answerphone message? From Leandro? Her contact.'

Elizabeth Young smiled. 'I don't know,' she said. 'But Ellie is very capable of making a message like that happen, if she felt she had to.'

Leme weighed it. Leme knew Ellie was a game-player. He trusted this Elizabeth Young, yes, but he also knew that Ellie could hoodwink. Maybe Ellie was all mouth, but that didn't explain what had happened yesterday morning and where the fuck she was now.

'What do you know about her private life?' Leme asked.

Elizabeth Young fingered her neck, looked at the ceiling. 'Ellie enjoys a social life. She drinks too much. Blacks out, forgets things, entendeu? Comes to work in denial of what happened. Not even knowing what *did* happen, sometimes. Nothing terribly awful, but there were some embarrassing moments.'

'What do you mean?'

Leme knew full well what she meant. In the months after Renata's death, Leme woke often with a knot of shame and fear in his stomach, a sharp string of memories pulled through his head, like ticker-tape, jarring hourly, shuddering as something new and fresh came back to him.

He'd wolfed beers for breakfast to quell that shame. He'd gabbed with men he shouldn't. He'd thrill-seeked to forget.

He'd schmoozed trim and paid them to sit with him for hours while he wailed and railed.

He'd threatened to roust the guys that ran the sequinned, pneumatic whores he'd taken pity on in American bars on the strip.

He'd come round more than once in an alley off Augusta, alone and damp.

Bloody.

He owed Lisboa a helluva lot.

Leme knew all about shame.

Blacking out was a relief at first. His anchor of ten years had gone. He didn't know how to behave. But the relief turned to fear pretty quickly. When you work on certainty as the basis of your life, professional and personal, missing hours are fucking terrifying. You can't live in that dark place too long.

But it's in the cracks where the light gets in.

'You're a very *human* human,' Lisboa once told him. 'Forgive yourself.'

It took time, though. Everything does, Leme had learned.

'She would make scenes,' Elizabeth Young said. 'In bars. Guys tried it on and she didn't like it. She would take their drinks and flounce. You know Brazilian men. She got a reputation in some of the bars near the office.'

'How do you know this?'

'I was there once or twice. Otherwise reports would filter in. A couple of colleagues were a little worried about her. Eventually I took her out on my own, gave her some advice.'

'And what was the advice?'

'I made a suggestion. A better way to meet men. A website.'

Leme raised his eyebrows.

'Don't judge, detective. It's classy.' She stared him down. 'It must be. I use it.'

'What's the name?'

'Single Gringa.'

Leme snorted. 'OK.'

'I don't know if she signed up, but I acted as a referee for her. It's a discreet, expensive thing, so there's no reason why I would know if she ever did.'

'And all this behaviour never threatened Ellie's job?'

Elizabeth Young shook her head. 'She's good at what she does, and the problems were never to do with colleagues. I just thought she was finding herself, figuring out the right way to live her life out here. It's a big change for a young woman, entendeu?'

Leme nodded. He did understand. Grief is all about exactly that process: trying to work out how the fuck you are ever supposed to behave again.

'Anything else you can think of?' he asked.

'Once – and this was horrible, but it does give you an insight into her behaviour – a van pulled up in Itaim. Three men jumped out and tried to grab her and a colleague she was with. Dangerous stuff, you know? When they take you off into some corner of a distant favela and bleed your bank account over five, six days? She had no idea. She was so drunk she kicked off. A mouthy gringa. They left it. She was lucky.'

Leme nodded. 'She did the right thing.'

Elizabeth Young made a face. 'I don't know,' she said.

Lisboa edged the door. 'Coffee?'

Leme shunted right to make space.

'Lovely office you've got here,' Elizabeth Young said to Lisboa.

Lisboa grinned. 'Room for two.'

He handed Leme the paperwork for the missing persons notification.

Leme glanced at it. All correct. Leme looked at Elizabeth Young. She'd told him everything she could, he thought. He handed the papers back to Lisboa. 'You take care of it,' he said.

Leme tipped an imaginary hat at Elizabeth Young. He stalked across the open-plan. The admin fuckhead would have printed what he needed by now.

Time to pay Carlos a visit, figure the play on the militars in Cracolândia.

Leme thought back. Leme remembered.

He understood that it had been instant with Renata –

He was chatting to a friend at a party at Lisboa's. The friend had waved her over. They'd embraced. Then Renata turned to Leme and they did a kind of double take.

Leme remembered –

His insides screaming, a surge in his chest –

A knowledge. That was it: he *knew*.

Leme remembered –

'Do you have a boyfriend?'

'Well…'

'What does that mean?'

'It means that you should take care.'

Clever girl. She was always right.

Leme remembered –

'Let's make it happen. I've never loved like this.'

'So leave him.'

'It's complicated.'

'Why?'

There's no good answer to that question. You either leave or you don't. There's no middle ground that isn't damaging for everyone. There's no middle ground. It's never complicated. Complicated suggests indecision. Leme was a fundamentalist in love. He just hadn't realised.

When they fucked, there was relief, sadness, a hint of joy.

A hint of joy to come. A reminder of the sadness he felt. Did she?

Leme remembered –

Months and months of desperate confusion.

'Let me be free of you,' he wrote in emails. 'Act, or tell me you're never going to.'

She did neither.

Later, she explained she hadn't known how to reassure him that one day they would be together without raising his hopes in the immediate term. Immediate term – he'd laughed at that.

Lawyer bullshit.

Leme heard her man had been fired, had a meltdown.

He did some digging. Not something he was proud of, but he was a detective for fuck's sake. Not exactly hard to get the drop on some cunt love rival, and dead easy when you're wounded, angry, to cross a perceived line.

If she'd been straight with me, I'd've never done it, is what he told himself.

But what did he do?

Just found out the prick was your basic nonce, that's all. Abused a position of power. Fuck, he'd been arrested even. Charges dropped, but still. No smoke, and he never got his job back. Leme could've found all that out by accident.

So that's all he did. Oh, and he let her know he knew. Not that it made any fucking difference. Of course it didn't.

But he understood. He had the soft heart of the forgiving and the diamond-hard edge of the jilted. Tricky balance that. Perspective and whatnot.

And it made him think. Why him and not me? What *was* all this co-dependent, abusive relationship, cowardly, head-in-the-sand, careless, malevolent fuckery? Seemed like a bad lot, a you-deserve-each-other scene. A shit-house of shame, that one.

Leme thought: *Fuck it.*

He had everything he needed to be happy.

But he never quite thought: *Fuck it.*

Silence is cruel in its non-resolution.

Leme remembered –

How she'd simply re-entered his life, fully formed, ready, wanting him. Wanting *them*. There was something supremely confident about it, bordering on the sociopathic, her almost wilful lack of empathy. Sweeping aside the past as if it hadn't happened. Which, in a way, it hadn't, to her.

Leme remembered –

He never forgot any of this, even in the light of what happened next. Easy to see love as overcoming obstacles, conquering; important to remember, Leme knew, that period of pain, darkness. It was a part of it.

Leme never forgot. He had only loved her. From that very first moment.

And now, yes, Antonia.

Prince Felipe, Cracolândia Drug Dealer

OK, I'll tell you what happened. Look, I don't want any more trouble, Dona Ellie, sabe? I been done had enough licks for this year, entendeu? I don't want to puke, get hit, take a fucking hard loss again for time, you know? I'm tired, I'm hungry, I'm a skinny Crack-land fuck. And I'm scared. That's why I'm talking to you.

I found out who you were and it weren't too tricky. You came down here with that black kid that time and we all knew 'bout it. And that snide militar Nelsinho – he fucking hate that nickname, think he the big Nelsão, entendeu? – scared you off? Well, we had a word with his burro goon, greased him with what dinheirinho we had, we got the number for your magazine, we figure why not talk to some gringa writer who might write something that help us, right? Então.

So what happened is not long ago when they start talking 'bout changing Cracolândia, clearing it like they clear the forest, moving in a few militars and whatnot, old Nelsinho and his boys pay us a visit. They know we run the rocks down here – there ain't much competition, entendeu? The noias like a bone-thin kid likes me to score from – makes 'em think I one of them, sabe? Comforting or some shit. So I get mine from – well, somewhere else. And slouch here and there and sell and make pretty much fuck all once the favela lot march down and take theirs. But now anything I do make, Nelsinho tells me, goes to him *before* I pass on to the favela lot now as they clearing the place and so the likes of me – which is *me*, sabe? – needs protecting from the law when they come in *and* the favela lot too when they do. Which they will. And you're not the law, Senhor Nelson? I say, and he say, querido, I am what *makes* the fucking law, sabe, so this is what it is, ta ligado?

We're being bled dry, haemorrhaging cash. Know what? We don't even never *have* it, so how the fuck we can bleed it? Entendeu? Lot of folk probably think we deserve it, good thing, save a few noias from themselves. You think that? Valeu.

Vou te contar alguma coisa.

A story. A joke, actually.

Want to know how they smuggle crack into the favelas from out of state?

Sewn up inside a dead baby. Not always, but it's one option, sabe? There's a lot of dead babies kicking around in cash-poor hick public hospitals in the interior, so they say. Life for life, ta ligado?

Want to know how a boy likes me get into this game?

You can guess.

No, I mean, go on: *guess*.

Crime pays. Can't you tell by my clothes and car? Where do you think they are? Same place as my teeth, porra: not with me. I didn't grow up hoping to be a Cracolândia hophead salesman stooge fucked over by police and thieves.

Did you grow up wanting to interview one?

Caralho, menina, you're funny, ta ligado?

OK, short version: militars is here to clean up, which means they hoover the cash we make before we moved on by them or burn on a favela hill in a stack of tyres when the PCC says chega, Felipe, this not working out.

Certo? Don't ask me why, but Nelsinho and his boys, and his big boss man with the tasty boots, they ain't playing.

And this ain't going to last too long.

You going to want some background, ne, menina? Learn how a boy become a man like me, ne? My life all because of those militars. I end up here, doing what I do, 'cos of them, 'cos what else you do when you have nothing, entendeu?

Osasco, you know it? That's where I was born. Yeah that place seen some darkness. Porra, ne? You know what happen? Where this darkness come from. So, when a militar gets snuffed by some gang-banger, they come where they think the shooter is. But it don't matter much they get the shooter, just some bad guys from the same bairro – it all comes out in the wash, sabe? They like terrorists, entendeu? Hoods, face masks, machine guns. They line the guys up, execute them. Or they spray the street. Either way, you're looking ten, twenty dead in a few hours. And for one reason: it a message – power, entendeu? These fuckers grew up same bairros, same problems, same jeito to earn, same methods at work, sabe? So they in competition, ne?

They all outlaws, no rule on the street they don't make. You kill one of mine, I'm taking ten, twenty, fifty of you fuckers. And these bullets don't discriminate.

Which is my story.

My daddy weren't a very good guy. But he wasn't a very bad guy. He was a poor guy. Short version: he was one of those ten, twenty, fifty, when I was eleven years old. And the bad news? My mummy ran cross the street to help him and gunned down she was too.

So, what do you think happened? My shack was quickly taken from me. Some bad guys just moved stuff in and kicked me out. That's how I ended up in Cracolândia. They welcoming here, if you can believe that – they really are. Safety in numbers. It weren't long I got a little grunt work running rock.

Something I never understood: how is that cheap rocks sold to slum-bum noias is what makes the money while the cash-heavy coke that go to the condos and playboy nightclubs, the baladas seems ignored?

But, yeah, that's why I do what I do. The PCC run me – they want to keep me in this shitheap desperate state, just enough change to live, to enjoy something and not complain; not enough to be tempted to go, you know, tipo, freelance. And now the militars are fucking me.

This ain't going to last long, sabe?

So, tell me about that poor black kid dressed up in cheap threads. Your turn, menina, sabe? Ah, it's no thing – only why he bring you here? Come on, I'm doing you a favour. No – this is about information: I have a bit, I'm a bit less fucking disenfranchised, entendeu?

So his name's Leandro, certo. But I'm not sure what 'facilitator' means. You mean helping clear the place? What, legally? Ha. Yeah, OK. And he knows some people who were there but ain't now, that what you saying? Yeah? Gotcha. So this young man is someone in this whole thing. You think old Nelsinho took a shine to him?

Relaxa, bolacha.

Who's the kid going to tell what the kid knows?

That's a saying to savour, menina.

Vai com Deus, garota. God be with you. You'll need him.

On the Way to Cracolândia

16 October, lunchtime

Leme sat in the back of the militar jeep. He watched Carlos fork rice and beans into his mouth, spear gristle-pork. Carlos talked with his mouth full. He drooled rice when the jeep turned too sharp.

'This is no bother, garanhão,' Carlos said. 'I'm just tick-tocking, waxing the day, entendeu? This'll be a pleasure. You want?'

He offered the foil container. Rice looked like maggots feasting on the cheap cuts of fatty meat. Squirming.

Leme shook his head. 'I ate yesterday.'

Carlos laughed and spat rice.

'You're going to *loooove* this shit, Mario. Dope fiends mandied up to the eyeballs, floozies brain-drained on crack. It's a playground and we're the bullies, entendeu? We vamp about a bit, high-heeled, king in the belly, roister doister with our weapons for the crack whores, and before too long some dedo-duro piece of shit grass will come forward to finger who we need. Cool in the cunt, my friend.'

'Charming,' Leme said.

'Ah, vai,' Carlos said.

Carlos barked instructions at the driver. 'Fifteen minutes,' he told Leme.

Leme'd called Carlos from the delegacia and told him what he knew. He'd looked over Ellie's notes again and pieced it together. A week before she disappeared she and Leandro went into Cracolândia. They were looking for a family that Leandro knew. This was for a story Ellie was researching. Leandro worked as a liaison guy for the law firm that was handling the residents' rehousing.

'Black kid?' Carlos asked.

'How did you know?' Leme said.

'"Liaison guy?" Right. They're going to find a nice middle-class Caucasian type to send down there into the fucking jungle? Too dark, too black, too many other animals. I've seen it before,' Carlos said. 'Favela intern to play the race card. Why the poor fucker got the job, I expect.'

'Very good,' Leme said.

The family's house had gone, Leme told Carlos. Three militars threatened Ellie and Leandro, robbed them and told them to fuck off. Leme wanted to know what the militars were doing in Cracolândia. Carlos said, 'Come and have a look.'

Leme told him that this Leandro was found sliced dead at home, gutted and glut, and that this gringa Ellie was off the radar.

'No problem,' Carlos told him. 'We can figure this.'

He'd picked him up half an hour later.

'When was the last time you went down there?' Carlos asked.

'A lifetime ago,' Leme said.

Carlos laughed – heartily. 'You're going to *loooove* this, my friend.'

The passenger seat militar swung his automatic out the window and adjusted his Aviator shades. Carlos opened his window and rested his handgun on the door.

The militar sitting to Leme's left cranked and jammed the magazine into his own automatic.

He nudged Leme.

'Locked and cocked, motherfucker,' he said.

Leme smiled. He groaned inside.

The driver popped the siren and they charged in bull-headed, riding the pavement.

A couple of stick-thin black men scarpered, but the rest of the deranged and the desperate got up slowly from where they lounged, dead-eyed. The militars with the automatics gave chase. They let off a round in the air and the skinny fucks stopped dead.

Leme watched. They turned and walked back to the militars, who collared them and strongarmed them back to the jeep.

Carlos elbowed Leme and whispered. 'This is just the bait. Sit tight.'

Carlos swung his thick legs out of the car and, still seated, addressed one of the skinny fucks in a boom-box bellow.

'Ah, Felipe,' he said. 'The English Prince. How you doing?'

Leme laughed. Prince Felipe. He tapped Carlos on the shoulder. 'Kid know why he's called that?' he asked.

Carlos grinned. 'Course not. Get out the car and watch this.'

Aviators pushed Prince Felipe forward. Carlos nodded. Aviators brought his nightstick against the back of Prince Felipe's head. He slumped, shocked, to his knees. His head stayed up.

He spat on the floor. 'Ah, vai, Polícial, filho da puta. Go fuck yourself, Carlão. What the fuck is this, eh? What I do?'

Carlos nodded again. Aviators moved in front of the Prince and jabbed him in the stomach, then again in the throat.

Felipe spluttered.

Felipe coughed.

Carlos nodded.

Aviators repeated the action but this time left his stick hard under Felipe's jaw.

Felipe gave a wet snarl and rasped, damp.

Felipe coughed. Felipe wet-retched and this time small plastic bags fell into the dust. Felipe pulled more from his throat.

'That's all of it,' he stuttered. He shook his head. 'No more, ta ligado? Leave it out, mate, please, ne?'

Felipe drooled.

Carlos puppet-showed it.

Carlos pointed at the other militar. Same moves. He night-sticked the other skinny fuck. Same result. In moments, the other skinny fuck was on his knees too, bags of crack dotted in mounds of maggoty vomit.

Carlos dipped his boot in the puked rice and fatty pork, the black bean skins.

'You bumfucks are eating well,' he said. 'For a pair of fruit dope-cunts. Parabens. Must be doing a lot of bone-work to stay that thin, entendeu? Which one's Alessandro and which one's Alessandra?'

Carlos winked at Leme. Carlos was playing for time. Leme smiled.

Leme remembered Ellie's first line.

He looked up:

Station clock, rolling balconies, green trees of the Parque da Luz, graffiti-free.

She was right. He could be anywhere in Europe.

Clever girl, he thought. Or very stupid girl.

Carlos sidled over to Leme. 'Any militars here, this'll flush 'em,' he said.

Leme looked around. Smashed windows and black, gaping doorways. Toothless and dust-rinsed women and men. Uglier than the devil sucking on a mango.

Carlos said – loudly, 'We hear there was a black kid and a gringa cunt down here a week or so ago. Some of our lot chased them out. Know anything about that?'

Carlos nodded Leme towards the addicts. One of them shuffled on his arse to the curb and slunk off.

The rake-thin dealers said nothing. Carlos motioned with his right hand.

The two militars nightsticked in tandem. Leme thought it was strangely balletic.

Carlos stood over the Prince and his companion. 'Hard out here for a bitch, eh girls.' He leaned down and eyeballed the Prince. 'I said, do you know anything about a poor negrinho and a gringa cooze coming down here last week?'

Leme squirmed. He trusted Carlos, but still. He and Carlos had logged some serious bar time over the years. More than that: he *knew*. He was solid, a good, dependable guy. But still.

Carlos chinstrapped the Prince with his own nightstick. 'How much you skim off of them? That why you're saying nothing?'

The Prince spat. The Prince breathed out hard. The Prince was defeated. 'Vai se foder, eh Carlão.'

Carlos looked at Leme. 'You wanna have a go? Won't be too long now, entendeu?'

Leme shook his head. He had none of the sadistic impulse you needed in the militars. In the civil police they were all amarelou, cowards, pussies, so they were told. Meting out punishment never struck Leme as especially uncowardly. Though if it ain't broke.

'Ah, meu Principe. Wrong answer.'

Carlos stepped back. He addressed the crowd. 'Anyone else know what the fuck I'm talking about?'

Leme noticed that the vagrant noia who had shuffled off was back. He gripped his right hand cash-tight. Leme smiled. Muito smart, old Carlos.

Carlos looked at Aviators and the other militar. He made a face. It said: hold tight.

Leme lit a cigarette. He watched the hopheads rubberneck,

craning jealously. He thought about throwing the rest over to the pack, watching them scrap. Nasty impulse, though it passed.

'Oi, Mario,' Carlos said, nodding down the road.

Three men were walking towards them. They wore militar vests. The two either side carried automatic weapons. The one in the middle rested his hand on his holster, flicked the top of his handgun.

They swaggered, cocks of the walk. The noias cowed, looked down, closed their mouths and faces.

Carlos looked at Leme and winked. 'Entendeu?' he asked.

Leme shook his head and took a step away from Carlos.

The three men in vests spread slightly.

Carlos and his men fanned back. Relaxed stand-off.

'E ai, Carlão,' Handgun said. 'Been a while, ne?'

Carlos grinned. 'Nelsão, meu. Didn't know you'd moved in?'

Nelson sucked his teeth, shrugged. 'Ah,' he said. 'Know what I mean?'

'Crystal,' Carlos said.

'What do you want, Carlão?' Nelson spat on the road. 'This is ours now, sabe? You come here, you ask us, entendeu? No offence, ne, but, you know.'

The four other militars rocked on their heels, trigger fingers extended but rested, composed but poised. Half-smiles, gum-chewing, jaws working macho sneers.

'Just a question,' Carlos said. 'Hear there was a young black kid visiting you with a gringa reporter. That true?'

Nelson jabbed a finger towards Leme. 'Who's this guy?'

'Friend,' Carlos said. 'Tourist, entendeu?'

Nelson examined Leme. Nelson sucked his teeth and spat again. 'Ah,' he said.

'Então? Know who I'm talking about?'

'Ô Carlão, sabe? Can't remember every little cunt looking to score, entendeu?'

'Word is they weren't.'

'So what? Do-gooders? Even less reason we'd run into them.'

'What about your guard dogs here? They know anything?'

The flanking militars bristled a moment, settled. Nelson shook his head. 'We only go out here together.' He nodded at the thinning crowd of addicts. He poked his foot into Prince Felipe. The stick-thin dealers were still on their knees. 'Know what I mean?'

Carlos laughed. 'So you don't know what I'm talking about?'

'Ah, Carlão, I'll ask around. Can promise you that.'

'Good lad. And good luck, eh.' Carlos winked and signalled to his men. 'I'll leave the Prince and his pauper for you to play with.'

Nelson gave Carlos a shit-eating grin. 'Kind of you. Later, ne.'

Carlos nodded.

Leme watched closely.

Nothing.

They all climbed back into the vehicle.

Carlos fingered cold rice. Carlos said, 'Então. You think?'

Leme shook his head. 'Guy was lying, right?'

'That or your gringa cooze is travelling, making shit up. She do that?'

Leme weighed this. Ellie played, but. 'Nope. Not like this.'

'So Nelson is hiding something. Not a surprise.'

Leme raised his eyebrows.

Carlos said, 'There are, in our fine group of militia men, a few, shall we say, *entrepreneurs*. So. Nelson likes to gamble. Got three kids, two different mothers. Money's got to come from somewhere. He runs puta out of a cheap motel on Augusta, I hear. Cheap escorts. Aspirational. Called: *Gash and Carry*.'

Leme balked. 'That's a joke, right?'

'Sadly not. Loyalty scheme tagline? *Same Bitch Different Day*.'

'Jesus.'

'He's a piece of work.'

Leme nodded. 'You think he might know something about where Ellie is? About why the kid was cut?'

Carlos said nothing for a while. He toyed with rice under his tongue. He checked his phone. He scratched his jaw.

Leme looked out the window. They headed south, across Augusta, shortcut up to Paulista. Leme saw the MASP museum perched on the hill, legs like a spider. Streets teemed with students and workers. As they came closer to the top, suits and shirts, heels and skirts.

'I'll find out,' Carlos said, eventually.

Leme nodded. 'Appreciate it.'

'You told me there was a lead. A guy. Last person to see Ellie apart from you.'

'Yeah,' Leme said. 'Fernando Melo. Lawyer for Zarzur Cabral.'

'You got his details?'

Leme wriggled his phone from his pocket. Copy-pasted the details into an email. Hit send.

Carlos's phone beeped. 'Porra,' he said. 'You're getting tech-smart, querido.'

'You tell me though you lean on this kid, entendeu?' Leme said. 'Respectable place he works at.'

Carlos snorted. 'He's a white kid?'

Leme nodded.

'The black kid cut to fuck work there too?'

Leme nodded.

'So,' Carlos said.

Leme understood. He felt a little ashamed. But he couldn't mention Antonia working there too, not yet. He hadn't told Carlos about the bag, the computer, and he wasn't going to.

They hit Paulista. Traffic lurch. Traffic tempo: shuffle.

Driver popped the siren.

Driver samba-ed left right left right and got across, tyres squealing.

Leme said, 'Leave me here.'

Carlos slapped him on the shoulder. They gripped hands.

Leme bounced. He headed down Haddock Lobo towards the delegacia.

Leme's phone yapped. Message from Lisboa:

Single Gringa. Jesus. Your girl was in. Young Fernando too. Your admin fuckhead got in. Correspondence *total.* Makes for good reading.

Leme scoped the traffic. Light enough.

Leme jumped a cab, flashed his badge. He wasn't sure how much of this correspondence he wanted to read. And this desire not to read it made him want to read it immediately. He messaged Lisboa:

Bring it to lunch. On you.

Lisboa's reply:

Rapido, ne? I'm starving here.

Leme smiled. He felt sure he was.

He figured it quick. With the Single Gringa evidence he could pull Fernando in, grill the fucker on where/when/what with Ellie.

The fact that he didn't much want to do *that*, made him want to do it immediately.

Antonia's Apartment

16 October, evening

Antonia was home when Leme arrived. She was in the shower. For a moment he forgot everything and almost joined her. Instead, he went into the TV room. He boosted the TV. He fished out the bag from behind it. He pulled out the computer. Same screen. Just as he'd left it. But the thread he'd placed inside as a marker had gone.

He wasn't imagining anything then.

Leme stood. Leme stared at the TV, dead-eyed. He killed the sound.

Little over two years ago, he thought, everything was different.

The day Renata was killed was like any other. For Leme, after he first met her, and then again after she finally acted on her promises and left the man who stood in the way, no day was *ever* like any other.

There'd been times when he couldn't understand what she'd done to him. Couldn't comprehend it. Just couldn't. It made no sense. None. Physical impossibility. Wouldn't register. Head-shake, head-rattling un-comprehension.

Nothing.

Constant.

Within weeks, she'd told him she loved him. Months after that she ended it with a one-line email, pleading a need for infinite space.

Disappeared, cut him off.

"I prefer nothingness" was all she'd tell him.

A grown woman. An intelligent woman. A good woman.

A woman who worked for others, solving legal problems for the disenfranchised.

A woman whose very professional being was rooted in deep empathy.

What? WHAT?

He simply didn't get it.

He went a little mad after that.

A carousel of bad decisions.

Her: email. Subject-line: **Fuck you**. Message: **You're a pig.**

She finished him, broke him. Pieces. She showed him how to hate himself. She was never wrong, *never* wrong.

A year or so later, she was back.

He was right to believe in her.

He was right to believe that there had been reasons.

A year is not that long.

Lisboa: 'She never deserved you.'

Lisboa: 'She was besotted with you. It *dripped* out of her.'

Lisboa: 'It's done. Over. Move on.'

The time evaporates.

The feelings never did.

Leme never gave up hope.

He didn't call it hope.

He called it: *understanding*.

Heartbreak, and then grief.

Her voice: hold tight.

Her voice.

Constant.

And now Antonia.

Leme needed to plant seeds. He popped the fridge. He tugged a beer loose. He cracked the can.

Balcony.

Lights glowed in concrete. Traffic thrum. Electricity crackle. Dark sky throbbing.

Clouds bulged, pregnant-heavy, waiting to crack.

Storm in one hour, Leme thought.

He shut his eyes. He breathed deep. He breathed out. He wanted to forget.

But he couldn't forget.

Earlier, his and Lisboa's lunch: bife a cavalo, two chopps, and a good thorough read of what Ellie and Fernando Melo had sent each other through the dating website.

'There's nothing incriminating here,' Lisboa said.

'Yes there is.' Leme eyeballed his partner. 'They didn't know each other until recently. They met online. Now she's missing.' He nailed the last of his beer. 'That's enough.'

'It's a lead. Not the same thing as evidence to pull him in.'

'It's not *a* lead,' Leme insisted. 'It's the *only* lead. And he lied to you about when he last saw her.'

They sat in silence.

Leme studied the words on the menu.

'Two options then,' Lisboa said. 'Visit him now. Informal talk, keep it vague, don't frighten him, blah blah blah. Or, give it a day or two and bring him in hard then.'

'Why?'

'I want to do a bit more digging. Informal talk might tip him off.'

Leme nodded. 'Makes sense. And a quick arrest might fuck a potential case.'

'So we wait,' Lisboa said.

He threw notes on the table. He slid his bulk out from under.

Leme guessed that this plan gave him at least that night to decide what to do about the bag.

He guessed it gave him that night to decide what to do about Antonia.

But as he sat on the balcony, he wasn't any closer to a decision.

He needed to plant seeds.

In the kitchen:

They sat. They ate.

Penne pasta. Tomato sauce. Parmesan cheese. Salad. A French baguette baked in the oven covered in crushed garlic and butter.

Leme picked. He chased cherry tomatoes.

'Good day?' Antonia asked.

Leme smiled. Tomorrow, he would move in.

This is what they did: they asked each other about their days.

'You know,' he said.

Antonia stopped chewing. She tilted her head. She raised an eyebrow. 'Not really,' she said.

'Ah,' Leme said, smiled. 'It *went*, entendeu?'

Antonia nodded and frowned. 'They do exactly that, our days,' she said. 'They go.'

It's not her fault, Leme thought. She doesn't know. When he and

Renata first lived together, she had to learn that he didn't like to talk too much in the early evening. He spent all day talking, all day solving other people's problems.

It's not her fault.

The bag though, and what that might mean.

'You?' Leme asked.

'You know,' she said, smiling now.

'You went to the gym?'

'I did. Usual scene. Fat old men – your friends, actually – walking, extremely slowly, on the treadmill for an hour. I don't know why they bother.'

'Stops them going to the bar too early.'

'I suppose that's one way to stick to a diet.'

'And keeps them out of the house, of course.'

'Charming.'

Leme winked. 'At least they run their mouths off when they're in there.'

'Well, that's all they run.'

They both smiled. See? We have fun.

But Leme needed to plant seeds.

They ate on.

The smack-riiiing of cutlery on china.

In windows across in the other condominium blocks, their neighbours moved about. Lights went on and off.

Black maids shuffled through utility rooms, dressed all in white, hefting baskets of washing. They stood over stoves tweaking pots of white rice. They eyeballed pressure cookers as they steamed and whistled, the beans pinging inside like microwave popcorn.

Black nannies toyed with children.

Women in gym-Lycra talking on mobile phones, directing them all with a flourish.

'You work with a guy called Fernando Melo?' Leme asked.

Antonia chewed. She nodded. She chewed and nodded. She swallowed. 'I do,' she said. She picked up her glass of wine. She looked at Leme amused-curious.

'Why? He in trouble with the law?'

She said *the law* in an American accent.

Leme smiled. 'Nothing like that. You his boss?'

'I'm senior,' she said. 'Our departments overlap. Not his boss *directly.*'

'What's he like?'

Antonia made a face that said: *really?*

'Go on,' Leme said.

Antonia made another face: *fine*. 'Playboy kid. Good worker. Rich family. Well, middle-class rich, entendeu, not *rich* rich. Clever, basically. Graduated GV. Fancies himself.' She smiled. 'Lives with his parents.'

Leme smirked.

'Why are you so interested?' Antonia asked.

Leme planted. 'Thing happened down in Cracolândia. Not a big deal. English journalist snooping. I thought about what you'd told me the other night about those property issues you were having. Had someone dig a little. This Fernando's name came up as one of the lawyers. Might be worth talking to him, apparently. What do you think?'

Antonia raised her eyebrows. She shrugged, made a face: *hmm?*

'He sorts out some of the liaison stuff, I believe,' she said.

'Liaison?'

'With the residents. Those we're helping. Lembra que eu te falei?'

'I remember. So he goes down there?'

'I fucking hope not. I wouldn't.'

Leme snorted. 'Who does?'

'We have people, you know, *that kind* of people.'

Leme got it. 'So Fernando runs them?'

'He runs them, yeah, that sort of thing, mais ou menos, ne? And a lot of contracts grunt work. Like I said, he's a kid, clever or not. Can be a bit of a jobsworth cunt actually, if I'm honest.'

Leme nodded. He poured them more wine. He thought that last bit was a nice touch.

'That enough, detective?'

Leme smiled. 'More than.'

'So we can talk about something else?'

'Anything you want, querida.'

Balcony.

Post-storm fresh. Air thin.

Antonia in her office.

'Email just came in. Need to use the computer to respond. Maybe make a couple of calls.'

Coincidence?

Leme smoked. He drank a cleansing beer.

Soon after, he went to bed.

Antonia slipped in warm next to him.

The silk/skin effect of her short black nightdress did the trick.

They didn't speak.

Her hands pinned down by his above her head.

Him biting at her neck.

Her: Oh God, said twice.

Her face: raw from his stubble.

They slept.

At five thirty, Leme's phone yapped loud.

Message from the delegacia:

Body.

And an address in the Zona Norte:

Close to Metro Parada Inglesa.

Inglesa.

Leme's first thought:

Ellie.

Fuck.

A Swank Restaurant in Itaim

One week earlier

After the debacle with Leandro in Cracolândia, Ellie decided that she needed to understand exactly why Fernando was helping her. Yes, *obviously*, there was the romance, and, well, the *sex*, but she'd met guys like him before, and she thought that, from her experience at least, a foreign woman was a holiday, an exotic bump in the road. Ellie wasn't sure that she hadn't missed something. Most of the time, this wouldn't be an issue – she was confident in her ability to measure what people want. She felt that Fernando liked her, was hoping to impress her, and passing the information that would help with her work was testimony to this.

And give Fernando some credit: at least he hadn't taken her to his mother's house for a feijoada completa cooked by her on their first date, like one memorable thirty-three-year-old teenage boy she'd kissed in a bar and swapped numbers with. He'd grabbed her face and pressed his lips against hers, thrust his tongue inside her mouth when she tried to say goodbye.

After that, she didn't return his calls. Nem fodendo.

For two months he rang or texted twenty, thirty times a day.

In the end, she told him that she'd been struggling with her sexuality and that she was now in a lesbian relationship.

It had worked.

'Oh,' this man-child had said. 'So it really *was* nothing to do with *me* then? Fine, no problem! That explains it. Maybe we can have a drink some time as friends.'

She never heard from him again.

Brazilian men. Nothing is ever their fault. Honking their car horns when she walked past, like a gaggle of Italians applauding when a pretty girl crosses a piazza. Knocking on a bar table, whistling. Honking their horns – literal and figurative, she thought.

She had to put this aspect to one side though. There was a fair bit at stake here with this story, and though she wouldn't admit it, the visit to Cracolândia with Leandro had shaken her up.

She'd reckoned that the militars would be more interested in him than her, which was one reason she'd fake-numbered him. The other was that she wanted things to remain filtered through Fernando for now. She needed to have Leandro help her, and not the other way around.

She called Fernando and they arranged to meet for dinner.

'I think I'll set up a dating app myself,' she told him as they waited for their starters to arrive. 'For rich, finance-types.' She winked, purred, 'Call it "Mobile Bonking".'

'Very droll,' Fernando said.

'You wouldn't get past the verification checks, querido.'

'I'll take that as a compliment.'

Ellie pursed her lips, raised her eyebrows and narrowed her eyes as if to say: *aren't we clever?*

Fernando looked down at the table. When he looked up at Ellie, there was an earnest expression on his face. 'You know,' he started. 'No. It doesn't matter.'

Ellie smiled. 'OK,' she said.

'It's just...'

He shook his head. 'No, it's silly.'

'OK,' Ellie said again. She leant back in her chair and drank.

'Aren't you even at all interested?'

He shook his head again, though this time as if clearing it.

Ellie softened. She laid a hand on his. 'You can tell me whatever you like, querido.'

Fernando gave her a thin, stubborn little smile.

'OK,' he said. 'I just sometimes worry you might be using me.'

The waitress arrived with their starters and Fernando ignored her eye sulkily. Ellie made a show of thanking her, which seemed to annoy him further.

'Explain,' she said, and squeezed his hand. 'I'm here, aren't I?'

He gave her a reluctant smile. 'True. I suppose I wonder if you'll still be here once this Cracolândia story pans out.'

Ellie laughed. 'Well, if *that's* true, then we'll still have quite a long time together, I reckon.'

Fernando's expression changed. 'Oh yeah? Why's that? What's happening with it?'

Ellie forked prawns into her mouth, carried on talking. 'You know I went down there with Leandro?'

Fernando nodded.

'Well, we were supposed to meet friends of his. But their houses had disappeared. Been levelled. They weren't there. And their mobile phone was out of service.'

'Drug addicts, right?'

'Not sure,' Ellie said. 'Leandro says no way. So.'

'The houses weren't there?'

'I know, right? Fucking weird.'

The waitress filled their glasses.

'So,' Ellie continued, 'three militar guys threatened us and told us to fuck off. I was going to leave it, but young Leandro turned out to be a little more resourceful than we thought.'

'Oh yeah?'

'He went back, managed to get a photo of one of them from one of the addicts. Apparently they run the place. We think we've got a match. Guy I know at the magazine ran it through a database. I told him it was a guy I met in a bar. He believed me.'

'Funny that.'

'Alright, settle down. Anyway, point is, that's why I'm meeting Leandro on the day after tomorrow to figure it out, see if it means anything. Slow progress, that's what I mean.' Ellie smiled – flirtatiously. 'You think you might be able to speed it up?'

Fernando looked serious. He nodded. He inched and wriggled his mobile phone from his pocket. 'I'll make a call. Hang on.'

Ellie grinned. Bingo.

She finished her prawns and mopped garlic and clove sauce with a hunk of French bread.

Fernando slid into his seat. 'Right, I've spoken to someone. Listen carefully, then we can talk about something else, OK?'

Ellie smiled. 'Please.'

'So, I'll tell Leandro tomorrow that you'll meet him at his place the day after. That keeps you out of direct contact with him in terms of phone records, at least. Which is probably a good thing.' Ellie nodded. Fernando said, 'I'll meet you a little beforehand here.' He gave her a piece of paper with an address in Lapa. 'Boteco, I know,' he said. 'Discreet, local place. Anyway, I'll give you Leandro's address then. I'll pull his address tomorrow at work. Then you go and meet him.'

'OK,' Ellie said. 'That works.'

'Another thing,' Fernando said. 'Then we really are going to change the subject. I'll bring his Carteira de Trabalho. We keep them at work. That'll prove his credibility, which might be helpful.' He paused and smiled. 'And this way we get to have breakfast together.'

Ellie nodded. She might need that to get the final green light from Elizabeth.

'Why are you doing this?' Ellie asked.

Fernando gave her a wolfish smile. 'Quicker this story gets done, quicker I really know you're going to stick around.'

Ellie smiled, blushed slightly. And Fernando looked pretty pleased.

Fernando's House

16 October, evening

Fernando jabbed a toothpick in his mouth and shouldered the phone. He speared it between his teeth. He John Wayned, flicking his tongue. He scratched the back of his left leg with the flip-flop that dangled loose from his right foot.

'Quem fala?' he asked.

'Any reason why a detective in the Polícia Civil might want to talk to you, Fernando?'

Merda. Antonia. Puta que pariu, he muttered.

'What was that?'

'I thought I asked you not to call me at home, Antonia, entendeu? Por favor.'

'I *said*, any reason why a detective in the Polícia Civil might want to talk to you, Fernando?'

'Antonia, I—'

'Because I have literally – literally *just this minute* – had a detective in the Polícia Civil asking about you.'

'I— '

'I don't have much time here, Fernando. Fala. *Agora*, viu? I'm in no mood.'

Fernando clicked his tongue. He'd had enough of this papo furado. This baranga Antonia was pissing him off.

She was giddy with a vagabundo sense of power.

Puta merda.

If he were still doing what she does when he was her age, he reasoned, he'd be pretty disappointed with the way life turned out.

'I don't know, Antonia,' he said. 'Why don't you tell me what he asked?'

'I don't much like your tone.'

'Gee, Antonia. I'm sorry. But if you want me to help…'

'He asked about a gringa journalist in Cracolândia. He said that they'd done some digging and your name came up.' She paused. 'This was interesting to me.'

'Look, I did exactly what we discussed, the work you've asked me to do.'

'And the English girl?'

'She's a friend.'

'That's all?'

'Well, you know.'

'I have to go,' Antonia said. 'There's a chance they'll come and find you, ask you some questions.'

'Right.'

'Remember, you're helping to run the liaison guys and doing some legal drafting. That's it.'

'Well, yeah, that's true. And Leandro?'

'We'll talk about him, not a big deal. There's one more thing you have to do for me though.'

Fucksake. 'OK.'

'Go to an address I'm going to send you in a text and pick up a file. Straightforward job. Important though. And someone's got to do it. You'll be an hour, tops.'

'Paid?'

'Cash, plus for receipts, tomorrow.'

'Combinado.'

'Ciao.'

'I—'

But Antonia had hung up.

Moments later Fernando's phone beeped and buzzed.

It wasn't far.

This would be easy.

He had to keep in mind why he was doing this, being this errand boy: money.

And there would be more coming tomorrow.

And it was worth it.

São Paulo, near Lapa

15 October, the day before, just after morning rush hour

Fernando pulled away from the boteco – tyres squealed, deliberate. Stylish. It was good to see Ellie, to help, to give her Leandro like he had.

His phone shook. What now?

Traffic lurch – pause. He picked it up. Text –

Him again. The fuck. Again? What does the tricky cunt want now?

Leandro's coat has been buttoned at home, entendeu? Keep that girl out of it, viu?

It took Fernando a moment to register this.

Fuck. Ellie. He just sent her to Leandro's. Fuck. FUCK.

He pulled a U-turn – reckless.

Porra.

He better get to Leandro's and sharpish.

São Paulo, Traffic

17 October, early morning

The address in the Zona Norte:

3332 Avenida Luiz Dumont Villares.

It was an approximate address. In the middle of the Avenida was a patch of dirty green, rust-coloured grass. Above ran the Metro line, a thin, concrete flyover heading further north to the city limit.

Parada Inglesa. How very fucking apt.

Leme pedal-to-the-metal floored it up there from Morumbi. He hadn't been that far north in a while. It was a residential shit-hole, most of it: the core at least.

Land was once a farm owned by an Englishman. Hence the name.

How very fucking apt.

He got on the police radio channel to work out the quickest way/ lightest traffic.

He took the Marginal: longer as the crow flies but early enough it was freed up.

Headed west, 100kph. Favela-flanked. Dirty men were bent and stoic loading junk into carts. Two or three yoked like oxen.

Leme curved sharp east at a tight right angle. Traffic heavier heading back towards the Centro.

Off at the Shopping Center Norte, past Estádio do Canindé. Leme's father took him there a few times when he was a kid. Home of Portuguesa: the team always a disappointment.

Memory shake.

Up through Carandiru. Following the Metro flyover. Into the bus lane. Some beeping and shouting, shouting and beeping.

Lurching, staggering forward alongside the mural of picnicking children painted on the low, crumbling wall.

Woman driver of a shiny new VW gave him the fisheye as he cut her up to get back into the main lane.

Leme rode it. Let her honk.

Gear-crunching time. Weave in and out, hand on the horn.

Leme spotted the lights flashing against the underside of the flyover. Couple hundred yards up.

Traffic snarled. Police tape and cars blocking, doors open like shields.

Three lanes down to one. Rubberneckers gawking. That slowed it right down.

Leme jumped the curb up onto the rough grass under the flyover. Dumped the car and hotfooted the rest.

In Leme's head, echoing: Ellie.

His heart zoomed, chest expanded.

A circle of white coats hanging doubled at the knee: leaning over, looking down at the ground, examining the body.

Leme flashed his badge.

Circle opened. Masked faces looked up at his. Eyes blank. Eyes expectant.

Leme dropped his badge.

Leme's chest swelled, jumped up into his throat.

Leme turned and vomited dry, red. Heaved chunks of pasta into his mouth.

Leme spat. Leme's head spun. Leme's eyes watered. Leme took a deep breath. Leme inhaled traffic fumes and cigarette smoke. Leme's eyes burned. Leme's throat burned.

Leme entered the circle.

He noted the position of the corpse. He noted the clothes, shredded.

He noted the angle of the arms and legs.

The body had been thrown from a moving vehicle.

He noted the angle of the neck, the way the head was attached. The way the head was detached. The thick, coppery line. The stain matched the dirt.

Leme noted the expression on the face of the body.

Fernando looked surprised, shocked. He looked like he might have had a moment, maybe two, to understand what was happening to him.

Leme noted this.

He hoped it hadn't been any longer than that.

PART TWO

Hate Fuck

São Paulo: 17 – 19 October 2013

Away

My mum emails me the same question every time she gets in touch:

'How's Brazil?'

A better question might be:

'What *is Brazil?'*

How long does it take to answer a question like that?

São Paulo's a start – what a city: rich in culture, dripping with cash, undermined by political corruption, marked by a rich/poor disparity which fuels desperation and a life-is-cheap criminal ethos.

And next year: the World Cup. And two years after that:

The Olympics –

A photo of a woman in a favela, slum-misery stamped on her face. She's saying: 'It's getting to the end of the month and I've only got Gold, Silver, Bronze medals in my wallet.' Gold=25 cents. Silver=50 cents. Bronze=5 cents.

I ask a colleague if she'll be going to Rio to soak up this Olympic spirit they've all heard about. She replies with the quintessential Brasilian shrug off: 'nem fodendo.' No fucking way. Or, and a better, more complete translation: not even if I were fucking while I were doing that would I do it.

They don't like to be patronised by the old world –

For them, this whole thing is inevitable. Once again, the lives of the many are plundered for the lives of the few.

That's Brazil.

Leaked Document Record: Land deal – Cracolândia
Recipients: Lagnado; Amaral-Gurgel
Subject: Changes to schedule

Zarzur Cabral, CASA, and the office of State Governor Machado hereby outline proposed changes to the scheduled development in the 'neighbourhood under consideration', now confirmed as the streets and squares in the Luz district known as Cracolândia and defined by the presence of users, or 'noias' as they are commonly known owing to the paranoid delusions to which crack addicts are prone, making them potentially violent and dangerous.

1. The development of the Luz district is to be postponed owing to opportunities that have arisen in the months since the initial development proposal was approved
2. The opportunities and their attendant logistics are to be overseen by the offices of Lagnado and Amaral-Gurgel utilising senior officers under their jurisdiction
3. Investors in the Luz district development proposal are to be informed that owing to bureaucratic and administrative hold-ups, the work due to commence in early 2014 will in fact take place later in the same year
4. This delay will allow the offices of Lagnado and Amaral-Gurgel to make best use of the opportunities that have come to light
5. The press and media are to be briefed on the grounds that the criminal element in the Luz district has made commencing construction according to the original proposal both dangerous and undesirable
6. The press and media are to be made aware of the dangers of the Luz district, and specifically the violence against women meted out by 'noias' and the vulnerability of female addicts and their children
7. The press and media are to be briefed on the actions of the military and civil police to combat these despicable crimes

8. The recent deaths of two [adjunct] associates of the development proposal project have been confirmed as unrelated incidents

Signed: The recipients.

Sorrocaba, Lago Azul, Fernando's Parents' Holiday Home

17 October, morning

Ellie was scared – *basically*. She'd admit to that, and admitting that she'd admit to that was something she wouldn't normally admit to. Christ, she thought, it's no wonder fear is momentary, temporary. I mean it's fucking crippling when it descends, no *paralysing*, but rationalising anything makes it disappear – *basically*. For the now, at least, and there ain't much else, really, is there, Ellie?

Oh no, there surely ain't. Fuck *me*.

For the last however many hours she'd been trying to work out if it had been fear – and fucking *guilt*, of course, the whole *what have I done* hideousness of it all – over the fact that Leandro was missing that had kept her stewing and drinking at Fernando's parents' holiday home, or was it, in fact, trust in Fernando, trust she hadn't really been aware she'd had? It didn't bear thinking about too much. Which was a problem.

She lay back on the lounger, adjusting the angle so that the sun warmed her face. She wore oversized dark glasses, a navy blue bikini and a huge straw hat. Her arm hung limp and her thumb was caught in the middle of a paperback copy of an airport thriller that grazed the ground.

'Dona *El*-lie!'

She turned towards the house. It was Maria, the maid, calling her. Ellie had been at the sítio for three days now and Fernando's housekeeper was doing a tremendous job looking after her, *distracting* her. What did she want now though?

Let her come and find me, Ellie thought.

She placed the book on her chest. The cover felt quite soft against her skin.

It was ten in the morning.

Fernando had said he would be back today, but she hadn't heard anything from him yet. She was beginning to think she should get back to the city. Fernando had said he'd tell Elizabeth and her porteiro where she was, so she probably shouldn't worry.

There was no one else, after all, that really mattered.

But, there was something else beyond the Leandro situation, and she'd spent the last two days in a spiralling, recursive, anxious funk over this – she hadn't told Fernando that she'd led Detective Leme to Leandro's house.

And that he'd likely be looking for her. Wouldn't he?

'Dona Ellie!' Maria shouted again. 'Cade você?'

Ellie breathed out slowly. She twisted her body towards the house. 'I'm here!' she called out. 'Outside. By the pool!'

Ellie heard Maria shuffle out to her, flip-flops slapping on the concrete, wet from where she had been mopping the kitchen and living room floors.

Maria stood over her, smiling. 'Oi, Dona *El*-lie, tudo bem?'

Ellie looked up into the sun's glare, squinting. 'Dona Maria. I'm good, thanks. You?'

'Graças a Deus, ne?' Maria replied, still smiling.

Servitude in this country, Ellie sometimes thought, seemed to equate with constant gratitude to God.

'Have you had any breakfast?' Maria asked.

Ellie shook her head. 'Ah, not yet.' She yawned and stretched, smiling, her body pushing up from the lounger, as if presenting itself to Maria to prove that, no, it had not in fact been nourished this morning. 'I'm lazy, entendeu?' Ellie lifted the book. 'I've been reading.' She smiled again.

'Would you like something?'

Ellie nodded – enthusiastically. She smiled, wide. 'I would *looove* something,' she said.

Maria smiled back. 'I'll call you,' she said, and scurried off.

Ellie sat up. There were voices drifting over from the golf course that cut this condominium complex in half. Men dressed smartly – their clubs wheeled along by caddies – hacking at the grass and swearing. She watched as a particularly ungainly squat man, dressed in a striped polo neck and ironed khaki shorts and with a cigar in his mouth, took a series of short swings before goosing the ball about twenty yards up the fairway.

The place was amazing though – she was grateful to Fernando for that. Quiet, a simple house, all dark wood and cold tiles, a swimming pool, a housekeeper who cooked. Cupboards of booze. Shelves of books, many in English. Comfortable sun loungers. A deep lawn next to the patio, which led onto the golf course. The neighbours were a hundred yards either side, hidden by the tall conifers which circled the property and whose smell blended with the cool, thin air, reminding Ellie of her childhood in Dorset.

And all fenced in and secure and patrolled by former cops – she couldn't really be anywhere safer. If that was even an issue, mind. This was the other thing that had been bothering her. She'd gone over it in her mind again and again. And she was still unconvinced that she hadn't missed something.

She heard Maria singing as she prepared the coffee and breakfast. Maria was very important – she couldn't talk to her about anything, so with her around she really could pretend she was on a sort of retreat. Rather than retreating, she thought. There: rationalisation. It's like compartmentalisation for the over-active mind.

Ellie lay back down and ran it again.

She'd pushed the door into Leandro's house and gone inside. It had been damp, smelled moist, rotten. She'd paused, let her eyes become accustomed to the dark, and had noticed the two doors leading off the corridor.

But before she'd had a chance to investigate further, even to call out Leandro's name, Fernando had sprung from the shadows, grabbed her wrist, and pulled her along the corridor and straight out into the tiny backyard.

'What the fuck?' she'd shouted at him.

He'd gestured for her to be quiet. 'We have to go,' he said in an urgent whisper.

'What are you doing here?' Ellie asked.

Fernando gripped her arm and looked her square in the eye. 'It doesn't matter. What matters is that we get out of here.'

Ellie was shaken. Fernando had looked serious, frightened, but also composed enough to communicate an authority Ellie hadn't seen in him before.

'You need to trust me,' he said. 'Leandro is missing. I've just been told. It's not safe here. You have to trust me.'

He'd looked at her. Imploring, desperate. He was shaking. He was genuine.

She nodded. She believed him. He took a padlock from his pocket and attached it to the door. He turned a key and pulled at it to ensure it was secure.

'Follow me. We have to leave all this, but it can't be clear we were here.'

Bewildered, Ellie had felt little choice and certainly no compulsion to argue.

But then she stopped. Patted down her dress, her pockets. Realised something. 'Wait, I had a bag. My phone. Leandro's Carteira. It's inside.' She pointed at the locked door. 'I must have dropped it when you grabbed me.'

'There's no time, Ellie. It doesn't matter. We need to go. We'll figure it out later. OK?'

She nodded. She remembered Leme. She could get a message to him. This did not look good.

He tugged at her wrist. 'Come on.'

What choice did she have? Fernando knew something of what she'd been doing, Leme didn't.

They pushed through the rusty gate at the end of the yard and shouldered through a tiny gap between two houses.

Fernando's car was parked on the street in front of them.

He opened the passenger door. 'Get in.'

An hour or so later, after barrelling down the Marginal towards Sorrocaba, Fernando was introducing her to the security guards at the gates of the country club condominium Lago Azul. Soon after that, Maria was cooking her lunch and she was lying on a lounger, dazed by the strong Caipirinha Fernando had made her before leaving – and by what the fuck had just happened.

It took a moment for Ellie to realise that Maria was calling her again.

'Dona Ellie! Ta pronto!'

Breakfast.

She sat at the table and poured herself coffee from a Thermos flask, adding milk from another. Spread out in front of her was fruit, yoghurt, bread, a hot plate of scrambled egg, sliced ham and cubed cheese on a breadboard.

Graças a Deus, she thought.

Fernando's explanation on the journey here was what still troubled her. It seemed hard to believe that she was in any danger. And how had he possibly found out that she was – or even might be – between handing over the address and Carteira and then whisking her away when she arrived?

Leandro was missing, he'd said. He'd been told by his boss. He'd been told to avoid Leandro's house. He got a call moments after he'd told Ellie to go there. He was worried. He arrived just in time. If Leandro was missing, he said, it meant something was up, something was wrong, that Leandro had said too much maybe, or spoken to the wrong man down at Cracolândia. Ellie had been there with him – it was best, and this was just a precaution, that she went away for a little while. That was what this was.

That is all this is, he'd said. Trust me.

She didn't tell him that she'd interviewed the Cracolândia dealer, Felipe, and that she'd told him something about what Leandro was up to.

It didn't bear thinking about. When she did, she felt a wave of nausea, of light-headed fear and guilt. No. She can't have – she *didn't* – say anything she shouldn't have. People knew.

And this was why Maria had been such a godsend. *Graças a Deus.*

And the plentiful booze. That didn't hurt.

She'd had time to consider everything over the last two days and she was ready with a whole load of questions when Fernando arrived today.

And then there was Leme. And this *really* troubled her. What on earth must he think of her? She'd literally vanished – at least that's what it would have looked like. What must he have done? Followed her in, seen she wasn't there, found her phone? Then what? When she thought of how she'd have to explain it all to him, she felt faint. The fact is that Leme didn't know about her visit to Cracolândia. Leme didn't know that she'd spoken to that kid dealer, Felipe. Leme didn't know that she'd been dating Fernando. And, most of all, Leme didn't know that Leandro was missing and that Fernando was panicked, and that meant that Ellie was panicked into leaving with him.

It was a fucking mess. The best she could hope for – and this was what she told herself every hour – was that Fernando had told

Elizabeth, and Leme had chased her up at the magazine offices and found out that she was OK that way. He'd be pissed off, but it might mean she wouldn't have to tell him everything.

She shuddered, shut it out, boxed it. For now.

Be present, Ellie, she kept telling herself. There is no future; there is no past.

She wolfed her breakfast, slurping coffee, Maria vacuuming and dusting inside.

After a while she realised the house phone was ringing. Ellie stopped eating for a moment.

The phone stopped. She could still hear Maria singing tunelessly and cleaning, the Hoover not quite drowning her out.

Ellie set about the cheese and ham, folding slices into a piece of French bread.

The phone again.

Fuck it. 'Ma*ri*aaaa!' she yelled. 'Telefone! Ma*ri*aaaa!'

The vacuuming stopped. The phone went quiet.

Ellie heard Maria's voice.

Then Maria went silent.

Ellie braced herself for the noise of the Hoover.

It didn't come though.

Instead, she heard an anguished wail, like animal grief.

Jesus.

She pushed her chair back, but Maria was already there, tears running down her face, her hands shaking, her head shaking.

Ellie held her by the shoulders and shook her gently.

'What is it, Maria? What's happened?'

She looked into her eyes.

Maria touched Ellie's left arm.

Morumbi

17 October, early morning

The cemetery hadn't changed.

The same toothless mendigos hanging around outside the gates, whacked out on cheap pinga and favela rock, laughing as the world passed them by. Leme felt something like admiration: you've really got to *commit* to be so uninterested in anything other than booze and drugs. And they *were* always entertained by something. 'E ai, playboy,' one of them shouted at Leme. And that set them right off: the thought that Leme might be a playboy. Through laughter, he tried again: 'Hey, play … *man*?' And that did it. They fell about, rolling around on the pavement, clutching their sides, hyenas in a Hollywood cartoon.

Leme smiled and shook his head as he passed.

He made his way down the path, past the Aviary. The birds turned to look at him, and they considered him with sympathy. Perhaps. They flitted from bar to bar inside their wire-mesh prison, nodded their beaks at him. Beaks? Was that the word? It didn't matter: he kept his fingers to himself.

The air cooled, the city's decaying stench dissipated and the flowers Leme carried seemed to visibly perk up. He raised his eyebrows at that. Examined them. Their petals had definitely opened out, inviting the cleaner air in, reaching to a light unimpaired by layers of thick smog.

Greenery –

Was it that simple?

The sun, fat, winked through the trees.

Trees. Leme looked up. Trees are staunch, he thought. They're there for you.

Renata's plot was tidy, recently swept, neat.

Leme placed the flowers by the headstone, knelt.

He always knelt. It wasn't to pray, but to try to get closer to her. To her ashes.

He closed his eyes.

He breathed – deep.

His mind went blank.

He let it clear.

He waited.

He waited for her voice.

His mind – clear.

His mind – empty.

He waited.

Nothing.

Her voice – no, nothing.

Nothing.

Like a punishment, or expression of disappointment, or, simply, knowledge.

Leme nodded to himself. He knew why. He'd killed. *He'd done exactly what he said he'd never do.* That was the phrase. He remembered.

He walked slowly back to his car.

They call it a bala perdida, a stray bullet, a *lost* bullet, that took Renata. Leme knew different. Leme knew it wasn't a random act of violence. Silva had found that out. Not that it went any further, *officially*. No evidence that could be called reliable, and no one wanted to know. Less said and whatnot. It all went nowhere. Do one, Leme, was the gist.

And so he'd taken revenge.

And *that* wasn't a random act of violence either. Far fucking from it.

He'd done exactly what he'd said he'd never do.

São Paulo, Delegacia

Same day, mid-morning

Briefing:

Delegacia. Airless room.

Five men in white shirts, sweating –

Five plastic cups of coffee, doubled up –

A plate of empanadas, untouched.

Superintendent Lagnado stood, palms on the table, tie pulled into a tight knot. Sleeves pinned and rolled, neat.

Thick, black hair –

Low forehead:

Violence restrained in a squat body.

'Então,' Lagnado growled. 'Some other fucker's had his coat buttoned then. Bring me up to speed.'

Leme eyeballed Lagnado.

Lagnado scouted the room.

He looked at Lisboa. 'This just some gash hound kid duped, or someone we have to worry about?' he said.

Lisboa squirmed. Lisboa looked at Leme.

Leme made a face:

What's the point?

Another detective, Alvarenga, gabbed. 'It's the second homicide in thirty-six hours. Victims are both young men. MO the same: cut at the neck with a jagged blade. Not too pretty. So far no clear forensic evidence. Killers left nothing, been smart. Both victims worked at the same firm. Both involved in the Cracolândia residents' project. Leme and Lisboa took the first victim, Leandro Bastos. Second, Fernando Melo, is up for grabs.'

Lagnado scowled. 'Let's assume there's no connection. For now. For the Melo kid, I want a division of labour. Alvarenga, you take the lead.'

Nodding.

Leme clocked this. Something wrong. He sucked his teeth: no connection? Porra. Fucker's under orders.

Lagnado continued. 'What about this missing gringa?'

Leme stiffened.

'Someone told me she used to spread for this Fernando Melo moleque. That true?'

Silence –

Lagnado roostered, indignant. 'Well? Leme?'

Leme tight-lipped –

Leme doodled on a pad.

Lagnado snorted. 'What is your fucking beef?'

He turned to Lisboa. 'Então?'

Lisboa gave Leme the sidelong fisheye.

Leme tapped the table with a finger.

Lisboa said, 'They knew each other. Dating website, you know how it is.'

'Fucking modern women,' Lagnado said.

Lisboa said, 'Yeah, well, they went out a bit. That's all we know.'

'This first victim,' Lagnado said. 'Progress?'

Lisboa nodded. 'Clocking movements over his last few days. Waiting for results. Forensics stripped, sparkled and spritzed the place. Nothing so far. No matches on the first sets of prints.'

'This Cracolândia connection,' Lagnado said.

Silence. It wasn't a question.

Leme fidgeted –

He weighed it:

He hadn't told anyone about his visit with Carlos.

Carlos didn't trust anyone else in the Polícia Civil.

Likelihood of Carlos telling anyone: zero, maybe zero point five.

'No one wants to contribute?' Lagnado asked.

Four men squeezed/cracked plastic coffee cups.

Four men examined spots on the wall.

Leme said, 'It might be above our pay grade, Superintendent.'

'Don't be a cunt, Leme,' Lagnado said.

Heavy silence –

Windowless room, throbbing.

Lagnado glared at each of the four men. 'Cracolândia is off-limits. Militars don't want to share. That's the word. Certo?'

Nodding.

'Updates tomorrow.'

Lagnado shouldered the door.

Meeting adjourned.

Ten plastic cups dumped in the bin.

Four men shuffled. Four men bit their tongues.

Four men watched Lagnado pop the lift.

'Papo furado,' Alvarenga said. 'Ta ligado?'

Grunting in agreement.

'What then?' Lisboa asked.

Alvarenga narrowed his eyes. 'Division of labour, right? So. We work together on the details. Forensics are looking for similarities. There's bound to be connections, points of reference. They're doing the lot.'

Nodding.

'This missing girl,' Alvarenga said.

Leme nodded. 'Leave that with me. Admin guys have something we can work with. Complications with both the Melo kid and Bastos.'

'She knew them both?' Alvarenga said.

Lisboa snorted. 'Good chance she was the last person to *see* them both.'

Alvarenga raised his eyebrows. 'Woah.'

Leme grimaced. 'Maybe she's doing something on Cracolândia. I'm figuring that with admin. We've got her phone and her computer. The fuckhead is flushing both, certo? Give it a little time. She may have got involved with some shutterbugs snapping the wrong people doing the wrong shit. Nothing more.'

Three men looked unconvinced.

Boteco near the Delegacia

Same day, late morning

'Fuck is this?'

Leme drew his finger along the list of figures.

'Fuck do they *mean*?'

Leme looked up at Francisco Silva. Leme figured Silva, his journalist friend, might have an in with the lawyers – or at least that his IT guy would *find* a fucking in – so he'd given him a bell, asked him to nose around.

'I asked you to look at Zarzur Cabral. This I don't understand, entendeu? What are you telling me?'

Silva was grinning like a dickhead.

Leme glared.

Silva's face was pouchier. His nose bulged. His suit hung crumpled, shiny, from his slouching, heavy frame.

Journalist.

Egg-stained tie. Coffee-stained cuffs.

Still grinning. Wolfing coffee and a mixto quente. Smothering it in mayo and mustard from plastic packets. Wiping his fingers on his trousers.

Licking his fingers.

'Mais um!' he shouted at the waitress, waving the sandwich.

Jesus.

'You *know* what this is,' Silva said. He stabbed with a finger at the top of the page. 'Your fucking name, Mario.'

'Not what I mean.'

'Então. Fala. You're telling me this is a surprise?'

'It's a head-scratcher is what it is.' He eyeballed Silva. 'This had better not be some underhand, bullshit stratagem you're cooking.'

Silva guffawed. 'You know me better than that.' He paused. He goofed. 'We're friends, porra.'

'OK,' Leme said. 'Just don't be snide, entendeu? Tell me why you have this, but not how you got it.'

Silva gave Leme one of his shit-eating grins. 'Ah meu,' he said. 'You know me? I'm fucking staunch.' He wide-boyed, bobby-dazzled. 'It's all good. Let me explain.'

'So explain, porra.'

Silva nodded. He looked left. He looked right.

'Turn it in,' Leme said.

'So you asked me to look into Zarzur Cabral, right?' Leme nodded. 'Well, where's the first place you should look when you're supposed to look into something?' Silva rubbed his finger and thumb together. 'Dinheiro. Cash, sabe?'

'Jesus,' Leme said.

'So my guy got into the accounts department files and pulled a bunch of transactions. Numbers, figures, got to know what you're looking for and my guy knows his shit, so. Anyhoo, one account keeps coming up, smallish amounts, then moved on, like a holding bay. Interest is minimal, but it's there, entendeu? Means the account is implicated regardless. Like a guarantee, bit of insurance. My guy reckons this might be a patsy account to cover up some shylocking either known or not known by accounts. Other option is they're kicking back and this means it slides over the monthly statements, something like that. Final option is it's just an extra leg for the money to run. Which means the account name is doing a favour.'

'Easy,' warned Leme.

'Hey. I'm just saying. Fact is it's your account, Mario.' He smiled, played concessionary, played the bigger man. 'So now we can rule that final option out.'

Leme nodded, breathed in. 'The fuck am I going to do then?' he asked.

'You never check your statements, right?'

Leme nodded.

'This has been going on, I think, like four months. Problem is, it's clearly about *something*. You say anything to the bank, your boss, your fucking girlfriend, whoever, there's a chance all we end up doing is sticking our hands up.'

'But I need to cover myself.'

Leme hadn't liked Silva's reference to Antonia.

He scanned it:

He ever tell Silva what she did?

No.

But Silva could know without that.

'You do. Like I said, you're implicated. Whatever, whoever is making those transfers – and remember, money is being moved *out* too, so this looks like you, whether it's you or not – is using you for a reason. Question is, if it's 'cos it's you, *you*, Mario Leme, for a fucking very specific reason, or just because, entendeu? My guy says finance stuff can be as random as fuck, so, you know.'

Leme squirmed. He grimaced.

He ran it:

He needed this on some sort of record. He needed to know: why him. He needed to know where this money was going. He needed to know for what purpose. He needed Silva to help with that. He needed to hear Silva say what he already knew. He said, 'What do you suggest?'

'Let's log it with your admin guy. Tell him the truth. Well, you know. But log it. It's set. Tell him it's part of an investigation and to keep an eye. Make the record and you're clear when it all gets rinsed.'

'Makes sense.'

'And I go after these numbers, figure out what it is exactly you're supposed to be doing for these lawyer fucks.'

Leme nodded. He didn't look at Silva.

He was thinking about Antonia.

Antonia transferred money to his account. Quite a lot.

Not the same thing.

Leme eyed Silva. 'Thanks. You know, I *suppose*.'

Silva laughed. Silva waved the paper. 'I'm on it.'

He left.

On the street, he keyed in Antonia's number.

She picked up. She said:

'Can't talk, meeting. Text me.'

He punched in a text:

Send your bank details. Need to settle up from a few weeks ago xx

He thought:

OK, let's see then.

Leme thought back. He remembered. Three months in. A relationship. This is how it starts. A surprise. He thought back to those early days and nights. Those early days and nights with Antonia.

There was a week, three months in, when Leme worked a late shift. Every day, at lunchtime, Antonia came to his flat. To wake him up.

She'd arrive, bottle of white wine in one hand, takeout sushi in the other. Leme *never* ate sushi.

He'd go down on her in the living room, barely taking her dress off. Then she'd lead him into his own bedroom – and *that* was never anything less than totally fucking erotic. He'd pin her hands way above her head and she'd wrap her legs tight against his sides, left foot hooked around the tops of his own legs, tapping, nudging, encouraging. And they'd turn around and the expression on her face when she looked back at him was always an astonishment: pure longing, pure presence, pure energy. Just thinking about it caused a shiver, a stir, a flutter.

It was, Leme understood, a form of knowledge, of recognition.

'When you're inside me,' she said once, 'it's like your cock achieves its essential cock-ness.'

Leme spluttered, laughing, wine everywhere. 'Oh yeah?'

'Oh yeah. There's something quite moving about it, you know, when something achieves its higher purpose and so on. I feel a sense of responsibility, a mentor's pride. Self-actualisation and whatnot. Textbook, really.'

Leme laughed some more. 'Sometimes I worry we perhaps talk a bit too much during these afternoons.'

'Well, querido,' she said, guiding him back inside her, 'just because we're laughing, doesn't mean we're not having sex.'

They'd eat their sushi afterwards, in bed. Leme was beginning to enjoy sushi.

'This is quickly becoming my favourite restaurant,' Antonia said.

'All you can eat, right?'

'I think, querido – I *think* – leave the jokes to me.'

He was leaving quite a lot to her, Leme realised around this time.

It was something like that week he'd spent with Renata, three months in too, but under the spectre of *him*. The feeling that was ever present: we are *stealing* this time. It exists only for us, and is therefore more precious as a consequence. This time, they said to each other, is really *ours*.

Leme knew now that this was a crock of shit.

A coward's way of letting you down is to make you feel deep gratitude even as it's happening.

The simplicity of time with Antonia.

Leme wondered why he was focusing on that painful period with Renata, why he was reliving a chapter he acknowledged but had also filed away within the narrative of their story. Love stories – all happy ones are alike, and blah blah blah, and Bob's your fucking uncle, entendeu? All unhappy ones too.

He supposed we did what we had to.

'You know,' he said to Antonia that week, 'everyone thinks they know you, but they don't, not really.'

'That's a funny thing to say.'

He propped himself up on his elbows, looked her in the eye. She paused, a piece of salmon sashimi held up by her chin, like a question mark. Her expression: this had better be good.

'I mean it's a privilege to get past your, you know, public persona, sabe? To know *you*.' Leme, mild panic, tried to find the right words, but the cupboard was bare. 'I'm happy, is what I mean.'

Antonia dipped the piece of salmon sashimi in soy sauce and wolfed it. She turned a crabmeat roll in wasabi.

'It's a compliment, porra,' Leme said, defeated.

She smiled. 'I know, babes, I just like torturing you.' She abandoned the crabmeat roll and kissed him. 'You've got a better way with words than you think.'

Point was, Leme had been around the block, and wasn't averse to a little self-protection. Common sense, ne? Doesn't take Freud to work it out, it's crystal: Leme needed to take a little care with himself.

He fell in love with Antonia that week. He was *in* love with her before, but that was when they fell, entendeu?

Only so much you can ever know anyone, though. All the post-coital bunny in the world ain't going to change that. This Leme knew. He'd been a soppy bastard before, and it'd come up roses.

Still, tread with a bit of foresight, ne? Triumph and disaster and whatnot.

Leme knew *this*.

Offices of Zarzur Cabral

17 October, late morning

Antonia pursed her lips and rubbed the top of her left foot with the sole of her right. *English client*. That had felt like a euphemism, though of course it wasn't really. He was waiting outside her office, about to walk in, her English client. She performed the same little ritual with her feet and then slipped her shoes back on and rose, wriggling around the desk so that she was in front of it to meet him when he walked in. She leaned back against the desk and tapped a pencil against her teeth in a cliché of nonchalance. She was self-aware enough to know that affecting the pose would not protect her from the nerves and the ominous feeling. She had got this far in her career by appearing outwardly composed, distant almost, but with just enough flirtatious interest in her colleagues – male and female – to engender trust and goodwill. It wasn't bluster – no, she'd leave that to the alpha types she worked alongside – but more like a projection of unflappable calm.

But today, she was unsettled, and it wasn't just Mario's odd request for her bank details – she could deal with that later. It was Fernando: where the fuck was he? And, more importantly, where the fuck was the file she'd sent him to pick up the night before?

She was about to look very stupid indeed.

There was a light knock on the door and her secretary held it open and smiled at Antonia, no idea how uncomfortable the next half an hour or so might end up.

'Sr. Abrahams ta aqui pra a senora,' Antonia's secretary smiled.

Antonia beamed and stepped across the room, offering her hand.

'Tom,' she said. And then in English: 'It's been a long time. You're well I trust?'

'Antonia,' he said and smiled.

He gripped her forearms in his hands, leaned back slightly and tilted his head to look at her, Antonia thought, as you might look at a niece or nephew you hadn't seen for a long time, measuring their appearance against the passage of time.

He nodded twice. 'As gorgeous as ever,' he said, satisfied, as if she'd passed a test that he'd set her but of which she was not aware, in the manner, Antonia imagined, of a professor at an Oxford college dealing with teenagers at interview.

'You flatter me,' Antonia said. 'And you don't look a day older than when we last met,' she lied. She wrestled her arms free and returned to the safety, the strategic high ground of behind her desk.

'You're too kind,' Tom said, laughing.

Antonia winced: she'd forgotten how he liked to shout. And she *was* too kind: he'd spread and his suit bulged in unseemly places, its pinstripes like a prison's bars, straining to contain him.

He sat down heavily. The chair jerked, squirmed underneath him, seemed startled, frightened; not used to the weight of old world entitlement, Antonia thought, and smiled to herself.

'Family well?' Antonia asked.

Tom waved an arm as if throwing salt over his shoulder, an English affectation Antonia had never understood. 'Fine, fine, you know.' He paused, shuffled forwards in the creaking seat, gave what may have once passed for a mischievous grin and said, 'I barely see them any more. Not that I'm complaining!' He let loose a deep, meaty, phlegm-rattled laugh and Antonia winced again and moved back into her chair. With the air-con glacial and tangible, these few extra centimetres were like a thin protective cloak.

'And you?' Tom asked, with what looked like genuine interest. 'Still single? Or have you packed that game in and settled down? No kids I'll bet, looking at you I mean.' He smiled.

Antonia thought of Mario. She wondered about this sudden desire to pay her back. What for? They were moving in together, officially, tomorrow. Maybe that was why, a sort of clearing of the decks, squaring up before things began properly. She could understand that; it was very him, actually. She'd think of how to play that later. She had enough to worry about today – and enough actual meetings – to warrant not replying with her details there and then.

Always easier to lie when you can't tell the truth.

'Actually, Tom,' she said, 'my boyfriend is moving in with me tomorrow.'

Boyfriend. She smiled at the memory of telling Mario that he wasn't boyfriend material. He hadn't liked that, had sulked for a few weeks. She'd meant it though – he wasn't. His wife – his angelic, fault-less Renata; though he'd seemed to forget the circles she ran round him, the pain and confusion she caused him before they actually got together – hadn't been dead that long, he was still clearly griev-ing terribly; she'd been sensitive, helped him through the process, provided a distraction, affection, love even. But that hadn't meant she was ready to commit to a man in that state. And as a line, it had worked. He *became* boyfriend material. It was an unintended con-sequence – she wasn't *that* well versed in this game and it had been an observation, not a prompt – but it was also a welcome one. She realised now that she didn't want to lose him and a feeling of longing coursed through her – if he were here now, all this would be easy.

It couldn't have been a coincidence though, could it? She hadn't been sure it was Mario she'd seen that day Fernando had handed over the English girl's computer, though it could well have been; and not long later Mario asking her questions about Fernando.

She gave a quick shake of her head and it was gone.

What was done was done.

'Congratulations!' Tom said, clapping his hands together. 'What tremendous news! We must celebrate later.'

Antonia wondered if he might be going deaf. She couldn't remem-ber him making so much noise when they'd last met a few years ago.

She made a face to say: *Thank you, that's awfully kind of you, and yes let's certainly celebrate at some point in the future.*

Tom gave another little wave of his arm, casting a smaller circle this time. 'To business,' he said.

And Tom's business was important to Zarzur Cabral. He'd owned land and stock and had been investing in Brazilian business for most of his adult life, which meant a far longer relationship with the firm than Antonia had ever had.

Antonia had been Tom's lawyer – specifically, individually rather than as part of a team – for over five years now. They got down to work. There was the usual admin, the signing of notarised docu-ments, the approving of the despachante's fees, the very English astonishment that such a job even *existed*; it was a routine Antonia had grown used to.

'I mean, I'm paying a man to carry my papers around, that's the extent of it, right?' Tom said – indignant. 'I could do all of this myself, or rather have someone do it for me, but instead you lot – and by you lot I mean *the Brazilian Government* – introduce another level of bureaucracy purely for the benefit of a class of middle-manager administrator that is utterly unnecessary. You've created a whole job whose only benefit seems to be the ability to jump the queue at the federal police, when that queue is only created in the first place because of all the despachantes trying to jump it! And by corrupt means!' he shouted. 'A job created *by* corruption, *for* corruption. I mean…' He let the sentence hang in the air.

Actually, Antonia thought as she pushed across the desk another contract to sign, the sentence didn't so much hang in the air as invade it, *possess* it, so that it might even take over more of it if left unchecked.

'Now, now,' she said winningly, and smiled. This seemed to pacify Tom.

'Those English roots of yours,' he said, smiling back. 'Means you understand me. I get that, and don't think I don't appreciate it!'

Antonia let that slide. She did have some English in her, of a fashion – her great-grandfather had come over to Brazil when the railways were being built; her grandmother had been educated in Europe; Antonia herself had attended the British School in São Paulo – but it wasn't something she was especially proud of and had never used it to secure any favour with people like Tom. In São Paulo society, she knew, this might confer glamour and status; she preferred to earn that for herself. And this English sense of humour, this dryness? That was just more Western entitlement, cultural imperialism: why the fuck should one miserable little country have a monopoly on being wry? Dickheads.

'Now,' Tom said, signing the last document with a flourish. 'We both know why I'm here, *really*. What's the news on the land?'

Antonia nodded. She felt her throat tighten. She could give a clear, simple overview, could report on progress, and the progress was all largely that, of course, *progress*, but without the file … well, without the file it was conjecture, hot air, anecdotal evidence. Not enough for Tom, no sir. Even if it were, she'd thought earlier, he'd make a point of it not being to establish quite how serious and professional he was.

She made a decision.

'There's a problem,' she said. 'Not insurmountable, certainly temporary, but a problem nonetheless.'

'Ah,' Tom said with the air of a disappointed, but unsurprised schoolmaster, each fingertip touching its opposite number, forming a squat pyramid in his fat hands.

'I decided to give you the bad news,' Antonia said. 'I could tell you how smoothly everything is going – and it *is* going smoothly – but I felt I should get to this first.'

Tom nodded – abstractly. 'Straight talking,' he said. 'Good, I like that. That's good.'

The change in his volume threw Antonia a little: he was practically murmuring now, relatively speaking.

'There's a file,' Antonia went on. 'An important file, a file we need.'

'Right.'

'The file contains the signatures of a number of residents who have already been moved on from the area, from the land. From Cracolândia.'

Tom smiled, thin – Antonia knew he didn't like her to use its colloquial name.

'The documents are evidence that you own not just the land but any shelter – officially or otherwise – that has been built on it. It means—'

He cut her off. 'That I can evict whomever and whenever the fuck I like,' he said – waspish.

Antonia nodded. 'That's right. The file does exist, that's not the bad news.'

Tom smiled again – thinner this time.

'But we don't have it here – *right now* I mean – to reassure you of quite where we are. You know, progress-wise.'

'You don't mind me asking why not?' Tom said, in such a way that he knew that she did, but that it really wasn't his fault.

'Not at all.' Antonia examined her diary and turned a page as if she were just checking on something. 'A colleague of mine – an employee, really – was sent out to pick it up last night.'

'And?'

'Well that's just it. He hasn't brought it in yet.'

'But he's come in himself?'

'Unfortunately not,' Antonia said. 'We're tracking him down as we speak. No one is too concerned.'

'I'm pretty concerned,' Tom said, raising his voice. 'Smacks of a little, well, careless? Unprofessional? Who is this colleague? He trustworthy?'

Antonia was nodding furiously. 'Oh yes. He's been with us a good long time, never let anyone down.'

'Before,' Tom added.

She looked at her desk and then up at him, resolute. 'Quite,' she said.

They sat in silence for a short time. Antonia affected to note down the next steps.

'Where might it be?' Tom asked.

Antonia nodded again. 'Well,' she said, 'there's an English girl, a journalist. There's a chance…'

Tom pulled a face. A very unimpressed face. 'Hang on a minute,' he began.

Antonia interrupted him. 'No, no,' she insisted. 'It's not like that. She's going to do a piece from *our* perspective, a positive thing. But there is a chance my colleague has taken it to her first. A slim chance, but still a chance.'

'English girl?' Tom asked.

Antonia nodded.

'Right,' he said. 'Good to know.'

'It'll be resolved by close of play today,' Antonia said, deliberately using the English expression, hoping it might soften him a little.

It worked. Tom smiled. 'Yes,' he said, 'it will be.' That sounded like a threat.

Antonia's phone rang. She pointed at it. 'Do you mind?'

Tom shook his head, generously, magnanimous to a fault.

It was Antonia's secretary. 'Pois não?' she asked.

'There's news.'

Antonia noted how her secretary had got straight to the point, none of the preliminary politeness. This was a good sign. Or a very bad one.

'Go on.'

'It's Fernando.'

There was a pause, as if her secretary couldn't quite work out how to form the words.

'Yes? Go on. You know how important this is.'

'He's been found.'

Antonia was nodding again. 'Good. When is he coming in?'

'That's not what I mean.' Her secretary let out a little gasp. 'He's been found – he's dead. It looks like he's been murdered. I'm sorry, that's all I know.' She spoke in a rush, clearly desperate to end this conversation. 'There'll be a briefing in fifteen minutes in the conference room.'

Antonia hung up. She felt dazed, suddenly, slow, distant, like watching the movements of her limbs under water.

'Everything OK?' Tom asked.

Antonia flinched, gave her head a little shake. 'News, actually, on the file. I need to go and look into it, but it's certainly something.'

Tom looked pleased.

She stood. 'I'll be in touch later today,' she said, holding out her hand.

He smiled – broad. 'Excellent.' He turned, stepped to the door, and called over his shoulder with a little wave, 'Always a pleasure.'

Antonia followed and closed the door behind him, leaned back against it. She breathed deeply, in through the nose and out through her mouth as she had been taught by the yoga instructor in her building.

A briefing. She'd be able to find out whether Mario knew about this, whether, God forbid, he'd been assigned to the case.

Christ, she thought. Fernando, dead. It didn't seem possible.

She breathed in again.

Antonia's Apartment

17 October, evening

Leme jimmied the service entrance. He thought he might off-guard Antonia. He ducked under hanging washing, lemon-scent fresh. He shouldered the door. It swung hard and slammed into the fridge. He swore and tripped through.

Antonia didn't flinch. She looked up from her phone. She'd been chopping vegetables. She smiled.

'Fish OK?' She jerked her chin at the counter. 'Wine,' she said.

She picked up the knife and gutted a red pepper, speared a lettuce, fast.

Leme plied her with a fake smile. He splashed wine into a fish-bowl glass. He wondered if this was a rigged game.

Antonia stopped chopping. She brought the knife to her lips like a finger, thinking. 'You OK?'

Leme, brusque: 'Why wouldn't I be?'

Antonia, dry: 'Now, now.'

Leme grunted.

Antonia gave him the bunny eyes. 'I can't cook dinner for my partner?' she asked. 'My *live-in* boyfriend?'

Leme smirked. 'Settle down, not quite yet, querida,' he said.

The knife thumped through the lettuce. Antonia's phone yapped and buzzed along the counter. She wiped her hand on a tea towel. She fingered a strand of hair behind her ear.

'Taking this,' she said. 'Quem fala?' She mouthed 'sorry' and Leme waved it away.

Leme nailed half the glass of white wine. It coursed through him, an icy-veined hit.

'Like doing drugs, white wine,' Renata once said, early days in, booze and food and sex, feeling each other out. 'Not that I'm turning myself in, detective.'

Leme had smiled. 'I never used to drink it,' he'd told her.

'Well, things change,' she'd said, eyes skipping, enigmatic, but not *so* enigmatic. 'Lots of new things, lots of change.'

He drank it now though. Great drink for a boozehound: smashes into you and separates your brain from your thinking mind, dislocates. Perfect drink for a professional, working person to torpedo, moments in the door, coat on, bag slung over the shoulder, rage dissipating.

Antonia turned half away from him, murmuring yes and no, that's right, fine, tomorrow. Leme leaned over the pan. A fish lay greased and spiced, glazed eye, scales coarse with salt and glinting in the evening light.

Leme heard Antonia end the conversation. 'Work?' he asked her.

She licked a finger. 'I didn't know you had a key,' she said, nodding at the door. 'For the service entrance, I mean.'

'I don't.'

'Ooh. Door open, was it?'

Leme nodded as if weighing the question. 'Yeah, it was. I took a risk.'

'You daredevil.'

They watched each other drink.

'You didn't send me your bank details,' Leme said.

'No, yeah, I didn't. Sorry.' A beat. Antonia focused on the salad. 'Online banking now then, eh?' She looked up, teasing. 'Dark horse.'

'It's the modern way, ne? I'll be on,' and his voice inflected the quotation marks, '"social media" next week. Dick pics and all that shit.'

'*Dick* pics?'

'New term, querida. One the admin fuckheads taught me. Means—'

'Yeah I can guess what it means, *querido*. Who says romance is dead.'

'Not the young people of today, that's for sure. Admin guy showed me this site, Single Gringa, place where you can find foreign pussy if you pay enough and dress up smart at the interview, apparently.'

'Jesus, Mario, *pussy*? You feeling OK?'

Leme laughed. 'Lifelong learner, sweetheart. Got to adapt, right?'

'Wait. *Interview*? What site is this?'

'It's posh. And feminist.' Antonia's lips thinned. Leme added

– hastily, 'Have to have a recommendation and an interview to, you know, make sure your intentions are honourable or whatever. USP is only the women can initiate chat once you're matched. See? Feminist.'

'Hmm.'

'But don't worry,' Leme said, 'I'm still moving in.'

'Lucky me, what with all this new learning.'

Leme smiled. 'Renaissance man, so yeah, online banking.'

There were shouts from the pool drifting up. Kids flirting. Kids playing some weird game Leme never got which basically involved the boys chasing each other in circles and then jumping into the pool – noisily. The girls watched. The girls pretended not to watch. The girls talked, were splashed, squealed, screeched. Leme pictured it in the quiet of the kitchen, the pan sizzling, spitting.

The air thinned –

The sky faded.

Leme scoped the apartments opposite, watched black maids, bustling.

'Hmm?' Antonia looked up at him.

'Online banking. We need to settle up a few things from the last month or so, and there's bills and whatnot. Makes sense, ne?'

Her back to him, manipulating the fish, Antonia said, 'That's not what "Renaissance man" means, Mario, by the way.'

'So you'll send me your details?'

Antonia, her back to him, nodded – just about.

'*Was* work,' she said. 'Earlier, I mean.'

'Ah, e?'

'A fucking headache actually.'

Leme said nothing. He felt a current in the room charge, pulse.

'More than that, if I'm honest.'

Leme: intrigue, alert, scanning her body language, tone.

'What?' he said.

'That playboy kid you were asking me about, Fernando Melo.'

Leme twitched, sucked in his cheeks: old trick to hide a tic, a tell.

He glanced away, quickly looked back: let her know he knew.

'You know what I'm going to say, don't you?'

He nodded. 'Why I came in the service entrance – to avoid you,' he lied.

'Are you going to be involved?'

What was the phrase they'd used in the meeting? Division of labour. He weighed it. 'Perhaps assisting, not the lead.'

Antonia nodded. 'Probably for the best. Right?'

'I'm sure it's for the best.'

'Right.'

'And your work call was about that?'

Antonia killed the heat under the fish. She moved it across the hob. She placed a lid over the pan. She turned to face Leme. 'Indirectly.'

'Right.'

'A client. He's connected to … what happened to Fernando. He doesn't know.'

'What's the connection?'

Antonia made a grim face. 'We were talking about it – Cracolândia.'

'And?'

Antonia tensed, brow furrowed.

'Hang on.'

She raised her hand, dropped her chin.

'What?'

'I don't like this. This, this way you're … *interrogating* me.'

Leme had played it wrong: pushy not concerned.

He dialled it back. 'You're right, I'm sorry.'

He tried a smile; a comforting smile to let her know this was about them as a couple, not as professionals.

'Force of habit. It's something I can forget, sabe?' he said. 'That I'm not questioning a witness, *interrogating*, entendeu? I'm really sorry. I didn't want you to feel uncomfortable.' A beat. 'That's the last thing I want.'

'OK,' Antonia visibly softened. 'But I didn't like your tone, sabe?'

'I know, querida, of course, and I understand. And if you want to talk, great, we will. If not, I understand that too. We'll eat, talk about something else, certo? Ta bom?'

Antonia nodded. 'The client is involved in the land deal in Cracolândia. So was Fernando, as you know, sabe, on a minor level.'

'OK, certo.'

'The client was in today. An English guy.'

'English guy?'

'Isso. He's had business interests over here for decades. Family stuff. Landowner, basically.'

Leme nodded. 'So why doesn't he know yet?' Leme asked. 'You know, if he even *needs* to.'

'He doesn't *need* to. And well, we don't want him to find out, not yet, at least, entendeu?'

'Not an easy thing to keep quiet. It's going to be in the news, com certeza. Nasty business and they *looove* that shit, the cunts in the press, believe me. And there's a connection with another murder.'

Leme paused. He examined a spot just above Antonia's head: another old trick. He looked her in the eye. He said, 'Another one of your employees.'

'What? What are you talking about?'

Leme noted: surprise, curiosity, confusion.

Genuine? He wouldn't swear it.

Compartmentalise *that*.

'You told me that Fernando was running the liaison guys in Cracolândia, ne?'

Antonia nodded.

'One of them. Kid called Leandro. Know him?'

Antonia shook her head.

'There were interviews down at your office.'

'These guys,' Antonia started, 'we don't employ them directly, exactly. They're connected to us, that's all. I've never … I've never had anything to do with any of them really.'

'People didn't talk about it? No gossip?'

'I haven't heard anything.'

'Not even today? After … Fernando?'

'Wasn't mentioned.' Antonia gave her head a little shake. She eyed Leme. 'OK? Enough questions. You're doing it again.'

Leme lifted a hand in apology and nodded, agreeing.

He thought: she's telling the truth.

He thought: what about Ellie's laptop?

He said, 'You want to eat? Stop this?'

Antonia shook her empty wine glass at him. 'I want to drink,' she said.

He smiled – rueful, empathic – and poured them both a hefty measure.

They nodded in a half-hearted, silent toast, glasses bowing to each other.

They drank long.

Leme said nothing. His silence said: your turn, when you're ready, I'm here to support you, and that's all.

'So our client's going to find out, you think?' Antonia asked.

Bingo.

'I think it's very likely, yes.'

Antonia was nodding, thinking. 'Could be a problem,' she said, 'if he finds out sooner rather than later.' She sighed. 'Nossa, que coisa, eh?'

He said nothing. He waited.

Antonia looked giddy.

She'd talk.

'That night when we were talking about Fernando, when you were asking about him,' Antonia said. 'I had to go to my study, a work thing, remember?'

He nodded. 'Claro.'

She was measuring her words.

'I spoke to him.'

Antonia licked her lips. Antonia gulped her wine.

He made a face: *it's ok.*

'I sent him on an errand, to pick up a file. An important one.'

He nodded: *it's ok, you were doing your job.*

'A despachante's office in the Zona Norte.'

Leme stood tight.

'The file's missing. That's the issue with the English client. Without the file…' She tailed off. 'Well, without the file, the sale can't go through.'

He thought: why is she telling me this?

He thought: and my bank account?

'We need the file before our client can find out about what happened to Fernando. I don't … that sounds so cold.'

Antonia's head dropped.

Leme watched her features dissolve. He stepped to her. He placed a hand on her shoulder, kissed the side of her head.

Antonia shuddered, breathed, composed herself. Leme wiped under her eyes, drew her hair behind her ears, kissed her again.

'Fernando had been knocking about with an English girl, a journalist,' Antonia said. 'We think she might know something about the file. We don't know. Fernando liked her, I think, was trying to help. I don't know.'

'Know her name?' Leme asked.

'Ellie something,' Antonia said. 'I can find out, I think.'

He nodded, tight.

'I told our client about her, that Fernando said she might be able to do something for us, a bit of positive press, nothing major, nothing controversial, sabe?'

'You tell him her name?'

Antonia considered this. 'No.'

Leme bit his lip. He ran his hand over the counter.

Chega, he thought. Enough, for now.

There was too much to process. He loved Antonia.

He took her hand and kissed her neck, softly.

Then more urgently.

She pulled him to her, brought his leg between hers.

He felt her hands under his shirt, his belt.

His own pulled at hers.

Grief, as he knew, was a powerful aphrodisiac.

The only response to death: feel alive.

The food was forgotten.

Leme woke. Eleven p.m.

Early.

The fuck?

He remembered:

Guilt.

His phone: insistent in the kitchen.

Antonia stirred.

He settled her with a soft hand.

He stumbled through to the kitchen.

His phone stopped, started again.

The name flashed:

Francisco Silva.

Leme groaned.

'Que isso, Francicso? Tou dormindo, cara.'

'I'm sitting in my car outside your building. Come the fuck down, you cunt, something's happened.'

Leme snapped awake. 'What is it?'
'Just come the fuck down.'
'Francisco.'
'I'm not fucking about here, Mario. We need to talk. Now.'
Leme ran it:
Best not to speculate with Silva.
Best get down there.
Tell Antonia a half-lie –
She knows Silva.
'Sit tight,' Leme said. 'I'll be down in five.'
Fuck.

Antonia felt the sheet sticky between her legs, the heat in the bedroom throbbing in time with the cicadas and the mosquito buzz and whine. Her head was flat on the mattress, nowhere near the pillow, her tongue hot and furry, her brain – it seemed – parched and raw, hair tickling her mouth. She felt Mario's hand on her arm. He rearranged the sheet around her shoulders and pulled the pillow down so that her head was propped up slightly as he knew she liked. Her eyes still closed, she said, 'What is it? Que foi?'

'Nada, não e nada. Telefone, só.'

Light from the street formed a yellow-white rectangle where they had left the door to the tiny bedroom balcony open. She was naked. Ah, she remembered: early night. Her mouth flapped like a fish, seeking wetness, freshness, finding only a sour white wine aftertaste. She should brush her teeth.

She should go and find out what Mario was doing.

Then, he was back in the room, pulling clothes on, talking.

'Ah fuck it. A journalist contact of mine is *actually downstairs*. Needs to talk to me. A case. That important, he's saying. Babaca. Fucking work. The guy's a pain in the fucking arse, but he's helped me out before, so, you know.' Scrabbling for socks, forcing his feet into his shoes. 'I shouldn't be long, entendeu? Go back to sleep.'

He left and she woke up.

She went into the bathroom, drank water straight from the tap – *now* who's the daredevil, she thought, and laughed – and brushed her teeth. She pulled on her nightdress and went through to the kitchen to get her phone. It was exactly as she'd left it: face down, a flashing light at the top showing mail, messages.

The sex had been a good idea, she thought: there was no way to finish the conversation they were having without some very tricky questions. She knew they'd both felt it, but still, she was pleased that she'd helped make it happen; made it happen. She'd done the right thing, and she'd enjoyed it.

She'd enjoyed it a lot ever since she thought she might have seen him outside her office when she was taking Ellie's computer from Fernando. There was an edge to him she hadn't seen before. And she enjoyed the doubts he was obviously having about her. She felt it gave her a certain power. Christ, that sounded pathetic, but there was something unarticulated, but definite.

But what now?

Fuck the bank business, she didn't have to worry about that. She could easily play a trauma card there; the forgetful grieving colleague, pestered by her client, no time, so sorry, yeah, no I promise I'll send it all soon, and don't worry I don't mind about the money at this point anyway, mi casa, what's mine, et cetera.

She'd mentioned this Ellie. Someone would have to tell her about Fernando, she thought. She didn't envy whoever had to do that. Welcome to São Paulo. Too awful. He was just trying to impress a girl, she thought. He had his moments, could be a piece of work, that was for sure, but he wasn't a bad kid.

Mario had said this journalist was outside the building. She went through to the balcony and leaned over as far as she could. There was a car parked with the lights on. Two men. Them, definitely. The lights were off behind her and so she decided to keep an eye on them. On him, really.

She got into her email and found the message she was looking for from Tom Abrahams and hit reply:

Don't worry – we have got specialists involved and we'll have the file shortly. Leave it with us.

Ax

She knew how Tom liked the informality of the 'x'. She smiled.

'Specialists': the Polícia Civil. Well, she thought, it was true.

Her boyfriend.

She could handle that.

Leme slammed Silva's car door shut.

'Give me a fucking light,' Silva snapped.

'Slow down, cara. No need to pirouette. Here.' He handed him his lighter.

Silva's hand shook as he lit his cigarette.

Leme looked on, amused-surprised. But worried, too.

'Então,' he said. 'I was in bed. With my girlfriend. You got a good reason for this, I fucking hope.'

Leme was smiling.

Silva looked him in the eye.

Leme stopped smiling. Leme saw:

Fear.

Silva's MO –

Tough guy, crusader. Been there, done that. Seen it all. Grizzled. Hardened –

Not an act.

First time for everything.

'OK, talk,' Leme said.

Silva reached into his inside pocket and pulled out a hip flask. He slugged at it, wet, wiped his mouth, breathing heavily.

He angled the bottle at Leme. 'Drink?'

'Não, just talk.'

Silva was nodding. Silva guzzled more. 'Puta, cara,' he grunted. He sighed.

Leme cracked the door. 'You going to talk or not?'

Silva leaned across him and closed it. 'Settle down, mate. OK.'

He turned in his seat to face Leme square on.

'I'm here because I was followed.'

'Woah.' Leme started. 'Sensible, nice one, thanks. You tailed?'

'No.'

'Certeza?'

'Absoluta.'

'OK. Followed by…?'

'Militars.'

'Militars?'

'Yeah. Two of them, on motorbikes.'

'You recognise them?'

'Never saw their faces. Helmets and shit. Visors, entendeu?'

Leme pulled his cap down over his face. 'Wait here.'

He hopped out and headed with purpose towards the bar across the road. He could see some of the old men from the condominium laughing, empty bottles filling the table like pieces in a game. The road towards Giovanni Gronchi and the main drag was dark, quiet: electric-buzz, the occasional shout, but otherwise nothing. Just beyond the last building was a patch of wasteland where the dealers from Paraisópolis came to meet the playboys to sell maconha and blow. There'd been incidents there in the past. Nothing too awful, in fact Leme kind of applauded it when the rich kids were ripped off. Never said that to his drinking partners in the condo bar though: it'd been one of their boys more than once.

Past the darkness of this patch of grass and trees sloping off down to the next condo development was a Habibs fast food place. The yellow sign a beacon for kids and workers on their way home, late. Leme craned, rubbernecked, trying to catch a glimpse of flashing blue and red. Nothing.

He long-strode it into the bar, straight through to the counter before his friends noticed him. He beckoned to the owner. 'E aí, meu. You alright?'

They slapped hands. 'All good, my friend. Entendeu?' He nodded at the tables. They were spread out over an old – and small – garage forecourt. 'Busy is good, right?'

Leme made a noise that said: Yeah, mate, I know exactly what you mean.

'Drink?'

Leme shook his head. 'Quick question. Any militars around tonight? Seen anyone?'

The owner clicked his tongue twice, waggled his finger. 'Seen no one. Just these babacas,' he said, smiling, nodding again at the tables.

Leme turned to look: cachaça shots in tennis kit – a warm down.

Leme nodded, knocked the counter with his fist. 'Be seeing you.' He winked and moved quickly back towards Silva's car. But he didn't get in. He waved at the segurança on duty outside. The segurança came over.

'Sr. Mario, tudo bem?'

The seguranças all moved with economy and certainty. Leme was always impressed by it. Unflappable, staunch –

Hard to read though.

'I'm OK, yeah, good. You OK?'

'Ah, you know. Surviving.' He chuckled.

'So, a question for you,' Leme said. 'See any militars around tonight?'

The segurança shook his head. 'Nope.'

'Ta bom,' Leme looked back over at Silva's car. 'He's going to park there for a couple days, certo?'

The segurança opened his arms. 'Claro. I'll let the guys know.'

'Friend of mine. Colleague. Going to stay at my place for a little while.' He winked at the segurança. 'Women, entendeu?'

The segurança gave Leme a broad smile. 'E isso aí.'

'Any militars show at any point, call me, ta?'

The segurança gestured with his hands, made a *Godfather* face that said: leave it with me, it's taken care of.

They slapped hands.

Leme opened Silva's door, grabbed his shoulder. 'Come on. Upstairs. I'll get you a proper drink.'

Leme dragged Silva up to his apartment. He got him a beer to go with his hip flask. He pulled a bottle of Johnnie Walker from under the fridge.

He let him sink into the sofa.

He grabbed a kitchen chair and sat opposite, too close.

He gestured: begin.

'I left the office, pretty late, about nine. Not unusual, but with no deadline it was later than it might have been, entendeu?'

'OK.'

'Traffic wasn't too bad and I was about ten minutes from home when I noticed a couple of militar bikes, lights off behind me. Thing is, I wouldn't have noticed them but I take a little shortcut that's no use to any fucker unless they're going to where I live, sabe? No reason for those bikes to have gone the same way. But they did.'

Leme asked, only half-ironic: 'Often get trouble from the militars, do you?'

Silva ignored him. 'I carried on, but took a right that I knew was wrong, that'd mean I'd have to double back on myself to get into my road, right? This little detour goes nowhere, I'm talking that little maze of steep up-and-down roads round the back of Paineiras, towards the Palacio, other side of the stadium from here.'

'Yeah, I know where you mean. Down the road. Clever, too, by the way. Quick thinking.'

'So the bikes followed and now I know they're following *me*. Or at least, there's enough chance that they are. So I swing back onto the main road when I reach the junction, double back, play lost, sabe? Stop-start stop-start kind of thing.'

'OK. This about when you came here?'

'No, I figured I'd have to try and get rid of them, so I head up to Morumbi, through Paraisópolis – at the edge, you know, not the middle of it – and swing into Shopping Jardim Sul.'

'Smart.'

'Right?'

Silva shook his beer can. 'Got another?'

Leme fetched two more from the fridge. They cracked the cans, knocked them together. 'So,' Leme said.

'I drove straight to the valet parking spot.'

Leme smiled. 'Very smart.'

'Guy took my car and I notice the bikes at the top end chatting to one of the seguranças. I go in, zoom up to that German beer and coxinha place, order one of each and sit tight in the corner, eye on the football, sabe? No one shows. I order another beer, to be safe...'

Leme smirked.

'...drink it and head back down. Valet guy fetches my car. I tip him and get in. And that's when I find this on the passenger seat.'

Silva tossed a thickish envelope onto the coffee table in front of him.

'Maybe valet wasn't such a smart move,' Leme said, fingering the envelope.

'You think?' Silva nailed the rest of his lager.

Leme studied the papers in the envelope. Silva drank and smoked – greedily. There were his own bank records, the exact pages that corresponded to what Silva had showed him was going in and out from Zarzur Cabral.

'Francisco,' Leme said.

'No,' Silva interrupted. 'Just keep looking.'

After his own records Leme saw another set: Silva's. 'OK,' he said. 'Someone's got into yours too.'

'Yeah,' Silva said. 'As you can imagine, I'm thrilled.'

'Why?'

Silva reached into his inside pocket and handed Leme a piece of paper:

Stop all this. Or you'll be next.

Leme nodded. 'A warning.'

'Thanks, Sherlock.'

Leme shot Silva a look. 'I mean this is telling us two things: one, they can implicate you if they please; two, I'm definitely implicated, in one way or another.'

'Makes sense.'

'Best thing you can do is stay here for a couple of days.' Leme waved the envelope and the note. 'We'll run these for prints. Not that we'll find any.'

'Mario? Militars, entendeu? Why?'

Leme shook his head. 'I'm going back to bed. Upstairs, entendeu? You'll find everything you need. Just don't drink all the booze in the house.'

Silva snorted.

'Anyone asks anything, your missus kicked you out.'

Silva nodded. Leme winked. 'You look the part, at least,' he said.

Delegacia

18 October, morning

Delegacia, first thing.

Lisboa, slumped over his desk –

Leme: 'Ricardo? Que isso, cara?'

Lisboa groaned. Lisboa stirred.

Leme laid a hand on his shoulder. He said, 'Você ta bem?'

He gave Lisboa a gentle shake.

Lisboa: 'Yeah, I'm fine. What the fuck? Calm down, mate. How about getting us some coffee.'

He patted the back of Lisboa's neck. 'OK, já volto.'

Leme crossed the open-plan office in the delegacia. Leme ignored the catcalls and hellos. Suggestion: Lisboa was having woman trouble.

Leme figured it:

Lisboa had slept in the office. Silva turned up on his doorstep, followed –

Not a coincidence.

Why had *he* heard/seen nothing?

The coffee machine rumbled, throaty, belched two steaming mugs. Leme double-bagged them, put two plastic packets of biscuits between his teeth. Breakfast: most important meal of the day. He smiled – wry.

Not like Ricardo this.

Leme shouldered the door to their office – a room for a couple of no-mark cunts, not detectives of experience and recognition. He'd never figured it, beyond Lagnado's instinct for violence, of any sort.

Lisboa wasn't there.

Leme studied his computer screen. Nothing. Email only. And it didn't look like it had been examined any time recent.

Leme sat. He picked up the phone, dialled his admin fuckhead.

'Então, cara. What have you got for me?' he said.

'Something, definitely. Well, maybe.'

'The fuck does that mean?'

'Just give me an hour. I'll be able to give you a few places she's been to – or planned to go to. Could be something. One hour, OK?'

Leme hung up.

Lisboa barrelled in, fresher. 'Men's room shower,' he said, waving his hands in front of his face, under his armpits, wafting the smell of cheap soap, pulling a face.

'Classy.'

'Yeah, well. Needs must.'

Lisboa slurped at his coffee. 'Christ,' he said.

Leme threw him a packet of biscuits.

Lisboa caught it smartly. 'Most important meal of the day,' he winked.

'So? Let's have it then.'

'Your friend Silva see you last night?'

'Why you asking that?'

Lisboa smiled. 'You first.'

Leme recognised Lisboa's look –

Chega, enough: end-of-the-tether situation.

So Leme went first. He told Lisboa what Silva had told him.

Leme finished his version, waited for Lisboa's response. Lisboa grinned. 'This is fucked up,' he said. 'Same thing happened to me.'

Lisboa pushed a thickish envelope across his desk to Leme.

He opened it. 'Fuck.'

He examined it. 'You do anything with this?'

'Nope. You going to tell me what's going on now?'

Leme nodded. 'Though, to be honest, I'm not entirely sure myself. Which is why I haven't said anything. Nothing to say, entendeu?'

Lisboa made a noise that said: yeah, I buy that.

'Forensics been in touch yet?'

Lisboa shifted forwards, changed gear. 'Funny thing,' he said. 'They're taking fucking ages. And know what? They're not being especially polite – basically told me to leave it, they're being fucked every which way at the moment and to concentrate on my own fucking job.'

'Charming. When'd they say this?'

'This morning. Early.' Lisboa gave Leme an ironic look. 'I couldn't sleep.'

'I still don't understand why you slept here?' Leme said.

Lisboa sighed, crunched through another biscuit. 'Two militar motor-cunts followed me. I clocked them pretty quick. I stopped for a beer, a pastel. Watched them peacock about outside the bar. Figured: fucked if I'm leading them home. When I got back into the car, the envelope was on the passenger seat. They weren't around – I couldn't see them – but why take the risk? I figured I'd be better off in a Polícia Civil delegacia than pretty much anywhere else.'

Leme barked a grim laugh. 'You'd hope so.'

'And the same thing happened to Silva?'

'Yeah, basically.'

'And the same papers? Bank records? Yours and his?'

Leme nodded.

'And Mario, you didn't know anything about this until Silva showed you what he'd dug up?'

Leme said, 'I'm working it out. It's … complicated.'

'Too fucking right. And Antonia?' Lisboa chose his words carefully. 'What does she know?'

'That's what's complicated.'

The phone rang, cut through them.

Leme picked up. 'Quem fala?'

A babble of excited chatter: Leme mouthed 'admin guy' at Lisboa, who nodded and leant back. His chair groaned. Leme raised his eyebrows. Lisboa blew him a kiss.

Leme was nodding. 'There in five minutes. Puta, meu, nice work,' he said.

Lisboa creaked forward. 'What is it?'

'Something from Ellie's computer. Connected to the maps function of her phone, apparently. Took them a while but they were able to recover any addresses anyone had sent her that she'd opened up.'

'That's straightforward, mate. I could have showed them that.'

Leme made a face. 'They'd been deleted, so they had to go through the computer side to get them. Anyway, turns out Fernando sent her more than one address.'

Sorrocaba, Lago Azul, Fernando's Parents' Holiday Home

18 October, late afternoon

It occurred to Ellie – once Dona Maria had calmed down and explained; once the shock had passed and the knowledge settled awkwardly within her, as if, she felt, she had swallowed something the wrong way, sudden sharp pains with periods of respite – that she was effectively stranded and that no one actually knew where she was.

'You mustn't bother Fernando's family, Maria, *really*, OK?' she'd said once Maria had finished wailing and sobbing, tearing at her clothes and invoking God's name and the name of a number of saints Ellie didn't recognise. 'You go,' Ellie continued, 'leave me here. I'll be fine. But don't mention *anything* about me, sabe? They mustn't be disturbed, entendeu?'

'OK, Dona Ellie, I understand. You're right, of course.'

'I'll sort my things out, clear up here, and call a friend to come and get me, OK? You go to the city when you can. You don't have to worry about me, OK?'

Maria sniffled something Ellie didn't understand.

'OK?' Ellie repeated.

'Let me first make you some food for today, tomorrow morning. Can I do that?'

Ellie smiled kindly. 'Of course you can, of course. That's very kind of you. You're a saint, Dona Maria.'

She looked pleased with that.

And, of course, Maria cleaned the house too before she left that afternoon, so Ellie was pleased with that.

But now, late in the afternoon, as the last golfers dragged themselves around the course in the setting sun, Ellie started to panic. She realised – with a degree of callousness that even she found a little distasteful – that she'd never slept with anyone who'd died before.

And, simply, she didn't know who to call. Without her phone, she didn't have any contact numbers. The only people she felt she *could* feasibly call were Leandro, Elizabeth or Detective Leme.

Leandro was out – there was no way she could get hold of his number. She could ring Zarzur Cabral, but he was rarely there and she doubted they'd give out employees' personal mobile numbers.

Elizabeth at the office was the obvious choice. She knew the number; Elizabeth knew where she was, at least according to what Fernando had said. But something was stopping her; she'd have to explain what had happened at Leandro's house and then what had happened to Fernando. She didn't much feel like doing that. And besides, she didn't really know what had happened. She'd been waiting these last couple of days for Fernando to come back and explain.

So that left Leme. He'd help, surely. But she didn't have his number and she didn't know the name of the delegacia where he was based and though she knew where he lived, she also knew that the seguranças wouldn't in a million years give out a number for him.

She didn't know what to do and this was a rare and unusual feeling: listlessness blended with a kind of hopelessness. Was this shock? Grief? Trauma? She felt desperate, but not sure in quite what way. She couldn't even shoulder the few things she had and get the bus back into town: the walk was miles, she didn't have enough cash for a taxi, and she'd left her own apartment that morning – that morning that seemed *months* ago – without her bank card or credit card, a precaution she often took when she didn't quite know where she'd end up.

There was nothing for it then. She went to the fridge and pulled out a case of beer, then to the liquor cabinet and an artisanal bottle of cachaça. She took the booze, a cooler, and the book with the soft touch to the one lounger that Maria hadn't stowed away, and she got drunk.

When she woke up, it was dark.

There were lights on in the houses around her and she could hear children's voices, so though groggy, she was reassured it wasn't late and she was fine.

The house was dark.

She rubbed her eyes and went inside to get the last of the food that Maria had cooked.

She didn't turn the light on and she realised – suddenly, with surprising clarity – that this was a very good decision.

Outside, in the half-moon drive at the front of the house, a car pulled in slowly and killed its lights.

No one got out.

'O Cara' (The Dude) – Society Drug Dealer

The fuck you want? I still don't really understand who the fuck you are? Yes, you've told me your name, Carlos, and I get that you're the militar big dog in ROTA and all that, yes, yes, that's crystal, but why are you fucking with me? That I don't get. Elaborate, please. Favor.

I *am* settled down, I am *not* wound up, I will not *get* wound up, I *am* relaxing the fucking lesbian, right in front of you, caralho. OK, so let me run this: one of your guys was the off-duty fuck who caught playboy Fernando and made the call to entice me out to where he and your other guys relieved me of fifty large. Entrapment, ne? Lucky my legal representation declined the case or you lot would be bent over by an eye-talian rent boy wrestler in a Frei Caneca basement about now, big dog. What? Yes, that's right, *Carlão,* it was fifty. Fifty thousand reais. What they tell you? Something a little lighter, no doubt. Boa, boa – bonito, eh meu, these loyal foot soldier fucks you run, ne? You wanna have a word, ta ligado?

What a joke: first thing that's made me smile in a month is a militar big dog boned by his own puppies. Sorry, Carlão, no offence, viu?

OK, easy, public place here, porra. I know that, I know, let's back the fuck up.

So, you're in charge of the guys that took my arrest-cash stash, which is one fifty-grand hole that is a *pouqiiiiiinhho* difficult to replenish. At least not quickly enough to guarantee I can stay out on the street, in my career, sabe, and not worry too much about the likes of you. Ta ligado? I need the insurance and it ain't easy to come by. The spics and the beaners need to get paid by my big dogs, so I need to pay them, entendeu? So. Like I said, this is a career. Look at my threads. Look at my style. Look at what I guarantee my clients. Do you know who my clients are? That's right: richer cunts than you. And they might not want any fuckery, church, but a couple of them might swing something for me. That worth the risk?

Então, porra.

Yeah, there *is* something you can do. Put the word out I don't have any fucking militar pussy fund on me and I'll be left well alone.

Oh there's something else? You're just going to give me back my money? No? I see, there's something I need to do for you. What a fucking surprise. I'm sure it's straightforward, meu querido, but forgive my skinny white bunda if I don't *exactly* trust the fuck out of you lot, entendeu?

How much we looking at?

Well, well, porra, if my arsehole could whistle, it would.

OK, I'm in. And all I have to do is show up at this place – a car park? Classy, Carlão – and finger the guy so you can be sure, and I get mine. Yeah, and I'll *owwwwe* you, yeah, understood.

Quid-pro-quo-type situation.

Look it up, porra.

We done? I assume this is on you? The generosity of our state knows no bounds when it comes to greasing mid-level losers like my good self, ne, Carlão?

It ain't humility: it's every man for himself and God for all, you know that bullshit line? Well, we done appropriated that nice little Catholic message for the criminal fraternity.

Beleza, Senhor, it's all good. It's us. It's very fucking US.

São Paulo, Marginal Freeway

18 October, evening

Leme jammed the brake. Leme shuffled lanes. Leme shunted, crunched gears. Leme cursed. It should have taken him about an hour to get to Lago Azul. He'd been stuck on the Marginal for nearly three.

Sorrocaba: Hicksville. Caipira: chicken coops and cheap exhaust, grimy pick-up trucks. Silent men in wide-rimmed hats sat stoic. The smoke from the road funnelled into a fat polluted cloud, pounded, beaten into shape by the heat.

Leme hit the dirt track early – get off this motorway queue.

Lago Azul – huge sign: a smiling blue fish jumping from a lake; a smiling blue fish playing golf; a smiling blue fish cooking at a barbecue, can of beer in his hand, smiling blue little fish playing close, smiling blue wife fish in a cute apron.

Can't miss this place. Family fun –

The air fresh. The air thin.

Leme thought of the pan at Antonia's, greased dead fish congealing. Leme thought of the fisheye. Leme shook his head. They'll talk –

Soon.

Leme fishtailed right and to the entrance.

He flashed his badge.

Seguranças scowled. They fronted. 'We'll have to call,' they said.

Leme nodded. Leme smiled. Leme played rule book.

Seguranças dialled the internal line. They grandstanded authority. They shook heads. 'No answer. No one in. Or no one there.'

Leme: 'There's someone there.'

Heads were shaken.

Leme: 'No answer equals more reason I go in, entendeu, porra?'

Heads were ducked in conference.

'We tail you though, certo?'

Leme: 'From a distance. And by distance, I mean *distance*, sabe?'
'Distance.'
Heads were nodded.
'Here.' Leme handed a map.
Leme ghosted into the complex. Leme passed mansions.
This, Leme thought, is what happens when you let new rich Paulistanos build their own holiday homes –
Architectural mish-mash, eyesore on eyesore:
American foursquare, French colonial, art deco, Creole cottage, Portuguese baroque, ranch house, Spanish colonial, Swiss chalet –
Cars shone in driveways. Kids roistered on quad bikes. Women pace-walked in Lycra, post-dinner.
Leme creeped slow, eyes peeled, lights low.
There:
A low house of some taste, dark windows, slight isolation –
Car in the drive. The fuck?
Leme dawdled – not expected.
Leme ran it back, what he'd been told:
Midday-ish. Leme scooted stairs to admin to talk to his fuckhead. He left Lisboa to argue with forensics and jumpstart Alvarenga to get some clarity from Lagnado. Leme felt this forensic delay was a tactic –
Someone wanted some time before young Leandro and the lovely Fernando were put on the slab and cut open. Autopsy boys running some tests –
Nothing yet. Only looking for drugs though. Autopsy boys know what they're looking for there.
Leme in and straight to his fuckhead.
'Here.' The fuckhead handed him an address.
'Que isso?'
'Playboy Fernando sent her this address a while ago. Fed her schmooze. Told her one day he'd take her there. Romantic weekend, entendeu? Snatch pad baited heavy for action. Booze and stars, that kind of shit.'
Leme snorted. 'Charming.'
'Ah, it is what it is. You jealous?'
Leme ignored that. 'You think there's a chance she's there?'
'I hacked into Fernando's phone using his account details and ID – there's a tracking device. He was there, day she went missing.'

Leme nodded. 'OK, makes sense. Anything else you can tell me?'

'On this? Only we've contacted the condo and there's not supposed to be anyone there at the moment. Last couple of days at least. No cars. Maid in and out. Doesn't mean the gringa's not though, of course.'

'Right.'

'Então.'

Leme nodding. 'You waiting for something?' he said.

The fuckhead: 'I thought you might blow me in gratitude.'

'Not your lucky day, son.'

Leme bounced up the stairs, briefed Lisboa. Three hours of bureaucracy, permission. Then –

Three hours of traffic.

No cars, the fuckhead had said.

Ellie's hands were spread in front of her, her head to the side, legs bent, in a parody, she realised, of someone ready to strike or defend herself or even a child playing move and freeze when the music stops.

She was giddy with recent drunkenness and deranged with fear.

So this is what it feels like.

Nothing moved outside.

She crouched and slid to the window – another parody, she thought; funny how much we rely on the cinema when in alien situations – and looked outside, square, at an angle she was sure meant she was hidden from view.

As she stood and watched, she became very aware of her breathing and the noise she was making. She tried holding her breath, but this seemed to heighten the silence around her and made her even more nervous. How we take the ordinary noises for granted! The low hum, natural and man-made, the families in kitchens and living rooms oblivious to Ellie's fearsome heartbeat, unaware of what was happening metres from where they sat and chatted and yelled and stropped.

Nothing stirred in the car.

The windows were blacked out, but Ellie could see the dark outline of someone in there, and it did appear to be only one person. This seemed encouraging, though she didn't know why.

Perhaps she should go out? Open the door and see what happened?

Or call the security gate?

Obviously that's what she should do.

She ducked under the level of the window and scooted, crab-like, across the floor to the interphone.

She reached up and unhooked it.

She tucked herself into the corner, just to the left of the second window that faced out onto the drive.

As she steadied her breathing and dialled, she heard a car door opening, saw a sharp flash of light.

She dropped the phone and pulled the curtains around her in – she realised even as she did it – an entirely futile gesture.

Leme sat and scoped the car, the house. Nothing moved. The house, dark, still. Leme studied curtains. Nothing. Leme killed his lights and edged forward.

Leme checked his rear view: seguranças followed –

At a *distance*.

Leme checked the perimeter. High walls ringed with barbed wire, security teams, CCTV –

At a distance.

Leme wondered about the security plan. In his own building, car jacking and robbery from the inside was the plot.

They had a stratagem in place though:

A pair of thieves stops you at a traffic light. One hops in the back with a gun trained on your head. When you approach the building, they crouch down low and tell you they'll kill you if you do anything suspicious. So you wave nonchalantly at the glass booth and ghost inside. Then, the thieves go from flat to flat stripping them of valuables. They load up and leave in the car in which they arrived.

It's a clever scam, if a little high-risk, Leme always thought.

The system:

If you drive in with a couple of ladroês in the back, you park in a special bay which the security guys have designated as a signal to them that you're in trouble.

Done.

Menus um, ou menos dois.

The ladroês don't tend to work again.

But in this hick condo?

Leme couldn't be sure.

Leme checked the glove compartment. Revolver, badge.

Leme holstered up.

Leme clicked the door – quietly.

At the same moment a man got out of the car in front. Leme sat tight. Leme rolled the car forward and hit the lights – full beam.

The man turned, dazzled.

Outside, a nasal cawing. Gulls –

They're a long way from the coast.

Otherwise, the thrum of evening and the dissipating heat.
The man raised his hand to block his eyes.
Gun.
Leme ducked down.
He heard a door slamming.
He heard the car starting.
He sat up, jumped out.
The car shot off.
Leme tried the front door of the house.
Open.
Leme heard a gasp.
Ellie. Thank fuck.
Leme hit lights.
Ellie sprang up and hugged him.
The man in the car:
Leme couldn't be sure, but it looked like one of Carlos's militars.
Fuck.

Leme sat. Ellie shook. 'Shock,' Leme told her. 'Perfectly natural.'

Ellie gave him an ironic look. 'He wasn't my boyfriend,' she said.

'Just a – what – lover?'

Another ironic look. Eyes blazed.

'Entendeu?' she added.

Leme said nothing. Leme knew what she was doing.

Leme had seen it time and again. Defense mechanism, strike out, attack, no weakness meant no pain: easier than trying to understand mortality, after all.

Leme thought of Antonia.

She claimed not to feel pain, *physical* pain. She made him dig his nails into her hand as hard as he could and she felt nothing, she said. Leme hadn't liked doing it – felt wrong, invasive, hostile.

Leme had felt forced into it; like he was the one it was hurting.

But Antonia did feel pain and Leme had hurt her.

And Leme would hurt her again. He was sure of that.

'Look,' Leme said, 'I need to know what happened to you after we got to Leandro's place. I'm going to assume you know what happened to him?'

Ellie shook her head.

Leme weighed it.

Leme told her.

'Fuck,' she said.

Disarmed. There – happens to us all.

'Fernando set you up with the meeting, right?'

Ellie nodded.

'Then what?'

Ellie told him. Ellie told him everything, she said.

Leme let it marinate –

Ellie had made a judgement, gone with the man that knew more – Fernando. She was protecting herself; at least she thought she was.

And it was a snap judgement –

Though it was very fucking likely the wrong one.

But based on misinformation.

She'd had no idea that Leandro was dead. She didn't know what scene she was leaving behind. They'd been working on very different assumptions on what the other knew. She was scared – and that was no surprise. She'd had *noooooo* idea who the fuck's feathers her little investigative jaunt had ruffled.

He believed her. Jesus. Poor girl. And lucky he'd played his cards so close. Lucky for her he got there when he did.

'And Fernando hadn't contacted you at all?' Leme said.

'No. He said he'd be back in a couple of days. That he'd be able to explain then. But...'

She tailed off. Her eyes misted – incomprehension.

Leme got that. But he needed to confirm what he thought he knew.

'So he meets you in that boteco, gives you the address, and then is already there when you arrive? You can understand my questions, Ellie. Leandro had been murdered not long before you arrived.'

'And Fernando?'

'Então.'

Ellie looked up – sharp; confusion or fear. 'What do you mean?'

Leme shook his head. 'Your phone,' he said. 'We have it. And your computer.'

'My computer?'

Leme nodded. 'Fernando lifted it from your apartment. He took it to a colleague of his, we don't yet know why. I was able to recover it. We used it to find you here. Tomorrow, you can come in and likely take it back.'

This was a lie.

'Why would Fernando take my computer?'

'Why would Fernando make you leave your phone at Leandro's place?'

Ellie measured her words. 'He didn't. I dropped my purse, my bag, when he grabbed me. Like I said before, he told me we were in danger.' She paused. 'He said there was no time, and I trusted him. It didn't seem important, my phone, you know. It made sense. I don't know.'

Leme nodded. It did make sense, when you factor in what she didn't know at the time, and what he now did know. Leme smiled, spoke – winding up: 'We need to get back and we need to let your editor know that you're OK.'

'Fernando told me he'd let her know where I was.'

'He didn't.' Leme stood. 'He also told you he'd let Leandro know, right?'

Ellie nodded – looked grim. Leme knew why.

'Então.'

Leme paced. He said, 'You better get your stuff together, make arrangements you need to with the seguranças. We can talk more in the car. You can stay at my apartment tonight, at least. There's space. Probably sensible, certo?'

Ellie nodded.

Leme remembered Silva. He smiled. 'You'll have some company.'

It didn't register. Leme said, 'I'll be outside.'

Outside, Leme smoked. The seguranças were dawdling, close. Leme lifted a hand, gestured: yep, it's fine. You can fuck off now.

The seguranças got it.

Marginal, night –

Traffic lighter. Leme drove fast.

Windows down. The air, cool. The air, thin.

The dank blash sludge of the river quiet and dark –

On a night like this it was almost river, not sewer.

Ellie's feet bare: propped up above the glove compartment.

Ellie slouched, buzz-tired. She talked fast. Hair pulled back, tank-top shoulders, three-quarter trousers.

Silva's going to *looove* this girl, Leme thought.

House-on-fire situation – no doubt.

Dark, deep vegetation crept up hills that banked either side of the motorway. Dotted lights thickened in concentration as they approached the outskirts of the city. The outskirts stretched; the outskirts a series of towns with no names, settlements trailing their way slowly to São Paulo: centred on fast-food warehouses and shit-cheap rodizio restaurants, the petrol station forecourts jammed with trucks, drivers in back rooms with state immigrant cooze.

Leme, stoic, watched the road.

Ellie yapped and gabbed, relieved.

Leme stopped her – sharp. 'Tell me about that little expedition you made to Cracolândia with Leandro?'

'Woah.' Ellie shot him a look. 'How the fuck did you know about that?'

Leme said nothing.

'Ah,' Ellie said. 'You've got my laptop, ne?'

Leme nodded. 'Então,' he said.

'Well, young Leandro was working as a liaison officer for Fernando's law firm. Idea was that he was keeping the residents there informed of what was going on with the sale of the land and what would happen to them next, entendeu? Sort of keeping things smooth, keeping them happy. At least the non-crackhead residents, anyway.'

'Makes sense,' Leme said.

'Yeah, ne? He had some friends down there and we were supposed to visit them so that he could show me how well they were being treated and that all was above aboard. Thing was, they weren't there.'

'They weren't there?'

'Neither were their houses.'

'Eh?'

'There was nothing where Leandro said their houses had been.'

'They'd just disappeared?'

'Exactamente.'

'How is that possible?'

Ellie shifted in her seat and turned to face him. 'They were favela houses, you know? Temporary, shit brick-and-plastic, that kind of thing, entendeu? But they'd been there for a long time. Legally, they owned the shelter, but not the land. Complicated as fuck, which is why Leandro was down there advising them all.'

Leme nodded. 'I know about all that.'

Ellie gave him a look. 'So we ask around. Well, Leandro does. Then three militars, real nasty bastards, turn up and tell us to fuck off. Unpleasant cunts. Not very constructed young men, shall we say.'

'They sound familiar.'

Ellie gave him another look. 'So we left. We were figuring out what to do next. That's when Fernando set me up to go to Leandro's house.'

'Why did you need him to do that for you?'

Ellie – indignant. 'Look, I'm not stupid, entendeu? I didn't want Leandro to know too much about me, and I didn't want to know too much about him. I fake-numbered him – oh, don't look like that, it is what it is – so he couldn't contact me if he wanted to. Fernando was helping me … expedite the whole thing, sabe? This way there was a bit of distance.' She made a face. 'Girl's got to be careful in this city, *detective*.'

'Night before you went to meet Fernando, before I followed you and took you to Leandro's, Leandro left a message for you at the magazine.'

Ellie frowned – interested-confused.

'It said: I'm worried about Fernando.'

Ellie didn't like that. She said nothing.

'Now why do you think he'd say that, Ellie?'

'I've no idea.'

'Ellie, Leandro is dead, shivved something awful when you go to meet him. Fernando takes you away from the scene. Whisks you away somewhere safe. Then he's murdered – same MO: shivved to fuck. You say you know nothing about it – and I believe you. But there are going to be some very difficult questions from some of my colleagues. Very soon.'

Ellie – terrified, in *waaaay* over her head –

Genuine. Honest reaction.

Leme was right to believe her.

'Describe the three militars for me,' Leme said.

She did. She described them spot on – detail-nailed.

Leme was nodding. 'I think I've met these militars,' he said.

The militars that scared the fuck out of Ellie?

Not Carlos and his mob. No –

Sounded like Nelson and his cowboys.

Leme had scanned the face of the man outside the house in Lago Azul.

'You see the guy in the car?' Leme asked.

Ellie shook her head. 'Fuck no. I was hiding behind the curtains. I saw an outline. Blackened windows, sabe?'

Leme believed her. Leme thought –

Carlos knew where she was.

How the fuck?

Carlos knew where Fernando lived – Leme had given him his details.

'We've got two homicides connected by two things,' he said. 'Three, actually: Zarzur Cabral, Cracolândia, and—'

Ellie jumped in. 'And me.'

'Isso.'

Leme tossed her his mobile phone. 'Call your editor. Let's at least clear that up. Number's in there. Contacts, under Elizabeth Young.'

Ellie made an ironic face. 'Oh yeah?'

Leme growled, 'Call her.'

Leme eased up the speed as they got closer to the city. Traffic thickened. Air thickened. Spots of rain –

Fat smog-storm in an hour:

Marginal flood. Mudslide heavy.

Should be home by then.

Leave her to Silva –

Fill him in:

Let him grill her.

He believed her, but –

You never know.

Ellie blathered. Ellie apologised for all the inconvenience and worry she'd caused. Ellie spouted English tones –

Leme caught bits.

Leme thought of Renata. Night-drive without her never the same. Leme felt a wave of sadness. Her voice –

Whispering.

Her voice –

Don't be afraid.

Her voice –

One day you'll get a real problem, and –

And?

Ellie's tone changed. Ellie played shocked. 'Christ,' she said. 'OK. I understand. I'll be in tomorrow.'

Leme looked across: and?

'Leandro left another message that night,' Ellie said. 'A phone number. It got lost in the in-tray pile.'

'And?'

'His friends in Cracolândia, the ones who disappeared. A new number, apparently.'

Leme nodded. 'Chase it tomorrow.'

Ellie – distracted. 'Yeah.'

Leme gave her the fisheye. '*And?*' he said.

'Something else. An English guy, older guy, was sniffing around the offices today, apparently.'

Leme thought: coincidence?

Unlikely.

Ellie said, 'Like a landowner, businessman. Something to do with the Cracolândia sale, though Elizabeth wasn't sure. Posh, polite, entendeu?'

'So why do you look so worried?' Leme asked.

Ellie gave a quick shake of her head – smiled. 'Ah, no reason. Interesting though, ne?'

Leme thought it was. Leme thought it was –

Very fucking interesting indeed.

Leme made a decision. He speared in a text message.

São Paulo, Antonia's Apartment

18 October, evening

When Antonia walked through the front door of her apartment – the front door of the apartment that, in a matter of hours really, she would officially share with Mario – her first feeling, when she called out his name and realised she was alone, was relief. Relief to know that, for an hour at least, hopefully more, she wouldn't have to confront the now undeniable fact that she would never measure up to Mario's first wife, Renata.

She'd always known that, but before now it hadn't been anything that *she had actually done*. She couldn't measure up simply because no one could. Death sanctifies quicker and more effectively than marriage ever could. Antonia knew Renata well, had known her since college, and while they had got on in the first half dozen years or so, and had continued a friendship of sorts – the competitive, faint praising, falsely modest, snide type of friendship that Antonia knew was the preserve of women complicit in its protocol and who extracted perverse satisfaction from it mores in the understanding that the souring of the relationship was *exactly* its appeal – Antonia had grown sick of Renata's self-righteousness and default position of indignant *goodness*, several years before her death.

There had been, briefly, an alliance as their other friends and colleagues from college began to have children and, it seemed, quickly renounced all rights and self-identity beyond their positions as mothers and wives. This area was a perfect fit for Renata and Antonia's caustic social commentary, though Renata always seemed to manage to stop short of the sort of hurtful character assassination at which Antonia was so adept, able to present herself as equal opportunities in terms of reproduction, avoid the accusation that she didn't have children because she couldn't find a man, that her perceived hostility to women who *chose* to have a family wasn't, in fact, hiding a desperate desire to have one herself, thwarted by her grasping, ambitions, and, essentially, *bad* character.

A character that couldn't cohabit –

A bad character.

Renata was never – at least as far as Antonia knew – a bad character.

And when she died, that became fact.

Of course – and here was the … paradox? – Antonia didn't ever intend to identify herself by her role in Mario's life in the same way that she had never done before with any other man, and in the same way that Renata never had with him or anyone else. So while she was fated by her own character to live in the same way as Renata, in the same way, in fact, that had been so attractive to Mario, she'd also be fated by the self-evident fact she was and never would actually *be* Renata.

She mixed herself a Martini, picked at an olive. She ducked into the fridge and wondered about something more substantial. She pulled a file from her briefcase and checked her phone. There were things she could – and while Mario wasn't here – should be doing. She sent him a text:

Dinner? Xx

That'd do it. No response meant work and she had plenty of time. Any other explanation and she'd have to be patient.

She sipped at her drink.

She smiled at the field day she'd have had if a friend of hers had ever got together with a widower:

All her bad habits will be frozen in that early stage when they're cute and not infuriating and all yours will be immediately infuriating – as they're not hers

He'll never have a bad word spoken against her –

All his friends will judge you –

You'll have rescued him from despair – with your feminine wiles

One night, he'll think he's sleeping with her, a dead woman, and then he'll wake up and see your face –

Anyway, she thought as she drained her drink, it might not matter in a day or two. She nodded – resolute. There was some satisfaction in knowing that now, after what had happened in the last few days, she would never measure up to Renata because of something *she had done.*

She smiled – yes, *fuck* yes, *that* really was satisfying, liberating, even.

She made herself another drink. Women aged better than men, she thought. The urge to romanticise the past that so defined men and their eternal disappointments disappeared with the better understanding women had of the present – of the reality of how things actually are, actually work.

Two drinks in and floating content on the warm, soapy, effervescent bath of alcohol, the doorbell rang.

Funny, Antonia thought, she hadn't been called on the intercom. Must be a friend from the building, a neighbour. She wasn't expecting anyone.

She unfolded herself from the sofa and skidded in her tights to the door. She checked the peephole: a man she recognised, maybe – though wasn't sure from where – as a friend of Mario's.

She opened the door.

A large man, bald other than wispy white hair clinging to the sides of his head just above his ears, opened his arms and smiled broadly at her.

'Querida Antonia,' he said. Seeing her confusion, he added, quickly, 'Carlos. A friend, *colleague*, of Mario's.'

He edged into the apartment, placed a bottle of wine in her hand.

'You don't remember me?' he said.

Antonia shook her head.

No, she didn't remember him, exactly.

She was pretty sure she would have.

His expression wasn't one you'd forget.

Antonia stepped back and allowed Carlos to come in, figuring, quickly, that the seguranças must have realised that he was in the building and, also, that they hadn't called her as he was known to them as Mario's friend. She decided that, for now at least, she wasn't in any danger. She'd spent most of her adult life composed and wary; she was used to situations in which she was, superficially, in the weaker position, on the back foot. In fact, she thought as she stepped into the kitchen to open the wine, being on the back foot usually worked out very well for her.

'Do you want a glass of this?' she called out, nonchalant as fuck, she thought.

'Something stronger,' Carlos barked. 'That was for you. Your fella'll have some whiskey around here somewhere.'

What a prick, Antonia thought. She fished inside a cupboard and found *her* bottle of single malt and poured two large measures into appropriate glasses.

She carried them through and handed one to Carlos.

'No ice?' he said.

She smiled. 'My *fella* asked me the same thing once,' she said. 'As I told him: you don't put ice in single malt.'

Carlos sniffed at it, like a bulldog, Antonia thought and smiled.

'Umm,' he grunted. He took a sip – begrudgingly, angrily – and nodded once.

Antonia sat down and gestured for him to do the same.

'No, if it's alright with you I'll stay on my feet.'

She flashed him a look that said: you're the boss.

'You're probably wondering why I'm here,' he said.

This time her look said: I was, but it's a nice surprise to see you.

'You've got something I need. A laptop belonging to an English journalist called Ellie something. She was fucking one of your colleagues and he gave it to you, apparently at your request.'

'That's not true.'

'Which part?'

'The bit about me requesting it.'

'No?'

'Fernando was taking the initiative there. He thought it would be useful. Might be. He … wanted to prove that he was doing his job properly. Let's put it that way.'

'And was he?'

'I think so, overall.'

Carlos took a step towards her and practically stood over her. 'I know all about him. Are you doing *your* job properly?' he asked.

Antonia smiled. 'Always,' she said.

He leaned closer. She could smell his hot breath soured by beer, his sharp, toxic aftershave. 'Didn't work out too well for Fernando though, did it?'

He stepped away and paced the room. 'Know where your fella is tonight?'

'No. Working. I don't know.'

'Very progressive relationship, is it? Must be hard in the shadow of that stuck-up bitch of an ex-wife of his.'

Antonia smiled. 'Not really,' she said. 'I knew her longer than he did. And you're right, she was a bitch.'

'Ooh,' he said. 'Easy.'

She made to stand, gesturing at him with her glass.

'No.' He raised his hand to stop her. 'Let me.'

Antonia handed him her glass. 'Thank you. What a gentleman.'

He glared at her, searching her face for irony. The point was – and this was something Antonia had learned when a little girl – if you only communicate irony, it is very difficult to spot.

He stomped into the kitchen. Antonia remembered that her phone was in there, on the counter. She hadn't checked it for an hour or so and fidgeted on the edge of her seat, fearful that some important email or text would be sitting there waiting for Carlos to read.

He poked his head around the door and tossed her phone across the room so that it landed on the sofa next to her.

'Thought you might need that,' he said.

She hit the power button and scanned the email subject lines. Nothing relevant. He was playing with her.

He came back, seemed to come as if through the wall itself with that compact but enormous body; that *bulk*.

'Here. Toma.'

'Saúde,' she said, raising her glass.

'Então, this laptop then: go and get it for me.'

'I can't.'

'You fucking well can.'

'No. I. Can't. It's at the office.'

'At the office?'

'Yes.'

'Why?'

'It's password protected. I couldn't get into it, so I took it in to the IT department to see if some bright spark might be able to help.'

'And?'

'No luck yet, but apparently just a matter of time.'

Carlos was nodding. 'OK,' he said. 'It's irrelevant now. I need it. Tomorrow. Meet me here.' He pulled a card for a restaurant in Pinheiros out of his wallet. 'At twelve thirty lunchtime. Got that?'

Antonia nodded. This was an interesting development. 'Why do you need it?'

'You don't get to ask questions, entendeu?'

Antonia felt her phone vibrate against her leg. Carlos turned another circle around the room. Antonia snuck a look. Mario:

On way home. Bringing the English journalist. She's going to stay at mine. See you in an hour or so. Bjs

As Carlos turned, Antonia tried to disguise her surprise.

'OK?' he grunted.

'Of course, I'll be there. One thing though—'

'Yeah?'

'What about the girl? What's going to happen to her?' Antonia should warn Mario, warn her, but she had no idea how. This girl … no, that would be too much. Too awful.

Carlos gave a grim, satisfied smile. 'One of my men is taking care of it as we speak. Don't even think about it. You don't want to know.'

Antonia nodded, then shook her head. So she was safe? For now, at least. She said, 'Yes, no, not another word, not another thought.'

'Very good.' Carlos sat down heavily on the chair closest to Antonia. 'Best you don't tell your fella about tonight, or tomorrow.'

'Of course.'

'He's chasing two crimes that will never be solved, entendeu? That young favela kid, no one will ever give a fuck about him. Fernando is trickier: his family are well off, might cause a stink, but it's easy, crystal. A mugging, a robbery, you know. He was fifty grand into a dealer we all know well enough: O Cara – the fucking Dude. No skin off anyone's rosy red behind if it's pinned on him, so that'll work, entendeu? Either way, forensics have been blocked by the superintendent. Ain't going to happen and Mario's going to be in circles.'

'Why are you telling me this?'

'To make sure you know what it is you should do. It all filters down, this construction business. Your Englishman buys the land, someone has to clear it, something has to happen to clear it, and someone has to deal with whoever doesn't like what has to happen. Entendeu?'

Antonia nodded. 'I'm a lawyer. Of course I fucking understand.'

'Alright, slow down. Just know this: the head of the Polícia Civil does not want these two murders solved. And that's because someone's told him not to solve them. No one does anything more, without the right authority giving them the nod.'

Antonia smiled. Her phone buzzed – this time she held it up to him. 'Mario,' she said. 'He'll be back pretty soon. You best fuck off, eh?'

That irony again –

Carlos knocked back the end of his Scotch. 'You're a lovely hostess. I'll look forward to having you and Mario round to mine one day soon.'

He clomped to the door.

'One last thing,' he said. 'You need a file. Legal permissions and whatnot. I have it. It's yours, for twenty-five thousand reais, certo? Tomorrow.'

He smiled and blew her a kiss, closed the door, gently.

Antonia stood and locked it behind him.

Mario had the English girl? And why did he tell *her*?

Did he know that she'd got the finance department to use his bank account to hide some of the Cracolândia payments?

That was the only thing she'd done that was really wrong.

She was beginning to realise she had no idea what was going on.

The file though: that was something.

So it wasn't with the English girl after all. Probably for the best if she didn't know how Carlos had come to it.

She'd be able to rustle the cash up at work without too much bother.

Leme's Apartment

18 October, night

Ellie surveyed the scene with a look that was part amused, part mock-appalled, part disgust – the disgust though was directed at the slumped, dishevelled, bulging form of a man; a man whose size seemed to creep out from within him so that the sofa, on which he lay, could barely contain him, barely prevent his flesh from following his limbs and actually slipping off, melting and dripping to the floor like one of those clocks in a Dalí painting.

'Makes quite an impression, ne?' Leme said.

Ellie smirked. 'Impression on your sofa, at least.'

'Drink?'

Ellie nodded. 'A beer would be great.'

She was feeling a lot better than she had only an hour or so earlier. She was safe here, and while she didn't exactly think that she was in danger, she was in too fragile a state of mind to be comfortably alone at home in a building that, frankly, did not have the security of this one.

There was only what Elizabeth had said about this older English businessman. And why he would have anything to do with Cracolândia.

'Here, get this down you.' Leme passed her a cold can of Bohemia and a glass.

She looked admiringly at the glass. 'Detective,' she said. 'How fancy you are: a frosted, bulbous beer glass with the *actual name* of the beer we're drinking emblazoned across it. I am impressed.'

Leme shook his head, smiled, winked and placed a can of beer lightly against Silva's face.

Silva grunted, sighed and let out a tremendous fart, as if the can acted like some kind of pressure gauge, flicked on to release gas.

'Charming lad,' Ellie said.

Leme nodded at the door to the balcony.

They arranged themselves on the plastic chairs around the plastic table, and Ellie traced the stains – red wine, tobacco, grease from barbecued meat, she thought – absent-mindedly with her ring finger. Leme offered her a cigarette and she took it.

They sat and smoked in silence for a few minutes. Ellie let herself grow accustomed to the background rattle and choke of the city that she had missed for the few days she was at Lago Azul. Silence was an odd commodity: on the one hand rare and delightfully simple in its desirability and effect, its suggestion of peace and calm and contentment; on another, the unnerving thought often occurred to Ellie that silence meant that nobody knew you were there, nobody could stop anything happening to you. At least in the city you knew you were not alone, and that people were *choosing* to ignore you, choosing not to come to your rescue. There was something reassuring about that essentially selfish exercise of free will, Ellie thought.

'Então,' Leme said. 'I'm going upstairs soon.'

'To see *Antonia*?'

'That's right.'

'Lucky you.'

'We could do this for a bit,' Leme said, 'it's very funny and so on, but I'd rather figure out our next moves.'

Ellie smiled, shrugged her shoulders as if to say, hey routine's a hard one to shake, entendeu?

Leme said, 'I want you to go the magazine's offices tomorrow – I'll drive you – and do two things. First, find out who this English guy is, certo? Your editor must have some idea. Second—'

'Wait. Why does it matter?'

'It might not, but it's worth finding out if it does.'

'The enigmatic detective.'

'*Second*' – Leme repeated, slowly – 'I want you to chase up these friends of Leandro. There's a number, ne? We need to know what happened to them. More importantly who did whatever it was that was done to them, entendeu?'

Ellie nodded and looked inside through the large windows. The beached sofa-man was stirring, scratching at his belly and jowls, coughing a meaty, loose, deeply unhealthy sounding cough. He cracked the can of beer and tipped his head back thirstily.

Ellie angled her glass towards him. 'I think the beast has arisen,' she said.

'That's Silva, Francisco, friend of mine. You'll like him.'

'Oh yeah?' Ellie was sceptical about that. She watched him rearrange himself in his trousers and the scepticism hardened into certainty. 'I don't know about that.'

Leme watched him and laughed. 'Believe it or not, he's something of a name, in your game, at least.'

Ellie raised her eyebrows, nodded. She'd read his work not long ago. It was what had set her off on this whole thing, really, to an extent, convinced her there was a story here.

'Journalist,' Leme said. 'Crusading type, no injustice too small, no politician too big, that kind of thing.'

'Jesus. You wouldn't get that from looking at him.'

'You'll see,' Leme said, standing. 'I'll bring him out here. We all need to compare a few notes. Another beer?'

'Fuck yeah, thanks.'

Ellie thought she'd need it – if she were going to be sitting up late with this Silva bloke, roommates for one night only.

Midtown

19 October, very early morning

Leme jacked another car from a different funcionario kook. Full-on piece of shit: rust-bucket. VW: green-brown, dirty windows –

Engine:

A growler.

Leme up lark-time and across town:

Pre-traffic.

Coffee from a flask from Antonia's –

One of those keep-warm silver cups.

Tongue-burn and mouth scrape:

Puta que pariu. And she'd been quiet, Antonia. More than normal. Box that.

Head tight, brain-fucked tired.

The plan:

Pick up Lisboa

Find Carlos's militar

Find Carlos

Glove compartment:

Gun –

Locked and loaded, porra. Leme gave a grim smile at *that* thought.

Night before:

Leme, Silva and Ellie played it.

Lisboa had made some calls. Lisboa had names –

Carlos's two militar stooges.

Leme's admin fuckhead ran them:

ID'd easy.

The fuckhead sent two photos:

One –

The stooge that followed Silva.

The other –

The stooge that followed Lisboa. The same stooge Leme saw

outside Fernando's place at Lago Azul – running scared. Amarelo cunt.

An address near Bela Vista –

Leme's old stomping ground:

Bixiga –

The bladder of São Paulo.

Leme's stomach lurching. Leme's head turning. The big question:

What the fuck did Antonia have to do with all this?

Leme drove – fast. The city filled with cars. The streets filled with brown faces waiting for buses.

Leme boosted Lisboa outside his building.

Lisboa popped his phone. 'Still time,' he said. 'The prick won't leave for half an hour,' he said. 'You OK?' he asked.

Leme said nothing. He grunted, 'Fuck knows.'

'And your English girl?'

Leme nodded. 'She's fine. A little shaken, but fine. Staying with me.'

Lisboa nodded. 'And today? What's she doing?'

'Chasing a lead. Cracolândia families. Friends of kid Leandro.'

Leme swerved and honked. He rode the anger of the taxistas he overtook and floored it up through Jardins.

'And Silva?'

Leme smiled. 'Holding tight at mine. Writing it all up. Getting his IT guy to check up on the lawyers, on the land, on—'

Antonia. Leme didn't say it though.

He pulled right into Bela Vista. The car gulped and roared. Lisboa raised his eyebrows. Sad-faced men and women hung from buses, doors open.

'You fed Alvarenga, Lagnado any of this?' Lisboa asked.

Leme snorted. 'Step by step,' he said. 'See what we've got first, ne?'

'Makes sense.'

Leme concentrated on the road. Tight corners with the carts filled with rubbish and the taxis jostling for the businessmen on their phones, in their suits.

'Nearly there,' he said.

Leme parked outside the stooge's building. They sat soft, saying little. The road was quiet. They were only a couple of blocks from

Paulista Avenue, but it felt like the place had emptied, that everyone who lived there had disappeared off to work already.

Leme scoped the neighbourhood. He knew the jobs the residents had likely gone to. Service-industry lackeys, the odd office boy, a few middle-class youngsters who worked in IT or some such, broken away from their parents' houses and set up alone or with friends in apartments furnished with cheap tables and chairs, stiff-backed, faux-leather sofas with plastic not long ripped off and discarded.

Leme knew, as Leme had been there himself. He eyeballed dead ahead. You leave a place like this but you don't escape it. This ain't the ghetto, no Senhor, but an honest, hard-working, working-class district – however fucking small it was – was a rare thing these days. This was a place you grow out of – literally. Roots remain. He didn't share this pearl with Lisboa, as Lisboa knew too. And Lisboa also knew where Leme got this half-arsed social commentary from –

Renata.

They sat and they smoked. The buildings seemed to bend over them, tall, swaying in the breeze, leaning in to touch, to connect, almost. Helicopters buzzed and whined like blood-hungry mosquitoes overhead, making drops, the fat smog cushioning the sound of their choppy, low hum-thrum, the sirens and reversing trucks piercing the pillow of pollution that softened, that settled, that *eased*, somehow, this whole inner city experience.

This, Leme thought, this need to observe, to judge, was just a way to avoid thinking about what he knew they were going to do –

And going to do very soon.

Lisboa checked his watch. 'About ready?'

Leme said nothing.

The gate of the building swung to with a slow creak. Both their heads turned.

Lisboa shifted forward. 'We're in,' he said. 'Look sharp.'

The stooge swaggered out, sunglasses and a Palmeiras cap, arm raised goodbye and good luck at the porteiro. No uniform –

Without it he looked like a stick-thin mummy's boy with an edge. Nothing more.

He walked, arm bent to his ear, chatting. Gesticulating –

Paquerando: cheeky-lewd and laughing.

Some poor cooze is going to get a shock, Leme thought.

Lisboa angled his head towards him. 'Go, porra.'

Leme hit the gas, pedal to the floor, riding the pavement.

The stooge turned, his face confused, arm dropped.

Leme swerved to miss him.

Lisboa swung out the passenger door – hard.

It smacked against the stooge – hard.

The stooge fell and Lisboa was onto him in moments, his bulk pinned him, his knee in his back.

Leme angled the car back onto the road. He watched.

Lisboa rested the barrel of his revolver against the stooge's cheek, while his mouth chewed pavement.

'Entendeu?' Lisboa shouted.

The stooge was nodding – fast.

He gave up his arms and Lisboa cuffed him.

Leme eyeballed the street. Nothing –

Early-morning light, crime-time quiet.

Lisboa strongarmed the stooge into the car. 'We're going for a ride,' he said, the stooge still nodding.

Leme gunned the car.

This might be over soon.

They drove to Pinheiros. Lisboa knew an abandoned car park, sheltered by the building site for the new Metro station, hidden from view. He kept his gun in the stooge's ribs. The stooge sat with his head bowed, sneering. Leme eyed him through the rear-view mirror. He wondered how much trouble he'd likely give them.

He wondered exactly what it was that they wanted to know.

They pulled into the car park and Leme aimed the car at a sorry-looking Portakabin in the furthest corner from where they'd ghosted in. The place was deserted.

Leme scoped it:

Surrounded by cranes and skips and piles of bricks –

Thick layer of chalk and dust –

No way to see in –

Or get out.

Leme pulled his own gun from the glove compartment and holstered it. He jumped, stood with his jacket open, gun-show cocky, waited for Lisboa to push the stooge through the back door.

Lisboa thundered out behind the stooge and strongarmed him towards the Portakabin.

Lisboa winked at Leme. 'This shouldn't take long,' he said.

Leme shouldered the door and they went inside.

Lisboa dragged the stooge to the far wall where a hook hung from the ceiling.

Under it was a wooden crate, about the size of a shoebox. Lisboa nudged the stooge and he stepped up onto it.

Lisboa snagged the stooge's handcuffed arms over the hook so that he was pitched forward, arms straining to stay upright.

Lisboa kicked the crate out from under the stooge, who sprung forward and was then pulled back, shoulders popping. He yelped, squealed –

Leme winced.

Lisboa took the stooge by the jaw, dug his fingernails into his cheek, twisted his head right left right left, snapped it back.

'Let's not waste any time, ne?' he said.

Leme stepped back and leant against the corrugated iron that just about held the thing up.

Lisboa said, 'Why were you following me?'

The stooge said nothing. He shook his head, spat.

Lisboa smiled. 'OK.'

He turned away from the stooge and looked at Leme.

Leme nodded down towards the floor.

Lisboa nodded in agreement. He turned back to the stooge and drove his fist into his gut.

Once, twice, and then, once, twice into his kidneys –

The stooge gasped.

Lisboa looked at Leme who nodded again.

Lisboa round-housed, heavy-bagged the stooge like an ageing fighter.

Leme called out, 'Chega, ne?' and Lisboa stopped, the stooge breathing heavily.

Leme: 'Why did you go out to Lago Azul? Who sent you to get the English girl? What were you supposed to do?'

The stooge shook his head. 'I'm not talking,' he said. He spat. He looked at Leme and said, 'No fucking way. Não vou falar.'

Leme nodded.

They stood in a triangle, quiet.

Then: a buzzing, a light flashing on and off like a heartbeat in the stooge's pocket.

Lisboa reached into it and looked at the display. He looked at Leme. 'Bingo,' he said.

He swiped and held the receiver to the stooge's ear, jabbed his gun into his side.

Lisboa fidgeted. Leme studied the floor.

The stooge said, nodding limply: 'Isso. Tudo bem. Yep. Don't worry. I'll see you there. Ta. Isso. Ciao. See you there, relax.'

The stooge was silent for a moment and then nodded and Lisboa took the phone back. A moment after that it buzzed again.

A text message.

Lisboa studied it and smiled. 'Carlos,' he said to Leme. 'An address. Instructions. One hour.'

Leme nodded. 'Best get a move on, ne?' he said.

Lisboa smiled. 'No need, cara. The address – it's right fucking here. Looks like I'm not the only one who knows about this place.'

Bingo.

Suplicy Café, Shopping Iguatemi

Same day, mid-morning

Ellie was early, but she didn't mind as there was something fascinatingly repugnant about Shopping Iguatemi, and she wandered the mall enjoying the aspirin-freshness of the air conditioning, the sharp fog of perfume from the beauty salons and the hordes of perfectly composed women with their straightened hair tottering on heels, stiff cardboard bags strung from their wrists like an odd sort of jewellery, bags which likely had obscenely expensive jewellery inside them, of course.

How very fucking meta, Ellie, she thought.

She sat at a table in the Suplicy café, ordered an absurdly priced espresso and picked at the tiny biscuit that comes free with it. It was nice coffee though, she'd acknowledge that, but to acknowledge that she now acknowledged the quality of her coffee made her feel a little queasy. She tended, she'd begun to realise, to start a lot of sentences with 'I'm not usually the kind of person who …' and more than once she had actually said 'I'm not usually the kind of person who cares about coffee or goes to Shopping Iguatemi, but Suplicy is great.'

Oh well. Denial, so the saying goes, is even better than smoking.

And anyway, it wasn't her idea to meet here.

And that was troubling her a little.

Shopping Iguatemi seemed like an odd place to meet a very recent former resident of Cracolândia, not at all, in fact, she now thought, the kind of place you'd expect a very recent former resident of Cracolândia to feel particularly comfortable.

She checked the prepaid phone Leme had given her until he could get hers back from the delegacia: she still had five minutes or so. She pulled her notebook from her bag and ran through the questions that she had prepared. She wanted to know how this woman knew Leandro, *if* she knew Leandro, and if she didn't, how she knew to contact Ellie at the magazine's offices. She wanted to know where this woman now lived, how they had been relocated, how much notice they had been given, had they had any choice. She paused, sipped at her coffee – fuck me, it really is *very* good – and smiled. What she wanted, she realised, was the whole story.

This was what that lump Silva had told her the night before, and she'd been kicking herself since that she had never really looked at journalism like that. *The whole story*. His point was so simple: find out *everything*, and then you'll write the best piece you can.

'But how do you know when you've *got* everything?' she'd asked.

He'd smiled. 'That's when you know you've cracked it and that you're a journalist.'

Leme had laughed at that and left them to it. He didn't want to sit around listening to a couple of *writers*, he'd said. 'Too much to *do*, entendeu?'

She was straight in to see Elizabeth in the morning, first thing. They both went through the prodigal daughter routine and it was nice, actually. Something else she hadn't thought she would ever acknowledge. Self-awareness: that was what her mum always called it, she remembered. Perhaps she was finding herself, she thought. Looking at Elizabeth's billowing floral dress and confident sashay down the street to the café for their breakfast, Ellie decided that finding yourself might not be such an attractive prospect.

But they'd got to the point pretty quickly.

'Phone call yesterday,' Elizabeth said, 'from a woman. I was expecting someone, so I asked her: "You want to talk to Ellie about Cracolândia, ne?" The woman's English was good, bit of an accent, but she made herself understood. I asked: "You a friend of this contact, Leandro?" She grunted yes. Anyway, I told her Shopping Iguatemi, at eleven. Nice and public, nice and safe.'

Ellie thanked her. Elizabeth was very pleased with herself. Leme had told Ellie the night before not to let on about Fernando, about Leandro. She might know from the papers – though it hadn't been a major story, yet – but if she didn't, don't help her.

As far as she was concerned, Ellie had gone to ground to research, to get to know the contacts a little better. It was, as Elizabeth said, 'all good'.

She'd remembered to ask, 'This English guy then, who was that?'

And Elizabeth had played coy, which Ellie thought was a defense mechanism for when she didn't know something. 'I'll figure that out by the time you come back,' she'd said.

Ellie smiled at the 'all good' as she jumped in a cab and called Leme to update him.

Leme was happy that she was meeting this woman at Iguatemi as this was no place for any funny business, but he'd made her promise him that she wouldn't go on anywhere else, that she'd call him once the meeting was done, and that he'd informed a couple of lower-ranking detectives who'd be at the delegacia what she was doing, just in case. Ellie had rolled her eyes.

'Why are men so keen to look after me?' she'd said.

'I think—' Leme had started.

'That was rhetorical,' Ellie had said. 'We *all* of us know, *very* well.'

And so here she was, waiting in a place as far removed from Cracolândia as could possibly be, and only fifteen minutes' or so drive, depending on the traffic. Not a bad start to the story, in fact, meeting in a sort of citadel of or monument to capitalism to reflect on an area about to be transformed into another one at the cost of ordinary people's lives, while flushing the drug trade down the plughole … or throwing the baby out with the bathwater – is *that* a clever little line or a very stupid one?

Her new dumb-phone beeped.

It was a text from Elizabeth. Of course it was: she and Leme were the only ones who had the number

It was an address in Pinheiros. And this:

New Cracolândia plan – the contact we talked about wants to meet you here. Two p.m. All above board. Good news xx

Guess I'll have to go to that address alone, she thought. And she *was* going to go: no doubt *at all* about that.

Prince Felipe

Porra, Carlão. You're being serious? You are? Caralho. OK, OK, I'm not doing nothing you don't want, entendeu? E noix, porra, you know that, viu?

And you promise this the last thing, the last trick I have to pull out my backside for you? You promise? You're serious, porra?

OK. So lay it out. Where you now? Settle down, mate – forget I asked.

You want me at that spot in Pinheiros at that time. Yeah, I can do that. But to do what? Give you a name? That's all. ID a fuck-for-brains Cracolândia rubbernecking meddler? Yeah, church, porra. Not a single problem. If it gets you out my arsehole…

Why me?

Yeah – I'm asking. No, I ain't getting precious, caralho, I'm asking. Fair's fair, ne?

What you think I the only one can do this pissy little job? Really? Meu, you're blowing smoke up me. Flattery, Carlão, is not stylish, entendeu? Yeah, I can chit-chat with the best, what of it?

Gotcha, amigo. E noix, just like I said. I'll be there. And then I'll be gone.

That OK?

I want no more of this, entendeu? *Entendeu*?

Portakabin

An hour later

The stooge's phone yapped. Lisboa swiped and laughed.

'E ai,' Leme said.

'Says, "Wait in the Portakabin in the corner of the car park until it's done."' Lisboa jawboned the stooge. He said, 'Until what's done, porra?'

The stooge kept it zipped – tight. He shook his head and spat.

Lisboa pushed the back of his head – hard.

The stooge yelped, shoulders strained and popped.

'Guess it doesn't matter,' Lisboa said. 'We can just watch, then give old Carlão a shout and bring him in. See how moody the cunt gets when he sees you trussed and skewered like the bitch snide grass you are.'

'How long?' Leme asked.

'Twenty, twenty-five.'

Leme nodded. He pulled out his phone and speared in a message for Ellie. No distractions, no noise. He'd call her after. He flipped the switch to silent.

The window was dust-caked and yellow. A straggly curtain hung from a bent rail.

Leme nodded at Lisboa. 'Go outside and check,' he said.

Leme arranged the curtain and stood slightly to the side. He could see easily enough, right across.

Lisboa barged back in. 'Perfect,' he said.

'One thing,' Leme said and nodded at the stooge.

Lisboa pulled a thick handkerchief from his pocket and waved it.

'Just the ticket,' Leme said.

Lisboa grinned at the stooge. He gripped his jaw and thrust the handkerchief into his mouth, forced it right to the back of his throat. The stooge gagged.

'You don't like that?' Lisboa said. 'Deep-throating motherfucker should be used to it. Chupa, ne? Better this than big Carlos, eh? Porra.'

Leme stood – stoic.

'Fifteen,' Lisboa said.

Leme checked the door at the back of the cabin. It opened with a crunch. Just beyond –

A thick plastic sheet, which pushed out onto the road.

Leme's car –

Fifty feet away.

Leme turned to look back inside. The stooge breathed heavily, nose-deep, dripping.

Leme worked it:

They watch –

Clock who Carlos is meeting.

Clock why.

Big question:

Do they leave the stooge as he is?

Leme weighed it:

Yes –

It made sense. He and Lisboa would scarper out the back –

Leme would follow Carlos once they'd seen him leave.

Leme would get him alone to get some answers –

Somewhere public.

'Five minutes,' Lisboa said.

The stooge gasped, gagged. There was a look in his eyes –

Leme noted it:

Anger. Something else too –

Knowledge, maybe understanding.

Leme put that in a box.

Moments later, two cars pulled in.

'It's on,' Lisboa said.

Carlos climbed out of the first car. From the passenger side –

A scrawny, scary-looking young man in a baseball cap, bone-thin, ragged.

Leme clocked him:

Prince Felipe, Cracolândia crack dealer.

From the other car, a smart-looking man holding a mobile phone. Gold jewellery, not too swank, not too flash. Leme knew him, too –

Posh dealer, well, deals to posh: known as O Cara, the Dude.

Well-known in Vice. Pretty good, considering his job, they say. Clever businessman, smart and reasonable.

Odd.

The three men stood and talked, shrugged, Carlos leading, pointing. He took them round to the boot of the second car, popped the trunk.

Carlos stepped back, indicated for O Cara to look inside –

Carlos yabbered on, giving instructions –

He took another step back.

Prince Felipe's hand went to the back of his waistband –

Revolver-glint.

The snap-pop of a small weapon, like a car tyre going, a champagne cork –

O Cara slumped. Legs eased apart, spread and wobbled.

Carlos nodded at Felipe, who leaned over the trunk.

As he did, Carlos's hand went to the inside of his jacket –

Felipe turned and smiled, nodded, drew his finger across his throat –

Carlos smiled back, pulled his gun, silencer-tipped, and popped Felipe in the chest, twice, and once between the eyes.

Pffft, pffft, pffft.

Felipe – dead-eyed, staggered to the floor:

Bewildered look, mouth open.

Carlos pulled a rag from the boot and wiped the gun down. Holding it inside the rag, he placed it in O Cara's hand.

He studied the car park and flipped his phone open.

The stooge's phone buzzed and rang, long blast short blast.

Carlos stepped towards the Portakabin.

Lisboa dropped the phone. 'We better skedaddle.'

Leme nodded.

They pushed through the door and plastic sheet. Leme ran it –

'You stick around, call this in. I'll go after Carlão.'

Lisboa nodded.

'Get yourself down the street,' Leme said.

Leme cracked the door of his car and climbed in. He pulled on a baseball cap, sunglasses and lowered the visor. Carlão didn't know about Leme's arrangement with his funcionarios. He waited.

Carlos was a friend.

He put that in a box.

Por Kilo Restaurant, Rua dos Pinheiros

Half an hour later

Antonia would not normally find herself in a por kilo restaurant as she didn't believe that buffet food – which is essentially what it was – could ever be as good as something ordered from the menu. It sat there congealing, neither cooling nor warming, each type the lowest denominator version, served up with no discernable joy or attractiveness, designed to be eaten in great mounds so that your body became like a car getting fuel – fill her up! – no doubt breeding germs, the greasy, oily base of most of the options appearing to multiply and spread as it remained – throbbing, oozing – in the heated metal and earthenware containers. No, Antonia would not have chosen this location for any reason at all. But she assumed that her meeting with Carlos would not last long.

She ordered a coffee and settled into a table near the door. She held her briefcase to her, feeling the wads of cash making it bulge as if it were full of paperwork, which, she supposed, in a sense, it was.

And then Carlos barrelled in. Antonia watched as he drew attention to himself, saying hello and a few words to almost every customer – though there were, to be fair, only about half a dozen – and chatting for a few minutes with the manager and one of the waitresses. As he caught sight of her and stepped towards her table, he turned and asked, loudly, the manager for the time.

'Just after twelve,' came the reply.

Everyone in the place heard it. Not, Antonia thought, a coincidence. Maybe these militars needed alibis pretty much all the time – it wouldn't surprise her given what Mario had said about them over the last year or so.

Carlos squeezed and puffed his way into the seat opposite Antonia.

'Hello again,' he said with a twisted smile.

The waitress brought him a glass of beer, which he bit into, taking a long, thirsty gulp.

'Needed that, did you?' Antonia said.

Carlos pulled a sardonic face. 'Stressful job,' he said.

'Let's get this over with, shall we?' she added.

Carlos smiled again. 'Suits me.'

'So, where's the file?'

'Money first.'

Antonia nodded and pulled the thick envelope from her bag. She pushed it across the table. Carlos felt the package and nodded.

'You know,' Antonia said, 'my boss was expecting me to ask for it this morning. He had the money ready. That strike you as odd?'

Carlos grinned. 'Not at all. I rang ahead. No point messing around, entendeu?'

'And the file?'

'Patience, querida.'

Carlos pulled his wallet from his pocket. Antonia listened to the gentle scrape of cutlery on china, murmured conversations, the sizzle of a frying pan out back.

Carlos handed her a piece of paper. She examined it. An address in Pinheiros, quite close by, she thought.

'What's this?' she asked.

'This, *querida*, is where the file will be at two o'clock. Make sure you're there.'

'What?'

'Best I can do. You're going to have to trust me.'

'I don't.'

Carlos grinned again. 'I don't think you've got much choice, meu amor.'

Antonia made a decision. He was right, she really didn't have much choice. Her boss had made it very clear that she needed to recover that file. Fucking Fernando. The little shit had really dropped her in it. Christ, she thought – look what had happened when she'd sent him to pick it up. Didn't bear thinking about.

She made up her mind.

'OK,' she said.

Carlos smiled. 'Nice one, querida. You know it makes sense.'

He pushed his chair back. Antonia stirred and re-stirred her coffee, thick, bitter and gelatinous, un-drunk.

'One other thing,' Carlos said as he heaved himself up. 'Don't tell your boyfriend any of this, certo? Apart from anything else, I'm looking forward to coming round for dinner.'

Antonia shuddered. She really didn't know what she'd got herself into.

Outside the Por Kilo Restaurant, Rua dos Pinheiros

A few minutes earlier

Leme sat in his car across the road from a shit-can, all you can eat, por kilo restaurant and watched Carlos walk inside. His phone yapped –

Lisboa.

The stooge ironed out – I witnessed it. Shot twice. Same gun the Cracolândia kid used, I reckon. I've called it in. Will sit tight.

Fuck. What a mess. Carlos had playbooked this nice. Muito smart, old Carlão. His old mate, big Carlos. Fuck this. Leme tap-tapped:

Don't say anything when the uniforms turn up. Will be in touch.

Leme breathed – hard. He closed his eyes. Her voice, whispering. Renata –

Now? Really?

He fought it. He opened his eyes –

Don't be afraid.

He shook his head –

Her face, smiling.

He breathed – heavy. He breathed again – freighted with portent.

He shook his head again.

Then:

Carlos sauntering out of the restaurant carrying a package he did not have when he went in. He was almost whistling. Fuck –

His old mate Carlão. Jesus.

He speared the key into the ignition and prepared to gun the engine.

He waited –

Moments later:

Antonia left the restaurant.

Carlos pulled away. Leme let him.

Leme decided to see what the fuck Antonia was up to.

His girlfriend, the woman he loved –

Jesus Christ.

The Address in Pinheiros

Just before two o'clock

Ellie opened the door to the apartment.

Oh. Fuck.

Pinheiros

Ten minutes earlier

Leme parked. Three cars up –

Antonia. She hadn't got out.

Leme had followed her from the restaurant to her office. She'd gone inside for about forty minutes. Then he'd followed her here. An apartment block on Joaquin Antunes, box-fresh, no one had moved in yet.

Security –

Lax.

But she hadn't budged from her car and Leme didn't know her destination.

He sat – tight.

His phone buzzed in his pocket:

Lisboa.

Crime-scene chaos here. I'm zipped up. No sign of what we did to the stooge. ID'd the bodies and no one seems to give too much of a fuck. Forensics, etc. Both in the frame for Leandro Fernando. And, vamos … abs.

Not a surprise. Best-case Lagnado scenario, this –

Two murders solved

Murderers killed each other/killed by a militar hero

Wrapped and sealed –

Tied off with a fucking bow.

And right after the offing, Carlos meets Antonia and she gives him a cash-heavy package.

Jesus.

Leme figured it, worst case:

The Leandro and Fernando slash jobs were hacked and run by Prince Felipe and the Dude –

Carlos:

The broker.

Carlos ties up loose ends with a Mexican stand-off-type whack job and Antonia pays him off.

Why?

Cracolândia land-deal complications, no investigation, no problem at all, porra.

Anyone else?

Ellie. Oh, fuck, Ellie.

He swiped at his phone and hit call –

Voicemail silence.

Fuck. He tried again. Same thing. He scrolled through his contacts and got the magazine's office number – she must be back there by now, that Iguatemi meeting can't have lasted too long.

He hit call.

Long blast short blast.

The fuck?

Engaged?

Come *on*.

And then, as if by fucking magic, Ellie walked past Leme's car and buzzed into the building.

Now *that* he wasn't expecting.

And right after that, Antonia got out of her car and made for the same place.

Right, Leme thought. Move.

The Street Outside

Just after two o'clock

Antonia –

'Mario?'

'You need to tell me what you're doing here – quickly. Entendeu?'

'I—'

Antonia: confusion, guilt; no fear though –

She didn't know what she was doing here, Leme realised.

'On the way, certo?' Leme said. 'You know which apartment?'

Antonia –

Mute. Nodded.

Leme said, 'I saw you with Carlos. He left with something he didn't go in with.'

Antonia nodded. 'It's complicated.'

'I fucking hope it is,' Leme said.

They buzzed. Leme held up his badge. The porteiro said he was expecting Antonia. That was enough.

Inside –

Landscaped garden, leather furniture with plastic covers, gravel paths leading to a tennis court, a barbecue area, a swimming pool, a squash court:

The usual.

'You know who you're meeting here?' Leme asked.

Antonia shook her head.

They stood in front of the main lift.

'And you still came.' Leme shook his head – bewildered. 'What number?' he asked.

Antonia fumbled for a piece of paper. 'Erm 602.'

Leme jabbed the number six. It lit up.

'You know why you're here?' Leme said.

Antonia nodded. 'To pick up a file.'

Leme smiled and shook his head. 'You see the young woman who came in just before?'

Antonia shook her head.

'I'll be surprised if there's a file,' Leme said. 'Put it that way.'

Leme's hands went to the back of his waistband. Still there.

Leme ran it:

'You go in first. Don't close the door behind you. I'll hang back. I have some idea who'll be in there, but I'm not sure. Certo?'

Antonia nodded. Her hands shook.

Leme felt anger, disgust –

Love, too. Love filled with resentment.

I love you and you let me down. Fuck you.

Love felt like that so often, he knew –

Disappointment.

Like when Renata got drunk and threw up red wine in their bed, on their walls, on his legs –

That was pretty much how he felt now.

Put it in a box.

The lift arrived and the door shuddered open. No one.

'Vamos,' he said.

He tried Ellie's phone:

It rang, once, twice, three times –

Leme tensed, expectant.

Then:

Nothing.

Someone else had hung up. She'd never done that before.

The Apartment in Pinheiros

Just after two o'clock

Ellie noted the twisted little grin on the man's face. This man, she was *not* expecting. He was sprawled on a cream sofa, legs wide and aggressive. Ellie stayed on her feet. She composed herself.

Ellie nodded at the file. 'That for me, then?' she asked, smiling.

The man's grin widened. 'Not exactly, no.'

'Mind if ask your name?'

'Carlos, querida. I'm glad you made it.'

'My boss sent me the address. I was expecting someone else. Some, well, friends of a friend.' She was smiling, kept her hands on her bag, gripped it so that this Carlos wouldn't see that she was shaking.

He smiled – not pleasantly. 'Friends of your Leandro's, I expect.' He paused. 'Yes, we know them.'

Ellie nodded, held tight. She looked around. The apartment was the model apartment for the new building, the one couples and families would visit to buy cheap while still being built – an illusion of wealth and comfort, Ellie had always thought, these apartments were. Who would ever buy a flat before it was actually finished? It was furnished as if in a catalogue, which Ellie acknowledged, it basically was – all exceedingly tasteful, plumped cushions, literally thousands of rugs and throws, a flat-screen fish tank – well, that's what it looked like – full of show goldfish and exotic plants. You can buy a sort of mini-shark in Shopping Morumbi, she remembered. It'd probably fit in this tank.

Ellie took it all in with a wry sneer and a quick shake of her head.

Carlos noticed. 'You don't like this place?'

'I don't like the *presumption*, entendeu?' Ellie said.

'The fuck do you mean by that?'

'Oh, you know.'

Carlos laughed and shook his head. He patted the thick package.

'Well, after we're … done, I'm investing in one. Management office downstairs. Cash is a very persuasive kind of deposit, entendeu?'

'Very original,' Ellie muttered. 'So why am I here, then?'

It dawned on her that she should be more afraid. It seemed an odd place, though, to be afraid *in*. Then again, there was no one really around.

'We're just waiting for—' Carlos started. There was a knock on the door. 'Oh, here she is. Just in time.'

Ellie turned to see a woman she didn't recognise.

'Antonia,' Carlos called out. 'So good to see you again after so long.'

Antonia, Ellie thought. Surely Antonia – Leme's girlfriend. She hoped so.

Antonia didn't respond. She stood with her back pressed against the door. Ellie noticed that she didn't seem to have actually closed it completely but from his angle on the sofa, Carlos didn't.

Then Carlos shifted slightly and Ellie noticed the revolver and silencer by his side.

Oh. Kay.

She glanced at Antonia, who was impassive, cold, distant to the point of vacuity. Though Ellie had always imagined she might look like that anyway. She smiled at that. She was doing what she always tried to do in difficult situations: forget any danger; keep noticing what she always did; smile.

'I've been wanting to get you two in the same room for a while now,' Carlos said. He snorted with laughter.

Ellie looked at Antonia whose eyes darted to the gun and the file and the package and back. Ellie caught something in her expression.

'We've met before, actually,' Ellie lied. 'Briefly. Her boyfriend introduced us.'

Ellie invested the word 'boyfriend' with something like meaning, looked at Antonia, squeezed her eyes as she said it.

Antonia's eyes flickered something back.

OK, Ellie thought, he knows we're here, at least.

Antonia spoke: 'Why did you need us in the same room, Carlão? You could have given me that' – she pointed at the file – 'earlier today. Saved me a little time, entendeu?'

Carlos smiled. 'I wanted this young Ellie here to know exactly what is in the file, and exactly what she can and can't do as a result.' He paused and stood, tossed the file onto the coffee table in front of him. 'And I wanted her to hear it from you, Antonia.'

He gestured for Antonia to go and look at the file. Ellie watched her closely. She placed her bag on the floor, stopping the door from opening any further. Leme must be right outside, she thought.

She made to go for the file herself, distract Carlos.

'Woah there, queridinha. Not yet, entendeu?' He nodded at Antonia. 'Age before beauty, ne?' He snorted again and fell back into the sofa, pointedly rearranging the gun and silencer.

Antonia picked up the file and sat down opposite Carlos. She opened it and examined it carefully, in, Ellie thought, almost a parody of a thorough, rigorous lawyer.

'What am I looking for here, Carlão?' Antonia said.

Carlos shifted to the edge of the sofa. 'Então, list of names, as you can see. Signatures. Addresses. The signatures are permission for relocation. The addresses are the new addresses, where the Cracolândia residents have been moved to. Certo?'

Antonia nodded. 'Some of these addresses are a very long way away.'

Ellie watched the door, watched Antonia, watched Carlos. But she listened. This was all adding up, she thought.

Carlos smiled. 'It's – how you say – social cleansing, entendeu?'

Ellie laughed. 'Social cleansing?' She shook her head. 'Jesus.'

Carlos glared at her. 'And you're judging what, gringa, eh? You're here, what, a year? Two? You speak a bit of our language, you fuck a few of our playboys – *dead* playboys – and you think you know us, can judge? Vai se foder.'

Ellie tensed. She didn't mind what he said; she minded the way he said it. No, she didn't *mind* it – it frightened her.

'Alright, settle down, Carlos,' Antonia said. 'She's just a girl.' She turned a page. 'So what you're telling me is that this validates the sale and administration of the land in terms of the residents. So we're done, right?'

Carlos smiled. 'Well, you know. Sort of.'

'Sort of?'

'Few things we need to sort out first.' He nodded at Ellie. 'Let the girl have a look.'

Antonia passed Ellie the file. 'So this is what got Fernando killed, is it?' she said, her head down, reading, heart beating – hard.

She didn't look up.

Carlos stood and grabbed her wrist. 'Fernando didn't get himself killed because of a file, querida.'

Ellie composed herself. 'This list of names is pretty short, *Carlos.* I thought there were a lot more people resident there – and I don't mean the noias, entendeu?'

'Well, you know, it's hard to relocate everyone, hard to keep track of everyone. People leave, people don't register. People can disappear. Not our problem.'

'People can disappear?' Ellie said.

'Ah, it is what it is. You're the boss, ne?'

'And Fernando?' Antonia asked. 'This other kid, Leandro? What about them? We know that *they* didn't disappear. We know exactly what happened to them.'

Carlos raised his eyebrows. 'I'm not sure you know *exactly* what happened. Point is, it's taken care of. Right now, in fact. The Polícia Civil have their men. Handed to them. It's done. Cases closed. Everyone's happy.'

'And what do you expect me to do with this?' Antonia said, taking the file back from Ellie.

'You do exactly what you were going to do anyway. And you will. Your Mario is implicated too, don't forget. Your fault – that money movement. You might not have done anything else wrong, but you did that. You don't want to get him into trouble, do you? You deliver the file, the land sale goes through, the politicos are happy, your bosses are happy, the money men are happy.' He opened his arms. 'What else is there?'

'There's her,' Antonia said, nodding at Ellie.

Carlos smiled. 'She's no problem,' he said. 'That's why I brought you both. I wanted you, Antonia, to see why you're going to do exactly what you're told.'

Carlos reached for the gun.

Ellie froze. A great surge of panic from within her chest left her short of breath. Her head spun. She thought she'd faint. Everything slowed down, and yet seemed to be happening very, very quickly.

Leme speared the door.

His hand –

Revolver-heavy.

'Chega, Carlão,' he said. 'Leave it. Step back.'

Carlos eased away from the sofa and the gun.

Leme nodded at the door. 'Out, both of you. Go to my car.' He tossed the keys to Antonia. He looked at Ellie. 'Meet me where we go on a Thursday evening, entendeu?'

Ellie nodded. Leme caught a flash of anger cross Antonia's face. Women.

They edged past him and through the door.

Leme stepped to the sofa and picked up Carlos's weapon.

'Então,' he said.

'Então,' Carlos said.

'I thought we were friends.'

'We are, porra. This isn't personal.'

Leme laughed. 'Original line, cara. I thought you were better than that.'

Carlos smiled. 'What was it your missus used to say? "People were born to disappoint."'

Leme felt a twang in his chest. He breathed – hard. 'What's next?' he said.

'What? You making this up as you go along? This … *rescue*? Porra. You're a disappointment yourself.'

'We saw what you did, Carlão,' Leme said. 'I was there, Ricardo, too. He still is.'

Carlos nodded, figuring it. 'Evidence will show a different story. I'll be the hero, solved the murders you boys couldn't.'

'Right.'

'Look, Prince Felipe sliced Leandro. The Dude did for Fernando. That's the truth. Forensics will prove all that. And that they killed each other, too. My guy? He was the one that tracked them – posthumous medal, entendeu? It's done. No one cares, mate. A poor black kid and a drug-using playboy buy it? A militar killed in service? Who gives a fuck? Certainly not your boss. And certainly not mine.'

Leme nodded. Muito smart, old Carlos. 'And you? What do you get out of it?'

Carlos pointed at the cash-heavy package. 'And there was a lot more where that came from,' he said. 'We've been running Cracolândia for years. That guy Nelson? Who do you think he was working for? And when they wanted to clear it, who do you think they asked? Porra, I thought you were cleverer than this.'

Leme nodded. He'd been right. But what now?

A deal –

'OK,' Leme said. 'You've played this bang on. But, I can still ask questions, cause problems. Agreed?'

Carlos made a face: maybe. 'Let's not forget what happened in Paraisópolis a year or so ago. Remember that? What you did to that gold-toothed fuck? Your wife's killer? A kid, porra. You're implicated, mate. We're in this together. Entendeu?'

Leme ran it – Carlos: spot on. He nodded at the door. 'You leave them well alone, and I'll keep shtum, certo?'

Carlos smiled, looked at the package. 'Like I said.'

'Yeah, you keep that too,' Leme said.

Carlos grinned. 'I knew you'd see sense.'

Leme holstered his gun. 'Got the keys for this place?'

Carlos nodded.

'Here,' Leme said, opening his palm.

Carlos tossed them.

'I'll see you around,' Leme said.

He turned and left, locking the door behind him.

He punched in '1' on the elevator pad. A moment later, the door slid open.

He left the building and waved at the porteiro, who gave him a funny look, but waved back.

He hailed a cab.

'Play Tennis, Itaim,' he said. Where he and Ellie hit up sometimes, played the odd set. She'd know.

And Antonia? He wasn't sure. They'd get through it. He knew that. He knew that was enough, too, for now.

He looked out the window.

Graffiti –

São Paulo is run by cunts

Leme thought that was about right.

One Month Later

A tall, swank building near Jardins

Leme stood by the lift. A fucking *lift* to go to a bar?

Porra. And a bar on top of the Hotel Unique –

How far have I come? he thought – sardonic.

A dolled-up, very attractive girl, who looked like she might be a student, smirked from behind her desk.

Leme looked her over and raised his eyebrows –

Então? he thought, but said nothing.

She smiled and went back to reading the paperback she had folded flat to the desk.

Nice job, amiga, he wanted to say, entendeu? Like the opposite of a siren.

She was supposed to send people *away*. Cowed, intimidated, tail between their legs –

Not Leme. He examined the lift and turned. 'What are you,' he said, 'like a bouncer?'

The girl raised an eyebrow. 'Ah, in a way.' She paused, smiled. 'Not that I'm any good at breaking up trouble.'

Leme laughed. 'No,' he said.

She tilted her head in a question. 'Então?' she said. She clicked her tongue against her teeth, muttered something.

Leme said nothing. He watched the numbers change. The lift stopped at the eighteenth floor.

'What's on that level?' he asked the girl. Proper, old-school charmer. Polite, but casual, he thought. He felt himself smile –

Involuntary reflex. Still got *that*.

'Hotel.' She smiled. 'Very expensive,' she said. Meaning: good luck, querido.

Leme nodded. 'Enjoy your book,' he said.

'Enjoy … the view,' she said, her smile widening. 'It's … unique.'

'Clever,' he said. 'Keep reading and you won't be here too long.'

He winked as the doors closed.

The girl gave him a wave.

Leme shook his head, grinning like a cunt.

They sat at a table outside and smoked. He ordered a beer. Ellie ordered a Caipirinha. Gringa ingénue –

The fucking complimentary peanuts are probably worth more, street-value.

He should take Antonia. She'd go for it. And fuck knows they needed some fun.

'Something wrong, detective?' Ellie asked.

Leme smiled. 'Nothing *wrong*,' he said. 'Just a thought, you know, another time. Blah blah blah.'

She laughed. 'Such a soppy thing for a macho Brasileiro, aren't you?'

Leme nailed half his beer and signalled for another. 'So,' he said.

'So.'

'You're working with Silva, then?'

Ellie nodded. 'I've left the magazine. He's taken me on. Like a research assistant.' She paused. 'Something he'd really like to know…'

'What a surprise.'

'You know him better than I do.'

'And I bet I know what it is he wants to know…'

'Então. Fala.'

Ellie leaned back and blew smoke above her.

'He wants to know if I'll give him Carlão. And if I can't – or won't – why I can't. Or won't,' Leme said.

Ellie raised her eyebrows. 'Very good, detective. And?'

'You're writing the Cracolândia story, but you don't have a conclusion, a happy – which means *un*happy – ending. Não e isso?'

Ellie nodded. 'He – and that also means *me* – doesn't really understand why it's all died down so quickly. He's got a hold of some leaked documents, his IT guy, you know, hacking and whatnot. Looks promising. It ties in some of the top boys in all this. *Maybe*. We've got the Dude,' she made air quotes with her fingers – sardonically, 'we've got the Cracolândia Kid – good name, ne? – but,' and here she switched to an Americanised English, 'we don't get what went down with you and the big bad wolf. Entendeu?'

Leme smiled.

'And fuck this place,' she went on. 'Look at them in there. Pushy playboy pussyhounds. Ugh.' She mimed being sick.

'Just your sort of place.' Leme winked.

Ellie smiled – rueful. 'It's São Paulo, ne? It's why I'm talking to you.'

'Explain.'

'It all just goes on. You give us Carlos. You don't give us Carlos. You explain. Or you don't. Entendeu?'

Leme nodded. 'Very perceptive. For a gringa.'

'How's your girlfriend?' Ellie said, pouting. 'Still got your bank details?'

Leme shook his head – smiling. 'Don't worry about us, queridinha. We're fine.'

Antonia hadn't exactly come up roses, though, that's for sure. Just your minor misdemeanour money-laundering through your boyfriend's account to smooth a few things over. Just keeping your semi-legal removal of Cracolândia residents ticking without too many questions being asked. Just your usual São Paulo elite/blind eye/high-ground business deal the likes of which upon our great city was founded.

Just that.

Leme could handle that.

Reason why?

Antonia acknowledged that she was wrong. Antonia thought about what he'd said, why he was angry, and she took his accusations and arguments with grace and understanding, thought about his side and admitted she'd been wrong, had *done* wrong. And then she did what she could to put it right.

Imaginative empathy, it was called, apparently. Course, she'd had to tell him that.

'Empathy, then,' Leme had replied.

'Don't be a smart-arse, querido,' she'd said. 'Empathy is recognising there are two versions of any narrative.'

He'd smiled at that.

Point is, the beginning of a relationship should be simple, happy, exciting. You should want to see, speak to, hear from your new lover. Leme wanted this with Antonia.

Point is, the more time he was with Antonia, the clearer he could see how badly Renata had treated him before committing to him. He'd *always* forgiven her flightiness, her duplicity, her manipulation, her controlling periods of silence, her emotional violence, her broken promises. And whenever he'd called her out on *anything at all*, normally in a moment of anxiety, or insecurity, or fear, and quite reasonably too, considering her previous, she'd attack, attack, *attack* him.

Renata had had Leme on a fucking hook. He knew that.

Yeah, he was glad – in the end. But good to dig it now, ne, for what it was.

And yet –

He had only ever loved her. There was never anything but love.

Funny old game, though, emotional abuse. You don't understand it, until you understand it.

And that was the other thing about his not-quite-corrupt lawyer girlfriend – she always helped him understand.

And it's no risk, after all, living honestly. And *that* was a sentiment Leme now understood.

'Oh, OK. You trust her still?'

Leme thought about this. 'Yes, I do. It's not worth you worrying about. She's doing the right thing.'

'And the Cracolândia deal remains in place. Everyone's a winner.'

'Winner, winner, chicken dinner.'

'You watch too much TV.'

They sat in silence and finished their drinks.

Leme stood to go. He nodded at the skyscrapers, then the low-level mansions, and then inside at the rich, suited businessmen and women. '*There's* your story,' he said.

'Ah, porra, stop being so … *profound*.'

'I'm serious. You don't need a conclusion, an *ending*. There isn't one, beyond what we already know. This,' he thrust his chin at the buildings, 'wins. And so does this.' He pointed inside the bar. 'All any of us can do is deal with the little stories, entendeu?'

He stepped away from the table.

'We'll be in touch,' he said. 'The fallout will happen. Sometimes it does. We can help make sure it goes right. As it should.'

Ellie waved him away. 'Fuck me,' she said. 'I'm drinking with fucking Yoda. You go, querido.'

Glossary

Acredito que sim	I believe so
Amarelou	In this instance, 'coward'
Amigo/Amiga	Friend
Até mais	See you later
Bala perdida	Stray bullet
Balada	Nightclub
Baranga	Derogatory slang, meaning 'ugly'
Batendo papo	Chatting, banter, literally 'hitting chins'
Beleza	Beautiful
Bem	Well, as in 'all well?' Also, as intensifier, 'well hot!'
Boca/Boca de fuma	Place in a favela where drugs are sold
Bonitão	Handsome man
Brega	Tacky
Cade você?	Where are you?
Caipirinha	Cachaça and lime-based cocktail
Cara	Dude
Caralho	Derogatory term, generally 'motherfucker' or 'dick'
Carteira do trabalho	Official document of employment history
Certeza absoluta	I'm certain
Claro	Of course
Cão de guarda	Guard dog
Chega!	Enough!
Coitado/Coitada	Poor thing!
Dedo-duro	Grass/snitch
Deus me livre!	For God's sake!
Dinheiro	Money
E aí	Hey
E isso aí	That's exactly right
Embora	In this instance, 'let's go'
Então…	So…

Entendeu?	Know what I mean/understood/you get me? Etc
Favela	Slum
Faz o que?	What are you going to do?
Feijoada Completa	Pork stew, with all the trimmings
Feliz	Happy
Filezinha/Filezão	Vulgar term to describe a young/older attractive woman
Filho da puta	Son of a bitch
Garanhão	Stud
Garoto/garota	Boy/girl
Graças a Deus	Thank God
Gringa	Foreign woman
Jeitinho Brasileiro	A shortcut, often used in terms of bribery/cheating
Jeito	Style/method/way
Limpeza	Clean up, in both domestic and other, senses
Louca	Crazy
Mais ou menos	More or less
Mano	Slang, 'brother', similar to 'dude'
Menina	Girl
Menina louca	Similar to 'wild child'
Menos um	In this instance, when a criminal dies, a shrug, 'one less'
Meu	In this instance, 'mate'
Nada	Nothing
Não e/Ne?	Isn't it/Innit?
Nem fodendo!	No way am I doing that!
Noia	Crack addict/paranoid drug user
Nossa!	Wow!
Obrigado/Obrigada	Thank you
Papo furado	Bullshit/nonsense
Pão na chapa	French bread fried in butter
Pastel	A deep fried pastry
Pegou?	In this instance, '[drugs] kicked in?'

Polícia Civil	Civil Police, which undertakes criminal investigation
Polícia Militar	Military Police, which polices the city
Polícial	Police Officer
Pois não?	Can I help you?
Porra	Literally 'semen', but used as a catch-all swear word
Pouquinho	Small amount
Puta	Whore
Puta merda!	Expletive, similar to 'Fucking hell!'
Puta que pariu!	Expletive, similar to 'Fuck me!'
Que porra essa?	What the fuck is this?
Que coisa!	Amazing!
Quem fala?	When answering the phone, 'Who's that?'
Quem quer crack?	Who wants crack?
Quem tem maconha?	Who has dope?
Quer provar?	Would you like to taste it?
Querido/Querida	Term of affection, similar to 'my dear/ sweetheart'
Relaxa!	Relax!
Rodizio	System that allows certain cars in the city at rush hour
Segurança	Security guard
Sem graça	Literally 'without grace', meaning gauche/ clumsy/tacky
Ta boa?	You OK?
Ta ligado?	Know what I mean/understood/you get me? Etc
Taxista	Taxi driver
Tudo bem?	How are you?
Vai com Deus	God be with you
Vai se foder!	Go fuck yourself!
Vai tomar no cú!	Up yours!
Vem ca	Come here
Vó	Grandmother

Acknowledgments

I'd like to thank the following –

The Arts Council England, for a grant that helped with the writing of this book.

Will Francis, Helen Francis, Martin Fletcher, Susanna Jones, Angeline Rothermundt, Kid Ethic, Luke Brown, Lee Brackstone, Sam Mills, Laura Barton, Jenn Ashworth, Wendy Thomas, Danillo Aguiar, Isabella Lemos, Karen 'Doula' Brodie, Rachel Mills, Martha Lecauchois, and, for helping me understand how to shape this into something like the novel I wanted to write, Lucy Caldwell.